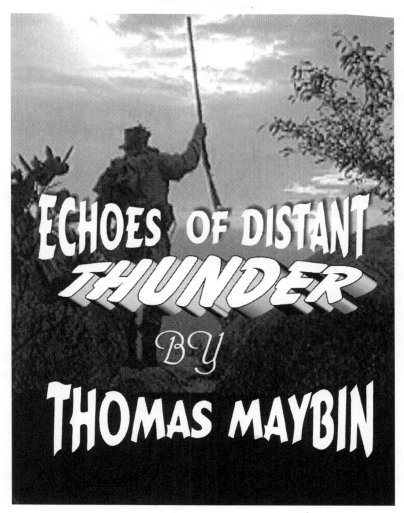

ECHOES OF DISTANT THUNDER BY THOMAS MAYBIN

Chapter 1

The old man's eyes were finally giving out. These days, only by placing his workbench in the direct sunlight filtering through the dusty window at the rear of his workshop could he see to do the fine details of his work. Even the best, brightest electric lights didn't illuminate as well as good old fashion sunlight. For this reason the old man only worked, as he put it, "when God saw fit."

But then it was not as if his slowly failing eyesight was not something he hadn't been expecting for a long time. Actually he felt lucky. At seventy-one, most men his age and long since been relegated to wearing glasses. Yet the old man, stubborn as always, steadfast refused to visit an optometrist.

It was hard enough to get him in front of a real doctor when he was sick, which wasn't often so it was a good thing his daughters had inherited his stubborn streak.

Between them, when it looked necessary enough to be worth the fight, the girls would gang-up on him. After a while, fearing that he might go deaf from hearing them fuss, he would allow them to make an appointment with the doctor.

Actually he liked Dr. Green who was semi-retired and treated only a few of his older patients, as a courtesy, from a small office he'd set up in his basement. Usually the two men spent most of the visit talking about trout fishing, or grouse hunting, before at last the doctor would send him home with a clean bill of health and a mild admonishment to start taking life a little slower. Advice which of course the old man staunchly ignored.

Other than his eyesight, he was in good health for his age. Here again he'd been lucky, seldom ever suffering from any long-term illnesses and only in the lingering heart of winter did he suffer from an occasional bout of arthritis.

On those bitter cold days it would sometimes flare up in his knees and occasionally in a couple of fingers that he'd broken, years ago, while snaking timber out of the mountains behind a pair of stubborn mules. That had been in his younger days when he'd been raw-bone tough and green as stump water, spending ten hours a day hauling timber down to the sawmill for five dollars wage.

These days, for the most part, his only ailment was an occasional winter 'cold' which could usually be broken up after a couple days rest and a few nighttime doses of his home grown honey mixed with a little a drab of the devils on libation, white liquor, Satan's Tears, wept through coiled lengths of copper tubing and collected in clear mason jars.

It was a spring water clear, jaw locking, breath taking brew, cooked off way back up in the hollow behind Sam King, his friend and closest neighbor's house.

Not that he ever got too deep in the cup, or on too familiar terms with old John Barleycorn. Oh no, his wife, May kept much too close an eye on him for that. She would get her feathers ruffled if he even so much as tried, as a preventive measure, to take a dose of this home grown medicine or in her words, **'that *vile brew.'*** But that was okay. May was a damn good woman, a looker too. Still was as far as he was concerned.

Over the years, he had never quiet figured out the

mystery of why a good looking, intelligent, gal like May had chosen to get hooked up with the likes of him. But she had, and not a day passed that he didn't thank the good Lord for his blessing. She'd stuck by him through some mighty lean times and never once complained, at least not to him anyway, and never failed to carry more than her share of the load.

Not much more than a girl-child when they'd married and younger than him by a few years, she had never the less, always been a rock in the river of his life. Without her strength, her will, to anchor him against rough, sometimes turbulent waters that life sent flooding his way, he would no doubt have been washed away and turned out...well... worthless.

These days he still worked with wood, but unlike 'the good old days' at the sawmill, now he was paid well for what he did. But with his eyes giving out work had become a more difficult matter.

Taking a piece of rough sawn, dense grained walnut and transforming it into a perfectly fitted, finely finished gunstock, required steady hands and more importantly, a close eye for detail. Now things had changed. His work was as finely executed as ever, but he could only work in the middle of the day when the sun was at its brightest.

On this day, Thanksgiving Day, sitting at his workbench with a small razor edged chisel in his right hand, he carefully pealed out tiny curls of rich brown walnut from the piece of highly figured wood in his stock vice. He knew that someone would shortly be coming to call him in to sit at the head of the table and give the blessing over the holiday meal.

4

As always, there would be a massive excess of food. Ham and turkey, a multitude of side dishes and deserts prepared in other towns, other kitchens, then carted here in Tupperware and aluminum foil covered dishes by his daughters and their daughters. It would be a feast of proportions impossible to sample, little alone be consumed in a single setting.

They would share the meal, the love and the warmth and comfort with family and friend, a time of reunion with children, grandchildren and great grandchildren. The old log home would be transformed into bustling beehive of laughter and conversation, warm enticing smells and a strange form of chaotic organization that only women seemed to understand.

After raising four strong-headed daughters and living over half a century with their strong-willed mother, he was smart enough to know when to stay out of their way. So until they gave the okay, he'd retreated to the sanctuary of his workshop.

After a few strokes with the chisel he would place the lock-plate of an engraved L.C. Smith shotgun over his cuts comparing the fit. It was slow, pain-taking work, shaping the wood to fit precisely around the metal, but was work he loved. He'd always had a talent for working with wood. A pastime he loved almost as much as he loved the woods themselves. He never tired of the pungent smell of fresh sawdust, the feel, the textures of wood from the various trees; no two pieces ever exactly the same. He enjoyed all the things that could be created from trees, things shaped by the skill of his own hands. He could not phantom a life in which his hands were not used for crafting of wood.

Over the years he had crafted a world of items ranging from baby cradles to homemade fiddles and banjos. He'd carved duck decoys and wooden toys not to mention most of the furniture in the log home where he and May had raised their brood of girls.

It was however the crafting of high quality gunstocks that he loved the most. It seemed only natural for there had been gun-makers and repairers in his family for generations and he'd carried a gun since he was old enough to wander off in the woods by himself. Then, even as now, the game he killed had been fare for the table.

The only time in his life when he could remember not working with wood had been the time when he'd taken a boat trip across the ocean to France. From there he'd hiked his way to Germany along with several hundred thousand young men.

He'd carried a gun then too. In that bitter two and a half years he saw a lot of the bright-eyed young boys fall by the wayside. Those who survived the mud, the rain, and the snowy frozen wastes of artillery blasted forests and bomb riddled towns and villages, or the seemingly endless nightmare of death and agony, might still wear the faces of young men, but inside they had become grizzled, heart scared veterans with eyes grown old beyond their years.

After what seemed a lifetime of fighting, marching, and fighting again, deep in Germany, he'd found himself on the outskirts of a place of horror called Ausiawisch. It was said there were worse places with worse atrocities, but if they existed, he had no desire to witness them.

He'd fallen to his knees in the mud and blood, making a promise to God that if he ever made it back to his beloved wife and the mountains of home, he would never again stray from their protective embrace.

I was not a hard promise to keep. After returning home in the spring of 1946, he eventually found peace of mind and forgetfulness in the healing arms of his wife and the bubbling laughter of their first baby girl and of course, in the swirling depths, the infinitely unique lines of fine burl walnut.

Over the years his skill as a gun stock maker had gained him considerable notoriety. Once he'd had taken on commissions from all over the country, doing custom work for wealthy and affluent customers. Yet never in all those years did he forget his roots. He might put off, for a few days anyway, doing a high dollar job in order to repair the stock of old single barrel shotgun that a neighbor used to hunt squirrels, or for that matter to replace a broken axe handle needed for splitting wood to help keep someone's home warm. There never seemed to be any lacking for projects to keep him occupied.

His girls were constantly after him to retire, to relax and enjoy life, but the very thought of retirement, of quitting the thing what he loved, never entered his mind. He would work as long as he was physically able. How long that would be only the good Lord knew.

This particular train of thought, one he tried to avoid as much as possible, always left him feeling a little melancholy. He knew his time in this world was limited, but he'd lived a full and rich life, at least in the things that mattered...his family.

His only regret, one that most every man could understand, was that he'd never had a son or a grandson to pass on his knowledge, the guarded secrets of his art and the hard-earned wisdom that can only be garnered from years of trial and error. Or maybe it was that he just wanted to have someone follow in his footsteps, to feel that his life's work had been worthy of example, that the things he stood for, prided himself on, did not simply vanish with the hollow sound of clumps of dirt landing on a wooden box.

It seemed as though his desire was destined to go unfulfilled for he had been blessed with daughters and granddaughters. It was not that the girls weren't capable or that he would not have been willing to teach any one of them. It just seemed that their interests were directed in other areas, which was okay too.

He'd always encouraged them to follow their own dreams and so they had, becoming teachers and nurses, lawyers and housewives, short order cooks, dental assistants and pharmacist. A list that always seemed to be adding new categories.

Some were married, some divorced, some single, some had been in trouble, some had caused trouble, but through it all they all had one thing in common; they were family. He was proud as hell of every single one.

It was not until just a few years ago, when the great grandchildren had started to come along, that any boys had been born into the family. Now there were four boys and two girls in that division, all within a year or two of the same age.

One boy, Lee the oldest of his great grandchildren was the one hope the old man held out for. The boy at only eight years old was quiet, thoughtful and seemed to show a real interest in what his "Pappa JC", was doing. Often when there were no other children around the boy would sit quietly watching as the old man did his work. Never saying a whole lot but seemingly fascinated by the deft movement of the old man's hands as he moved from tool to tool to accomplish his job.

Of course, like any child, when there were other kid around to play with he was like a wild Indian, a seemingly inexhaustible supply of energy and mischief. A trait that reminded the old man of himself so many years removed.

Almost as though the thought had conjured the image, the door to his workshop swung open with a clang and in rushed half dozen noisy, laughing, quarreling kids. They ranged from four to eight years old, four boys and two girls and brought to mind the old *'Our Gang'* theme from the **Little Rascals**. The look of determination in their eyes bespoke of a mission of major fledgling proportion.

The old man tried to keep the merriment he felt from showing in his eyes. He was, after all, the all-wise, all-knowing monarch of the family, the venerable old guru to whom they all turned for answers and advice, for the sage wisdom of his years. Well... at least the small children did ...anyway.

"Pappa JC," said Lee, seemingly the self appointed leader of this nestling mob. "Will you make us some guns and some bow and arrows, so we can play cowboys and Indians?"

"That's a mighty big order on such short notice," the

9

old man said, placing the stock he'd been working on a shelf behind his workbench and knocking off the wood shavings from his much patched shop apron.

"And just how do you plan to pay for such an extravagant array of weaponry."

"Oh Pappa J", piped little Kimberly, the younger of the two girls. "You know you wouldn't make us pay. You love us."

"Yes I do love you," he said, reaching down and taking hold of the girl and placing her on his knee. "But I would make you pay... In kisses."

He hugged the girl tight and kissed her on top of her adorable little blond head.

"Pappa J. You know kisses are always free."

"Even from a beautiful Indian Princess."

"I don't want to be a beautiful Indian," she pouted, all the while winding one finger round and round in one truss of her silky blond hair." I want to be a cowboy."

"Okay. And why is that my little cowboy princess."

"Indians are bad. They cut off your hair."

"Oh, I hadn't heard," the old man said trying to keep serious look on his face.

His statement started a landside of bantering and arguments among the troop of pint sized adventurers. They all wanted to tell their own Indian war stories, at the same time.

The old man felt a sudden empathy for the hawk sitting in the top of a tree and suddenly finding itself surrounded by a whole flock of screeching, harassing bluejays.

"Pappa JC," Lee said, again asserting his seniority over the brood. "What she means is that they scalp people. Sneak up on you in the middle of the night; take a big knife and *WHAM* cut off the top of your head."

The old man felt the little girl shiver, sinking deeper against his side. He figured it was time to put an end to this narrative of over imaginative speculation before the child ended up having nightmares, and he thought wryly, before he could be held accountable and severely chastised by the gaggle of over-protective women-folk he'd helped sire.

"Listen Little-Bit," he said, hugging the little girl but speaking loud for the other children to hear. "Indians are just people, no different than you or me or anyone else. The truth is we have Cherokee blood mixed in along with Irish, English, Dutch, Scotch and German."

"What about the hair," Kimberly asked, running her tiny finger along the edge of her blonde trusses in the pantomime a scalping knife?

"Well, Little-Bit, that was a long time ago. It don't happen any more," the old man said, trying to find the best way to phrase what he needed to say in terms that a child would understand.

"No matter what color someone happens to be, whether it's red, white, black, brown or yellow, there are always a few bad people in the bunch that turn out to be mean. Those few always manage to cause trouble and do things that give everyone else a bad name. That's the way it was with the Indians. It's the way it is with everybody.

11

Hopefully over time things have gotten a little better. Nobody gets scalped around here anymore, so don't you worry your sweet little head about it."

When the old man looked up, he was surprised to see Katie standing in the doorway listing to his narrative. Katie was the youngest of his granddaughters. She was a slender little wisp of a girl with elfish features, reddish blond hair, a few freckles and a twinkle in her eye.

At fifteen, fiercely independent, intelligent and cute as a button, she was also a bookworm and something of a recluse. She would as soon be locked in her bedroom with a book as to be hanging out with her friends at the mall. And at times she looked so much like her grandmother had at that age, it made his old heart skip a beat.

"Okay kids," she said in a more grown up manner than seemed required of her age. "It's time for all of you children to get washed up and ready to eat."

"Ah, shoot. Pappa JC was going to make us some guns and bows," Lee moaned with all the typical impatience of youth. His tone leaving no doubt as which activity he held in higher esteem.

No arguments," Katie said with such an air of authority that the old man had to once more suppress a grin. Heaven have pity on the poor boy she chose to marry.

The children almost as though of a single mind turned to the old man, each tiny face looking for the world like a condemned prisoner appealing to the warden for a stay of execution.

"Okay kids," said the old man. "Its time to go. Best get along like she says."

Like a group of grumbling dwarfs from a Walt Disney cartoon, the children, in single file, trooped out of his workshop, muttering and complaining about the unfairness of how they were treated by 'grown-ups.' He could sympathize with them. Sometimes he felt the same way.

Katie walked over and draped her arm across his shoulders then kissed him on his cheek.

"Love you Pappa," she said

"Love you too, Pumpkinseed." It was a nickname he'd given her when she was two years old. At that time she had spent most her summers there. Now she was busy with school, writing for the school paper and working on the school yearbook staff.

"What you said about our family having Indian blood was it true or were you just trying to keep Kimberly from being frightened?"

"Both."

"Cool."

"Cool"? He knew full well the new 'hip' meaning of the word; he just liked to play the role of the back-woodsy old mountain man. Of course she knew that he knew. It was an old game.

"What you were telling the children...about people being the same... no matter where they live of or what color they are...I think that was good. It sounded like something my teacher, Mrs. Johnson, would say."

"Cool,"

"Pappa, why are you out here working? It's a holiday. You should be resting."

"I was just keeping out of the way of the women folks. You know how your mother and her sisters get at times like this. A man could be trampled underfoot before you know it. Besides this is not really work. I was doing the final fitting on a gunstock I'm making."

"Another one of my teachers, Mrs. Crawford, says that guns are evil, that they should all be destroyed. She says without guns there would be no more wars or killings."

The old man paused, then ran his hands through his bushy white hair to shake out any stay wood chips, and then took off his shop apron as he tried to piece together what he wanted to say. It was important to convey to his granddaughter how he felt about the right, the freedom to own guns. How did he pass on the feeling he got when he held a finely crafted firearm in his hands, his appreciation for the workmanship, the art of the gun maker? How do you relay the memories of days spent in the woods, the smell of autumn leaves, of gun oil and spent cordite? Or the warm coziness of sitting near a fire as a rabbit roasted on a hickory spit. Or how the feel of a worn single-shot .22 rifle at your side could offer comfort against the darkness in the woods at night.

No, he was not at all sure he could put into words the complicated swelter of emotions he felt concerning guns.

Of course, there were even some guns he did not care for. Assault Rifles, ungraceful, ugly and blunt, and of no beauty or grace and yet these too he knew had their purpose, though not for him. To fit within the realm of his personal aesthetic value, any gun needed to be dressed in wood.

He had never been one for using a lot of big words. Now he wished he knew more, or at least the right ones to use. In his heart he had the feeling that what he needed to say was vitally important.

"I'm sure your Mrs. Crawford is a smart woman...and good person, but what I want to know is how you feel. Do you think she's right?"

"I'm not sure. There is so much violence in the world, so many people being killed. Sometimes I don't know what to think."

"The world *is* in turmoil, no doubt. Bout as bad as I've ever seen. But it's never going to change, get any better until people start taking responsibility for their actions."

"I don't think I understand, Pappa."

"Okay, let's break it down this way. Your teacher says that guns are evil." The old man reached over on his workbench and picked up a wood chisel and handed it to the girl.

"What's this," he asked?

"A chisel, of course."

"Yes, but more generally speaking, it's a tool."

"Okay."

"Now, if in using this tool, I let it slip and stab myself in the hand. Is it my fault or did the tool suddenly take on a sinister aspect, a mind of its own, wishing me harm. Or is it still just a tool ?"

"It is still just a tool."

"Right, nothing but a tool. A tool yielded by human hands. Without someone to direct it, someone to take responsibility for its use, is no different than any other tool. It has no will of its own. With out someone to load and pull the trigger on a gun, it is as simple and harmless as this chisel."

"But, Pappa, the chisel was made to be a tool. Aren't guns made for killing?"

"Not always, but yes for the most part they are. Sometimes it is necessary to kill."

"Why?"

"For food... of course with all those burger joints pooping up on every corner that probably doesn't qualify much these days, but it once did. Sometimes though it becomes necessary to defend ourselves, to kill for survival."

"Have you ever had to kill anyone, Pappa?"

"Once, in a war, a long, long time ago, I did. And I hope none of us ever have to again. But the possibility is always there."

"It's confusing sometimes. I don't understand how people can be so cruel to each other."

"Baby-girl, I don't know the answer to that either. But it's like I was telling the younger children, no matter where you go, no matter what race of people you deal with, there will always be both good and bad. And always among the bad there will exist the very worst of the lot, evil men and women who would rob, murder, oppress or enslave or worse, annihilate entire races, even their own families, all in the name of greed for power or even from racial hatred or just plain meanness. For these reasons it is sometimes necessary to use force, to protect ourselves."

I still don't think I could ever kill anyone."

"I pray to God you never have to, but being prepared, ready to defend ourselves if that need ever arises, is the best deterrent against those who would do us harm."

"Do you think things will ever change? Get better, I mean. Do you think people will ever stop hurting one another?"

"Oh, I reckon things are improving all along, though sometimes it seems a mighty slow process and folks has still got a long way to go. That's why we have police and armies to protect us. And it is also the reason why some very smart men put in the Constitution that we all have the right to "keep and bear arms". Or simply put to own guns so that we can protect our loved ones and ourselves."

"I think I understand what you are saying. Maybe you should come to my school and explain it to Mrs. Crawford."

"Baby-girl, if I thought it would do any good, I might give it a try, but you know that's another great thing about this country. Those same smart men, the ones who laid out our constitution, also added a section that guaranteed we all have the right to our own opinions and beliefs. Besides all this palavering don't amount to more than one old man's rambling thoughts. Nothing you should be fretting yourself over anyway."

"How did you learn all of this stuff, Pappa? I mean,

Momma says you never got to finish school. Where did you learn all the things you know?"

"Well, Baby-girl, schooling was not as important in my day as it is now. Back then a man had to learn by doing, by living, educating himself ever day, sometimes by the hardest way possible, learning from mistakes. But those days are gone, now it's important to get a proper education. The more time you spend in school, the more you learn, the easier your life will be."

I like going to school."

"Frost."

"Frost?"

"Better than cool."

"I want to go to college, study to be a writer."

"So I heard."

"Do you think I will make it?"

"Don't think. I know you will. You will do great at whatever career you decide to pursue. If you chose to become a writer, then I have faith your words will have great meaning. That's why I've got something to give you. Something I've been saving since I was a young man, since the day my father gave it to me."

"What in the world is it, Pappa?"

The old man stood up from his chair and walked over to a huge bookshelf covering almost the whole wall. The shelf was filled with hundreds of volumes, with subjects ranging from history to doing your own plumbing, biography to fiction, with authors ranging from former President Jimmy Carter to H.G. Wells, Hemingway to

Louis L'amour. There was even a volume of poems by Edgar Allen Poe and paperbacks of –Tarzan- by Edgar Rice Burroughs. He had read them all. For more than fifty years he'd been a voracious reader, but that too had changed with the dimming of his eyes.

From the shelves assortment of books he plucked a single dust covered volume. Carefully he blew the sanding dust of walnut and cherry from the ragged leather bound pages.

"It's a diary, written over two hundred years ago by the first member of our family to come to this country. Your great-great grandfather, many generations removed."

"Who was he?"

"His name was Matthew Maybin," the old man said, placing the book gently in his granddaughter's hands. "I've been waiting until you were old enough to take responsibility for its care. This was written over two hundred years ago. The pages are very fragile."

A yellowed piece of paper obviously used as a marker was sticking out slightly at the top about half way into the ancient ledger.

Gently she opened the pages to the marked spot.

The loose paper turned out to be more than a simple page marker. It too was very old. The words written on paper were smudged, water stained, and written in a flowing, flowery kind of script that at first was hard to read. But then her eyes and her mind adjusted to the unfamiliar style. What at first seemed gibberish became words in her mind?

"This is a hand written copy of The Declaration of Independence," she said, unable to keep the awe from her voice. "We studied it last year in my American history class."

The old man didn't speak, but a smile warmed the features on his craggy face and brightened his eyes as he watched his granddaughter reverently studying the aged paper.

"On the back of the paper there seems to be a map. The lines are so faded it hard to tell.

"It is a map," he said not hiding his pride in the girl.

"A treasure map," she asked, excitement rising in her voice?

"Let's not get ahead of ourselves," the old man said, his voice carrying an air of secrecy."

"Read what's written on the marked page."

Looking down at the page, her eyes again had to adjust to a different flowery script....

Camped this night on the banks of a river called thee French Broad....

A look of wonder spread over her face as she read the words aloud.

"The French Broad River runs right in front of our house in Etowah," she said.

That's the reason I marked that spot in the diary," he said, reclaiming his chair.

"Did you know that the name of your town, Etowah was once the name of a   Cherokee village?"

"No, I didn't. How did you know?"

"History," he said, his smile smoothing out the crows feet around his eyes. "History is all around us, usually right under our noses, if we just take the time to notice. Take for example, the town where your Aunt Kay lives. Old Fort. It has that name because it sits on the original sight of Davidson's Fort from way back in colonial days."

"Pappa, why do I get the feeling that this history lesson and the discussion about freedom and the Constitution is tied in with what's written in this diary."

"Ah! You're found me out. My secret's out of the bag," the old man said, his smile seeming to melt away a few of the years written on his face. "I had hoped that one day you might take the words written in those pages, transform them into a story. A story that sings with the truth of how things really were in those by-gone times, of how people lived and loved, of the struggles and hardships they endured. It is a story of how they fought and died for what they believed. Maybe you can bring to life the story, not only of our family by of all the families who struggled to make this country what it is."

"Pappa, I'm not sure I'm ready or that I have the skill for something like this."

"Maybe not now," the old man said, laying his hand gently on her shoulder. "There's no hurry. It has waited for two centuries. One day you will be ready. Only you will know when that time comes."

The girl looked once down more at the words written so many years ago. Her mind was awash with a mixture of emotions…awe… wonder, but mostly pride. It was hard to believe her grandfather had entrusted her with the care such of a treasured family heirloom. She was amazed by his remarkable knowledge of the world present and past. But she was also filled with doubts, unsure that she would ever be able to accomplish such a formidable task

Fortunately she had a great abundance of one of the blessings of youth, a sense of wonder. She was enthralled with the idea that recorded history was there, held in her hand, waiting to be brought to life. Her mind was filled with unanswered questions.

"One thing, Pappa," she asked. "The map. Where does it lead?"

The old man smiled. A long thoughtful silence passed before he answered.

"They all lead to the same place. The map on one side, the Deceleration, the words written in this diary, all eventually lead to the same destination. And there in lies a most wondrous treasure, but not the kind you think. It is a thing you must find for yourself."

Sensing that she would get not further answers to her questions from her suddenly mysterious grandfather, she placed the map back in the diary.

Before gently closing the book she once more read the words at the top of the page.

Camped this night on the bank of a river called the FrenchBroad….

Earlier today I saw a most remarkable

and disturbing sight........

★★

Eight years later.

A young woman looks down at the stack of white papers sitting neatly on her desk. Her heart is filled with conflicting emotions. She is proud of what she has accomplished and at the same time sad that her grandfather had not lived long enough to see her work finished. He had passed away two months earlier. He had started her on this journey years ago. It seems as if he had known her better than she had known herself. His memory brought a swell tears to her eyes, one of which managed to finds its way on to the first page of her manuscript. She didn't bother to wipe it away. It would dry with time with barely a stain, besides her grandfather would not want to see her sad. He would have been proud of her, she knew.

He always had.

Chapter 2

Camped this night on the banks of a river called the FrenchBroad......

Earlier today, saw a most remarkable and disturbing sight...

The Cherokee territory, in the early spring of 1776 was no place for a man to travel carelessly or without good cause. Anyone willing to risk venturing into that vast, sprawling wilderness of untamed dark forests and swift flowing rivers, and wishing to live long enough to boast of his exploits, had well better keep one eye on his back-trail and one hand held close to his rifle.

The French Broad River, its tributaries forming as tiny trickles in the mossy tree covered slopes of the southern Appalachians, flowed for only a surprisingly short distance north before becoming cold and deep, a formidable obstacle to the westward intrusion of colonial expansion.

At that dark and bloody time in history, the river marked the current eastern boundary of the lands claimed by the Middle towns of the Cherokee nation.

From the very beginning of their involvement with those strange, pale skinned interlopers from across the great river of salt, the Cherokee had met with only treachery, deceit and tragedy. Their vast woodland domain, once encompassing thousands of square miles, had been reduced to less than a third of its original size.

Could it be any wonder that young hot-blooded war-chiefs, like Double-Head, Little Owl, Bloody Fellow and Dragging Canoe, were to determine, at any cost, to stop the encroachment of their lands?

Tomahawks and scalping knives grew ever more stained with the blood of white settlers. And yet for each scalp taken, for each homestead burned, it seemed that ten more arrived to take their place.

Each day the ships arriving in ports like Charles-Town, Wilmington and even as far away as Boston disgorged a steady stream of immigrants.

From around the world they came, dreamers searching for the utopia of this new Promised Land or refugees fleeing the tyranny of the old, failed Promised Land.

Matthew Maybin had once been among those new arrivals, making his way on unsteady legs away from a ship whose crew and captain had treated their passengers more like prisoners than paying customers.

Walking along the crowded wharf, Matthew had taken one last look at the Pennsylvania Farmer, the ship where he'd spent two months crossing an ocean seemingly bent of destroying them all.

The day was December 17th in the year 1772. Matthew stepped of the salt-slicked walk boards into a new and unfamiliar world. All he owned was carried in two small canvas bags, other than the flintlock rifle slung across his shoulder. He did not dwell long near civilization, for he had fled England with a price on his head.

In less than a day he headed west, making his way into the wilderness. At times, that day seemed a lifetime ago but in fact had only been four years.

Now, sitting on the western bank of those dark churning waters of The French Broad, he was very much aware of the danger his present position accorded. Four years of living in the wilderness, of trading with and at times dwelling among the Cherokee, surviving by his own wit and will, had forged him into much more than an ordinarily cautious man. He had learned to, as his Indian given name implied, drift through the thickest forest without making any sound, seemingly able to vanish into thin air on a wisp of wind. Among the Cherokee, he was known as Smoke.

On this day Matthew sat on the bank at an intersection where another sizeable stream flowed into the river. A long pole, one he'd cut from a stand of river-cane, stretched out over the conflux of the two waters. Dangling from the end of the pole, on a line made of braided hair from a horse's tail, dangled a hook. The hook he'd shaped out of wire from a roll he carried in his pack.

He had hardened and tempered the hook in the coals of his campfire earlier that morning. It now held one of a hand full of wiggling red worms he dug up on the bank. Because the current was swift, he'd had to use his belt knife to split one of the round lead balls for his rifle half way in two, then crimped it on the line with his teeth a few inches above the hook. The added weight kept the bait down deep where the fish darted across the sandy bottom in their constant search for tidbits of food curried by the river current.

Six of the brightly speckled trout, already dressed, hung on a forked sapling at the waters edge. Fishing with a line and pole was something the Indians found amazingly hilarious, not nearly as efficient as their traps and wicker woven baskets. But it was a method and a pastime that Matthew had perfected in his homeland of Ireland.

Despite the relaxing effect of fishing, Matthew never, for even an instant, dropped his guard. Unlike the deer skin coat he wore, his survival skills were so well honed, so much an intricate part of his make up that he could not have shed them, even had he chosen to do so.

For that reason, when a kingfisher flew down the river voicing a piercing cry of alarm, it was not unnoticed by a pair of piercing green eyes shaded by a floppy, broad-brimmed leather hat. By the time a pair of woodducks, wings whistling with the speed of their hasty retreat, had passed overhead, Matthew knew someone was approaching from up-river.

When the first whispering sounds of a canoe slicing through the water or the faint noises of wooden paddles being dipped into the river could be discerned, there was no sign that Matthew had ever ventured near the riverbank. Vanished. Smoke.

As the two canoes drew closer, Matthew watched from where he lay, flat on his belly, in the same patch of river cane where he'd cut his fishing pole. The dense maze of green foliage had collected a topping with winter-dried leaves. It offered perfect camouflage for his

27

brown buckskins and leather hat. From the depths of this cover, no one could spot him unless they were deliberately looking for him. And as far as he knew, no one was aware of his presence...

His first real surprise was the construction of the canoes. They were built of birch-bark tied over a framework of willow saplings, the seams covered with pine pitch. These were the boats of the northern tribes, perhaps Ottawa, Delaware, even Shawnee or any number of other tribes of the Iroquois Confederation.

Matthew had heard of this type of boat from other woods runners, like himself, who had ventured further north than he had traveled. How these two canoes had come to be here in this river in the southern mountains was more than a little mystery. At some point, he knew the two canoes had been portaged over a vast expanse of hard to travel land.

The Middle Town Cherokee used dugout canoes. Big cumbersome boats, burned and carved from the trunks of trees, built for fishing or moving cargo. The two boats coming down the river were built with one thing in mind... speed. And while he was sure local Cherokee possessed the skill necessary for their construction, he'd never seen any in his wanderings among them.

As the two boats drew abreast of his hiding place, the mystery took on broader, more perplexing aspects. The occupants of the canoes were not Cherokee.

A white man rode in the front of the first boat. He was dressed like a colonial settler, a frontiersman, but Matthew could tell, even form a distance that his demeanor did not match his attire. For one thing, he made no move to help with the paddling of the canoe.

Instead, he gripped the rails of the boat with well-manicured, spotless white hands that showed not the least trace of having ever preformed menial labor. Like a statue, the man sat with an air of imperial superiority, his nose pointed perpetually upward, a sneer on his face, as though disdaining the whole idea of wasting valuable time on his present task.

In the past, Matthew had seen enough of the type to recognize him immediately for what he was. An Englishman, either of the so-called *gentry* holding some politically appointed title, or an officer in the military. Matthew leaned toward the latter. The man just had the snobbish look, the overbearing haughtiness of a career military officer.

The two Indians in the canoe, behind the disguised British officer, were Shawnee. Matthew knew beyond a doubt that they were either foolish or very fierce and brave warriors, journeying, as they were, so deep into the stronghold of their longstanding, blood enemies, the Cherokee.

The second boat held an even bigger surprise, a young girl, or rather a young Cherokee woman, nineteen or twenty years old. Matthew could not tell a whole lot about her, because of the way she was tied. Her head was bound down to the rail of the boat by a length of leather strap wound tightly around her neck. Her raven black, shoulder length hair dangled down almost to the waters edge.

Even from a distance, Matthew could see the fear written across her young face, the desperation in her large brown eyes. She might have been pretty. It was hard to tell. A gag in her mouth kept her from crying out and the way she was bound almost insured that if she kicked out, somehow managing to sabotage the boat, she would drown.

The two warriors paddling the second canoe could have passed for copies of the first pair. Their stern faces showed no emotion as they dug paddles deep into the river, pulling, straining bronze muscles glistening with the sheen of sweat in the dappled sunlight.

Matthew had no idea why the girl was being held captive, especially in the presence of the Englishman. Had the Shawnee been on a simple raiding party for slaves, they could have picked much easier location and target. No, none of it made sense.

As the canoes swept by, for only the briefest instant, the brown eyes of the girl locked with pair of green ones concealed in the depths of the cane thicket.

Matthew knew with out a doubt the girl had seen him. He was so startled that for an instant he could only blink back at her before dropping his head, concealing his eyes under the brim of his hat.

The two light weight canoes virtually flew along with the aid of the current. In a matter of seconds they were beyond his limited sight.

When he was sure the boats were gone, Matthew stood up, returning the .40 flintlock pistol he had been holding in his hand, back in the leather belt at his waist. A rifle of the same bore hung in the cook of his arm

"None of your bloody business," he mumbled to himself, as he gathered up his gear and the fish. In a few steps he'd disappeared completely among the myriad of giant sycamore and white oak trunks

As he slipped along, like one shadow among many, following the faint traces of an old deer trail, Matthew was troubled. The camp he made earlier that day, under an overhanging rock shelf, shielded by a giant hemlock that would break up the smoke of his campfire, lay about a mile west of the river. He wound his way there, by a different route than the one by which he had left. A caution he had come to rely on.

His thoughts kept straying and he knew this was s dangerous thing to let happen. He should be concentrating on his surroundings but something kept gnawing at the back his mind, like an old toothless hound worrying at a bone, a bad feeling nagged at his thoughts, somewhere just below the depth of awareness. Despite his pretension that the strange occurrences at the river had been none of his concern, the thought of the girl being held against her will bothered him more than he cared to admit.

Winding his way silently through the lonely forest, wading through a sea of fiddle-back ferns and dog fennel, a pair of large brown doe-like eyes, pleading for help, seemed to haunt his every step.

Chapter 3

Laurel tried desperately to hide her pain, to be strong and not show any weakness in front of her captors. She would not give them the satisfaction of seeing her pain. It was hard.

When the men were occupied with maneuvering the canoes around rocks or fallen trees, she had pulled and tugged at the leather straps binding her wrist. Now her arms were raw and bleeding and the straps seemed even tighter than in the beginning. Another leather strap kept her head pulled down tight against the willow framework of the canoe and another cut into the flesh around her ankles.

The men who had bound her were experienced warriors, tying her in such a way that assured she could not kick holes in the birch bark covering the framework of the boats. Nor could she cause it to overturn without running the risk of drowning herself.

It was all she could do to keep from gagging on the foul tasting, filthy rag the men had roughly stuffed in her mouth and held there by greasy rawhide thongs. They tasted like old grease and rancid meat. She had to breathe through her nose and try not to think about the churning in her stomach or the pain in her bladder.

She had been bound in this manner for the better part of the day, only able to do two things...watch the riverbank passing by as each paddle stroke carried her further from the security of her village... and think.

Trying hard not to think about where she was headed, she instead pondered on all of the dark possibilities of her future. This too, she soon discovered, was a treacherous trail on which to be traveling. It was a path leading downhill into an even deeper valley of despair. Instead she concentrated on ever detail she could gather about her captors, looking for any weakness that might help her escape. So far there had been none.

This day had begun like any other. The first rays of morning sunlight filtering around the deer hide covering on the door of her grandfather's cabin had not offered up the least hint of the tragedy soon to befall her.

Every morning at first light she went to the river's edge to fill a hollow gourd with fresh water for brewing tea.

Gray Fox-Killer, her grandfather, had acquired a taste for hot tea from his long time friend, John Stuart, the superintendent the English King assigned to her people. That had been many years ago, before her mother and father had been killed and before her people had been forced further back into the mountains. John Stuart was gone. His deputies, Cameron and McDonald had been good men as well, but they too had been replaced by Stuart's less competent younger brother, Henry.

Her grandfather traded fox and mink hides to the traders for tea, but she had boiled the last of the tea-leaves so many times that they barely darkened the water. Gray-Fox would soon have to return to drinking tea brewed from bark of the three leaf trees or make the journey over to the *Flat Rock* to deal with the trader Smith. Unlike some of the greedy, deceptive white men who traded goods among her people, Smith was part Indian and always dealt more than fairly.

Undoubtedly the warriors who captured her had known about her morning trips to the river. Concealed behind the trunks of huge water oaks along the riverbank, they had waited until she had passed before jumping her. Obviously at least one of them had been watching for a long enough time to pattern her routine. This unsettling revelation gave birth to an even more disturbing question. Why?

Still befuddled by the night's sleep she had been unaware of impending danger until a strong brown arm snaked around her neck, pulling her head back, forcibly locking her jaws shut. Unable to scream, she had tried to kick her way free, only to find herself surrounded by a hand full of tall muscular warriors.

One of her assailants, a fierce looking, scared and scowling brave, she would later learn was the leader of this band, had backhanded her hard enough to momentarily knock her unconscious. In a matter of seconds she found herself bound and slung over the shoulder of a heavily muscled warrior who trotted along with the others as though she were no more than a minor encumbrance.

A line of dark-skinned phantoms, like a disjointed snake with a frog in its belly, slithered its way between the shadowy timbers and morning fog, heading north by

34

east, away from the river until it too was swallowed by the vastness of the dark forest.

Her captors took no pains to cover their footprints as though holding the warriors from her village in such scorn, such contempt as to be of no concern, defying them to follow. This self-assured arrogance of her captors sent icy fingers of dread inching their way down her spine.

The first fuzzy impressions to cross Laurel's mind, after the daze of being brutally backhanded by one of her attackers began to fade, was that these men were from her own tribe, that they were Dragging-Canoe's warriors. It was not unheard of, in the past, for a warrior to kidnap his intended wife, especially if he and his followers were strong enough to not fear reprisal from the girl's family.

Dragging-Canoe had long let it be known that he wanted Laurel for his wife. It was not a case of mutual desire. Out of courtesy she had not out-right rebuked his continued proposals. After all Dragging-Canoe was a powerful and respected chief and she wished to bring him no shame, but then neither did she have any intention of accepting his offers. And neither would her grandfather ever force her into accepting such a union against her will. Her only hope was for the war-chief to grow tired of waiting and turn his attention elsewhere.

It was not that she had any feelings of animosity toward the war-chief, but rather that she had no feelings toward him at all. Most young woman among her people would have felt honored to be the mate of Dragging-Canoe. The wife of such a prestigious warrior, a chief of

35

his own village, tall and handsome and son of the greatly revered chief Attakullculla, or **Little Carpenter**, as he was called in the worlds of the white men, would hold great status of her own. But Laurel was not willing to trade status for and empty heart.

Now draped, like the carcass of a white-tailed deer, across the shoulders of a huge warrior, she could only see the ground passing under his feet or catch an occasional glimpse of the one man behind her. She wondered if Dragging-Canoe had been even more ruthless than she had believed.

It was during one of these brief glimpses that she came to the fearful realization that these men were not Cherokee. They were instead Shawnees, sometimes called Seneca, long-standing enemies of her people and while these men had painted their faces and adorned themselves in the manner of her people, she knew it was some type of disguise, and what was even stranger; all the warriors wore leather boots, not moccasins.

Looking backwards, Laurel was shocked to realize that the tracks they left so carelessly in the soft forest dirt would appear to be made by a group of white, rather than red men.

What purpose did this disguise and trickery serve? Laurel tried hard, but could not seem understand this strange occurrence. She did however know that whatever the reason, for her, it held ill portent...

Laurel's despair deepened. The sudden realization of haven fallen into the hands of her people's worst blood enemies, that she would likely never see her grandfather or her village again and that she could end up dead or worse a slave, tore at her spirit.

By comparison, as bad as that thought had seemed, being kidnapped by Dragging-Canoe would have been like a walk in a warm spring rain.

Chapter 4

From a hundred yards out, Matthew made a complete circuit of his camp, and then stood back for several minutes in the darkening evening shadows, observing the camp and the surrounding area. A fairly large man, at 6' 2" and 210 pounds, he, never the less, moved with the quiet grace and sure-footed certainty of a mountain lion. His moccasins made no betraying sounds as he moved among the undergrowth and forest detritus. His green eyes missed nothing, from the gray squirrel, thinking itself hidden behind a limb on a gnarled old chestnut tree to the new dotting of fox tracks on the path leading his bivouac

. Small footed visitors, looking for scraps of food around his campsite were not what concerned him. It was two legged variety of varmints that made him wary, but as far as he could tell no one had come near.

He was not sure how many wood-runners, red or white, knew this particular camping place. Not many, he figured. He had been shown this secret campsite long ago by his friend Thadis Smith. Also known as Silver Hair or Gray Wolf, Thadis was the son of a Dutch trader and a Cherokee mother. His father had been killed in the war with the French, leaving Thadis to be raised among his mother's people. But he'd inherited his father's looks and so lived the half-life of the mixed breed, not fully accepted in the world of either the red or the white man.

Thadis had named the place Buzzard's Roost. Why, Matthew had no idea. In all the times he and Thadis had camped in the spot, he'd never seen any sign of even a single buzzard living there. Of course, in dealing with Thadis, you never knew, it was just his sort of perverse senses of humor to refer to himself as the old buzzard who came there to roost.

The Roost was at the end of the little out of the way cove, nestled between two steep ridges where an outcrop of granite offered a dry camp even in the nastiest weather. It was one of the first places that he and Thadis had stayed after they met. Matthew had been new to the mountains and green as swamp moss when he first ran into Thadis. It had been a stroke of good fortune on his part for the grizzled old long-hunter had taken him under his wing and had become a mentor, teacher and friend.

As a young man, Thadis had married Whistling Bird, third daughter of Old Raven, but more importantly the great niece of the famous chief, Old Rabbit. She had died trying to give birth to Thadis's only child, a stillborn son.

Thadis had placed Whistling Bird and their son, whom he'd given the name Little Blue Sky, in a burial mound, high atop a rocky faced mountain that Thadis called Looking Glass.

Each spring, for over twenty-five years, in April, Thadis made the trek up the steep mountainside, to the secluded spot to spread white dogwood blossoms on the moss covered mound.

Matthew had accompanied him only once. After seeing the tears in the eyes of his old friend, a man normally as unyielding and tough as a gnarled old oak tree, he figured one time of intrusion into his grief was enough. Thadis seemed to understand this as well and never pressed him to return.

For reasons, possibly known but unspoken, the old trader had taken a liking to the young overgrown Irish boy. Perhaps it was because he sympathized with the pain. the sense of lose he saw hidden deep in those smoldering green eyes or a bitterness stemming from some deep seated sorrow that ripped at the boy's heart and darkened his soul. Whatever the reasons, the two men had formed a strong bond of friendship.

Because of his relationship with Thadis; Matthew had been granted access into the mountain towns of the Cherokee.

Before moving in on the camp, Matthew walked over to fallen oak tree. The huge old monarch, hollowed by age had toppled years ago. Now the bottom of the cavity in its base was filled with dried leaves, chestnuts, pinecones and acorns, a place where, squirrels and chipmunks stored nuts for the raccoons to steal. It also held other items of no consequence to the local wildlife but of vital importance to Matthew. The hollow log made a convenient hiding place for two canvas packs that held not only his camping gear but also his means of making a living. His future.

For the past few years he had moved among the settlers and the Indians alike, making his way, earning what few coins he had collected by repairing broken guns, knives and other things and by trading items from his packs.

**

Matthew had been born in Northern Ireland in the year 1752. Son of William Maybin, a full blooded, hard drinking, harder fisted Irishman, who loved the sea almost as much as he loved Matthews's mother, Amanda Doyle.

Amanda was the daughter of a prominent English family of some means, with both political and social connections. Their relationship was a never-ending source of gossip for months following their scandalous and unsanctified marriage.

How a young, well-schooled and refined English-woman like Amanda had ended up married to a rough and tumble rapscallion like William was a mystery.

Some people, primarily Amanda's mother and older sisters, even went so far as to claim Amanda had been kidnapped, that William was in reality a pirate and a cutthroat and that he used the guise of an honest ships-captain to cover his illicit activities. They ranted that he should be imprisoned, or better yet hanged.

If William had been a pirate, he was a smart and cautious one, for never once was there a wanted poster showing his likeness and offering a reward for his capture. And not once did the sheriff come knocking at his door with a warrant for his arrest, or at least not for anything any more serious than breaking up all the furniture down at the local pub. And as to being a kidnaper and a cutthroat, it was rubbish. Amanda had followed William of her own free will. She loved him dearly

. As for William being a cutthroat that too was untrue. He always remained a gentleman, even as he relieved English see-going merchants of their gold filled purses, treating them with the utmost respect and courtesy.

These things, Matthew knew about his parents, not from experience, but from what he was later told by Alex Doyle, Amanda's older brother.

William and Amanda had perished at sea, their ship broken apart on rocks in a terrible storm. All aboard had drowned. It was rumored that William's ship was running close to the rocky coastline, along the southern tip of the Isle of Man, trying to out maneuver a pursuing British Man-o-War.

The year was 1756. The year of Matthew's fourth birthday, also the same year he was sent to England to live with his Uncle Alex and his wife and three daughters.

As he grew to be a young man, old enough to comprehend the fate that had befallen his parents, Alex had taken his young nephew aside and explained as much of the past as he could. Matthew sensed that his uncle did not hold the animosity toward his parents that the rest of his mother's family seemed to exhibit. In fact, though saddened by her death, when he spoke of his sister and William, of the freedom they had know, his voice seemed filled with a distant, lost sort of envy, as though he too longed to live life free from the constants of English aristocracy.

Alex Doyle was, at that time, one of England's premier gun-makers, specializing in the building of firearms for the wealthy and elite customers from London to Belfast. His guns were masterpieces of the

42

gunsmith art, often ornate and gaudy at the purchaser's request, but well built and masterfully executed.

At the age of fifteen, Alex had convinced his father to allow him to travel to Liege, Belgium to learn from the Master Gun-makers there. Alex had spent eight years in his own apprenticeship. It had been a worthwhile endeavor, for now his work was so much in demand that he could name his own price. When Matthew showed aptitude as a gunsmith, Alex, having no boys of his own, was more than happy to apprentice his nephew. So at the age of ten, Matthew went to school with his cousins during the day and helped his uncle in his shop during the evenings and on weekends. He proved a quick study.

Matthew quickly learned that to be a Master Gun Maker, you needed to master a number of different skills. First you needed a good grasp of mechanical engineering and principle. You had to know wood, to know the different types, the grain structure and how to work and finish them. You needed to be a metallurgist, a chemist, machinists and a blacksmith and an artist all rolled up in one. Of course at the time these things were not considered separate skills, only part of what had to be learned. And more than anything else, Matthew had found that he needed a steady hand and an immeasurable amount of patience.

In a few years, Matthew was proficient enough to begin taking some of the workload around the shop. By the time he was sixteen, he was approaching his uncle in the level of his craft.

**

After building a small fire out of dried wood that would give off very little smoke, Matthew centered a frying pan over two rocks on either side of the fire. As the pan heated he used his belt knife to slice off a couple strips of salted fatback, dropping them onto the hot surface. As the grease began to melt, He laid the trout he'd caught in the pan. When the fish began to sizzle around the edges, he opened his pack, taking out a hand full of ramps and sprinkling them across the cooking fish. He had discovered a patch of the small wild onion like plants earlier that morning, and dug up a double hand full. They would add flavor to the fish as well as being a tasty addition to his meal.

The meal he was preparing was a veritable feast, one he'd been thinking about all day. His stomach was grumbling and his mouth should have been watering over the aroma of the cooking food. It was not. He had lost his appetite. Instead of the contentment he'd anticipated, he felt only a disgruntled kind of restlessness, almost verging on anger, as if he wanted to lash out at something or someone.

He knew full well, could not deny the source of that anger. It was the girl.

It went against the grain, against his very nature to stand by while someone else was hurt or abused. But what could he do, by now the two canoes were miles down stream and he had no idea of what he could have done anyway.

"Damn it," he grumped, mumbling under his breath. .

44

"This land is full of folks a hurtin' and anyway, who appointed you to save the world? Remember what happened the last time. Remember the rabbits."

He ate directly from the pan, with little enthusiasm, pulling the bones from the fish and tossing them into the fire. As he'd prepared his meal, the sun had slipped behind the thin blue line of the distant mountains. The light fading from the western sky, turned from orange to mottled shades of ever darkening purple, until at last, the night shadows reached up to draw the world into its grasp.

Matthew sat with his back against the rock wall of the overhang, watching as the fire burned down to a bed of red glowing embers. He knew better. Looking into the fire did away with his night-sight. It would take several minutes for his eyes to readjust to the darkness if the need arouse. A dangerously long time, especially so since it only took a few second for your enemy to slip up and slit your throat, or drive an arrow through your chest.

He was not particularly worried about that possibility right at the moment, but little lapses could become bad habits. Bad habits got you killed.

Despite his own admonishment, Matthew's thoughts seemed to have a will of their own and somehow had the power to drive back the darkness, not of the night by in his heart, to dispel the melancholy, to block away the loneliness.

For four years living in the wilderness, with exception of a few weeks spent in Indian villages and some time in the company of Thadis or a few other traders, his nights had passed in much the same manner. In loneliness.

Four years of running. From what he was not sure. Maybe he was running from himself. For that matter, he was not even sure why he ran? He was a wanted man, but not in this country. So why did he inflict this self-imposed exile?

He was sure of one thing, it was not his destiny be a great leader or a hero.

Once more his eyes moved to the bright embers as though the glowing red coals held some hidden answer.

"What could I have done," he mumbled under his breath. It was not his place to save the world. Hell, he had not been able to save his own little world. Nor had he been able to save the life of the one girl he had tried to protect. Truth was had he not interfered, she might sill be alive

As the night deepened, the loneliness in his soul regrouped for another assault. Neither the slowly dimming embers of his dying fire, nor the steadily brightening light of a million stars spread across the night sky offered up any answers.

Chapter 5

Six years earlier.

England, May of 1770

From the very moment she stepped through the door, over which hung a sign that read: Alexander Doyle Gun Maker & Associate Esquire, Matthew's life was to be forever more changed.

Introducing herself as Michelle Annette Marcella, she was, without a doubt, the most beautiful woman that he had ever seen. The bright smile warned the lines of her face made his knees feel as though they were made of rubber.

From the bright dress she wore, flowing downward like yellow waterfall over mounded layers of ruffled petticoats, to the way her golden blond hair was whipped up like a halo, and then bound around her head, she was the picture of loveliness. And that smile. She reminded Matthew of a cluster of daffodils, poking their delicate leaves and bell-like blossoms up through the last fading traces of snows in early spring. The yellow flowers a striking contrast to the whiteness of the snow and the piercing blue the sky.

So captivated was Matthew with her beauty that when she first spoke, he found himself tongue-tied. It took a couple of swallows to ease the sudden dryness in his throat. He felt like a bumbling fool when she had to repeat her request. Surely she must view him as some kind of a gawking lummox or slightly touched in the head.

"I should like to speak with Missouri Doyle. Please. If it is possible," she asked for the second time?

"Ah...I'm afraid my uncle is out of town;" Matthew finally managed to get out, fighting not to let his discomfiture make him stammer. "He has gone to purchase some new equipment, won't be back for a couple of weeks."

Upon hearing this news, the girl looked so unhappy, so crestfallen that Matthew felt bad for her.

"Is there anything I can help you with," he asked, finally allowing a few of the butterflies in his stomach to flutter away. "I run the shop when my uncle is away."

"Alas, I do not mean to belittle your skills," she said with a sigh, "but I have been told that your uncle is the only man in this city to whom I can trust to help with this problem. You see, I foolishly managed to drop my gun and now, I fear it is broken." Having said this, she proceeded to reach into her purse and pull out a very small, delicately made flintlock pistol.

Matthew was astounded both by the fact that such a delicate slip of a girl, such a tiny damsel, could or should possibly be in such distress as to have need of such a weapon and also by the unique design and execution of the work involved in its construction.

At the same time, he could feel his face growing a little heated by the fact that a woman, no mere girl, one whom he'd never seen before, could possible presume to

48

pass judgment on his skill. His uncle had enough faith in him to leave him in charge. That of itself would have been credentials enough for an ordinary customer.

Just as quickly as she had ruffled his tail feathers, the girl smoothed them away by simply flashing another of those disarmingly beautiful smiles. And as simple as that, she handed him the little pistol.

"I'm sure your skills will be more than sufficient," she said. "I am afraid that I am more than a little desperate."

The gun felt tiny in Matthew's hand. Again he marveled at the craftsmanship and balance of the diminutive little weapon. The name, Phillip Chesspite was engraved on the barrel. Matthew had heard the name before. He was a French Gun-maker of some renowned.

"My great uncle," she said, watching him read the name. "It was a gift, given after a lengthy discussion failed to dissuade me from coming on this trip to London.

He was worried for my safety, but the chance to perform in a play before the Royal Court, perhaps even the King, was much too grand an opportunity to pass up. He said that since I refused to listen to reason, to remain in France, then the least he could do was give me a weapon to defend my virtue from English barbarians. I had no idea he would be proven right, so quickly."

"I suppose, since I am only half English, then that makes me only half barbarian," Matthew said a little sardonically.

"I must apologize," she said, her expression truly contrite. "I did not mean for my words to come out in such a manner. My grasp of your language is at times, struggling at best. I did not mean to imply that all Englishmen were scoundrels, only that there are bad men in any country where you might find yourself, even France. And I must admit my current problems stem from the uncouth actions of one from my own country."

"I suppose you are right," Matthew replied, mollified but not understanding what he had been thinking. It seemed that he was trying to find some reason to pick a fight with this girl. He was normally easy going, never this testy, on edge. What kind of effect was this girl having on him? It was crazy. It was not in his nature to behave in such a boorish unseemly manner and especially not around women.

To cover up his discomposure Matthew gave quick perfunctory examination the gun. He spotted the problem immediately. The trigger moved back and forth of its own violation.

"The sear spring is broken," he said, maybe just a trifle too smugly, but glad to be back in his own element. "I can make you a new one, but it will need to be hardened and tempered and it needs to be covered with powdered lime so it cools very slowly, overnight. Then tomorrow morning I can fit it to your gun."

"Oh well," she said, obviously disappointed that he could not affect immediate repair to her pistol, but smiling none the less. "If I must wait till tomorrow, then it is as it must be. If that scoundrel, Rafael chooses this evening to accost me, then he will have to wait till tomorrow to be shot."

While her words suggested that she wished to make light of her worries, Matthew was suddenly bothered by an uneasy feeling that her flippant manner was in truth, a cover-up for a genuine sense of fear. He had no idea, could not imagine, why anyone would wish to cause harm to someone as obviously innocent as this very lovely young woman. He felt a sudden flush of anger directed at anyone villainous enough commit such an atrocity, followed by a wave of embarrassment at his newfound protectiveness of someone he'd just met.

"I have a gun you could borrow," Matthew said, struggling to overcome the butterflies in his stomach. "It's a little larger than yours, but I'm sure you could handle it well....That is...I mean if you would like too."

"Oh, that is very sweet of you, but I would not wish to imposition you."

"It is not an imposition. I would feel better if you took it," Matthew said. "In fact, I think you should let me walk you back to where ever it is you are staying...I mean to make sure no one bothers you."

"I think I should like that very much," she said with a smile that turned Matthews's legs a little rubbery once again. "But what of your work? I do not wish to take you away from it."

"I can finish it when I get back," Matthew said, a little more confidently than he really felt. It would take him into the night to fashion the spring for her gun, but at the moment it seemed of little importance when compared to the chance to spend time in her company.

Reaching under the counter, Matthew took out a .36

caliber flintlock pistol. It was a gun he had built in his spare time, under his uncle's supervision. Master Doyle had accorded him high marks on it construction and finish.

Tucking the gun in the waist-ban of his pants, and then taking the keys from a wooden peg, he held open the door for the beautiful young woman. He hoped she had not noticed the shaking of his hands.

Locking the door and placing the key in his pocket, Matthew had to hide his surprise, as well as his pleasure, when Michelle looped her arm around his.

Walking down the street, the last rays of evening sun gave her silky blonde hair almost radiant glow.

Her smile reminded Matthew of a painting he'd once seen of a Greek goddess. He felt giddy, his heart racing and his head swam as though he'd spent too much time in the local alehouse.

In no hurry for the moment to end, he walked as slowly as possible, he hoped...without being too obvious in his lagging. Had anyone asked, he would have freely avowed to being in love, and strolling through heaven with an angle on his arm.

Chapter 6

The small fire Matthew had used to cook his evening meal had long since burned down to a few faintly glowing embers. In the sky, the position of the stars told him that it was still a few hours until dawn. Anyone looking in the direction of those few glowing coals would have seen only the reclining figure of a man, his back against the rock face, a buckskin jacket pulled up over his shoulders like a cloak, a leather hat slouched low over his head.

Matthew had been awake for several minutes now, but as yet had not moved a muscle. Instead he strained every available sense, surveying the night, trying to determine what had awakened him, what had the alarms clanging in his head

A small sound, muffled, nothing really, a dry twig snapping ever so faintly under a layer of winter dampened leaves, had riveted his attention. Suddenly Matthew was acutely aware that he was not alone.

His ears told him that someone or something was stalking up on his campsite, sixty yards out, but stealthily inching ever closer to his sleeping spot. The faint wisp of a smell, a combination old wood smoke and sweat soaked leather, reaching his nostrils, told him that this was no animal but rather a human predator stalking his position.

More than twenty feet away from the small cedar bush that he'd cut to drape his coat and hat over, Matthew eased out from under the wool blanket where he'd actually been sleeping. His moccasins made no sound as he, like a spectral apparition, disappeared among the dark labyrinth of night shadows. Nor did the weak starlight give any betraying glint from the knife gripped firmly in his right hand, one whose blade he kept deliberately tarnished for that very reason.

As silently as a cat, he moved away from the camp, making a short circle, coming up to the left and slightly ahead of his stalker. Against the trunk of a huge hemlock, pressed against the rough bark, he stood erect and rigid, no more than a slight aberration of the trees original shape.

Time slowed, taking on a surreal quality that gave greater definition to even the tiniest sounds. The fluttering tiny insect wings, the chirp of a cricket, the noise of a falling leaf tattling through bare branches, seemed to rumble as loud as thunder. Even the starlight seemed to take on a peculiar disrupted quality, moving slower, like individual bits of sparking dust falling from the sky, only to be absorbed the flowing ocean of darkness.

Suddenly a bit of night gloom, detaching itself from the rest, flowed into the dark form of a man. He was standing directly beside the tree where Matthew waited. After another short pause, noiseless as river fog the figure glided a few steps forward, its movements seemingly more fluid than mechanical.

As thought he melted and become a part of the primal forest giant, a thing of wood and bark rather than flesh and bone, Matthew watched and waited. When the interloper started forward once more, he took one silent step behind, then bringing his arm around, he placed the six inch length of razor edged steel against the front of the mans neck.

"Getting a little careless in your old age ain't you Thadis," Matthew asked, in a quiet whisper? "If I'd been looking for hair, I would have had yours before you ever knew it was gone."

"Careless hell," the man grumped. "Thought I never would break enough damn sticks to wake you up. You must have been sleeping sounder than a wintering bear."

"Well this bear's been a hearing you blunder around for the past hour and smelling you for two," Matthew said, unable to keep the grin off his face or out of his voice. "Besides, I think we see who is the better man. My blade tells the tale." To make his point, he applied a little pressure to the deer antler handle of his knife. Not much, for he had no real desire to hurt his long time friend and teacher.

"Yah, the blade always speaks the truth," said the man, Thadis Smith, also applying a little pressure to the knife in his own hand.

For the first time, Matthew became aware of the delicate touch of a foot long length of cold steel blade pressing upward into his straddle. Then the pressure eased up. Without as much as a whisper of noise, the big blade disappeared back into its deer-hide sheath.

"It's good to see you Thadis,' Matthew said lowering his own knife. "Figgered you would have gotten tired of lugging around that damn big knife. You know, if you ever slip into a deep hole in a river, all that weight's gonna drag straight to the bottom."

"It'll take a lot of water to drown this ol' boar coon," Thadis grumped.

This was a game they had played often the past couple of years. The verbal bantering, as well as the testing of each others physical abilities was a long established a part of their relationship, a ritual as familiar as shaking hands. They were student and teacher, although, over time, that distinction had begun to fade.

"How did you know I'd be here," Matthew asked?

"Remember who showed you this spot?"

"Yah, you did, but you couldn't have known I'd be here."

"Ran into William Timberlake. He passed by my place a couple of days ago. Said he'd run into you a few days ago, south of Davidson's Fort. Said you fixed a broken frizzen spring on his rifle. Also said you was headed over this direction. Just guessed you might be camped here."

"I am camped here...You know, a few more years practice and you'll get the hang of this tracking and trailing business."

"Is that a fact, well then, being I am such a greenhorn, do you mind lowering that mean little sticker, before I hurt myself laughing at it?"

"Good to see you, Thadis," Matthew said, lowering and sheathing his blade.

Ten minutes later, after rekindling the fire and putting

56

coffee beans supplied by Thadis, in the pot to boil, the two men sat watching the approaching dawn as well as savoring the warmth of the blaze. Neither designed to speak as the coffee boiled. In the past they had spent much time together in this same manner. Neither man feeling the necessity to disturb this short time of quiet contemplation.

A great deal of emotion passed, unspoken between these two friends. Feelings that neither man could have expressed had either been a willing to speak the words. Things that the veneer of civilization had clouded or erased and yet here in the wilderness were the only true virtues by which a man could be judged. Virtues like honesty, loyalty, and unfaltering trust, things that could not be conveyed with spoken words, but were proclaimed by deeds.

In the wilderness friendship was far more that a shallowly spoken word. It was a code of honor that men lived by. Having a friend meant having of an extra pair of eyes to watch your back or a hand to help if you stumbled and fell. It was someone to simply sit across the fire from, listening to the sounds of the wilderness at night.

An unspoken flood of emotions passed between the two men with as little disturbance as the movement of the stars in their eternal trek across the firmament. It had been three months since they had last parted company, yet both men slipped easily into an old and familiar routine.

The strong coffee not only tasted good, but it felt good too, warming his fingers through the tin cup and an giving warm glow to his insides, helping fight off the early morning chill.

"What brings you over this way," Matthew asked as he divided the remaining coffee between the two cups? "Thought you were still be working on the cabin you were building over near the Flat Rock."

Flat Rock was large outcrop of granite, several acres in size, fairly level, surrounded by towering pines and hemlocks, located along the Estatoe trail, about thirty miles to the east, near where the Blue Ridge Mountains dropped suddenly into the foothills of South Carolina. Estatoe was the trade path between the Middle and Lower towns of the Cherokee and was a central meeting place where they gathered in the spring and fall to trade furs and vegetables among themselves or for tools and trinkets from the local traders.

Thadis, the son Dutch/English trader, Preston Smith, and Cherokee mother, Sara Longleaf, had grown up among the Cherokee and though he looked more white than Indian, his heart was of the People…as the Cherokee referred to themselves. He could pass for a white when visiting white settlements or cities like Charles-Town. But if you cut deep enough, penetrated to the heart, Thadis's blood flowed red, in more ways than one.

Normally a lighthearted and easy going, Thadis loved a good prank or a long swig from a crock of ale. When angered the gnarled old frontiersman could be as tough and stubborn as a hickory stump and as mean as a sow bear protecting her cubs. Matthew could not think of another person in the world whom he would rather trust with his life.

Thadis emptied his cup then wiped his mouth on his buckskin sleeve.

"Trying to stop a war," Thadis said at last. The tone of the old trader's words, the look in his steel gray eyes conveyed the same seriousness as if he'd said he was tracking a wounded bear or side-stepping the buss of an angry timber rattler.

This was another thing about Thadis Smith, when angry; he was one of the most dangerous men Matthew had ever known. Never mean or bullying, always soft-spoken and slow to anger, he had a very defined sense of right and wrong and if you did manage to incur his wrath it was prudent plan to stay well of his path. In his younger years, Thadis had been known among his people as *waya gago vtivhiluhiyui geluhvsdi* (the wolf who never howls). As the years passed and his hair began to turn, this name evolved into simply *Gray Wolf.*

"The war with England," Matthew asked? For the past year talk of war had hung like dark ominous thunderclouds on the horizon. Like wildfire, rumors raged up and down the frontier. He'd heard that colonist in Boston, dressed like Indians had tarred and feathered the tax collector, John Malcomb and dumped a shipload of tea into the harbor. It seemed only a matter of time before hostilities broke out. Hell, for all he knew it might already have. He had been in the wilderness for some time now, cut off from any news from the east.

"Not with England," Thadis said, his tone somber. "That war is coming and I don't believe anyone can do a damn thing stop it. What I am trying to head off right now is another war, one with my people."

59

Although Thadis was half white, Matthew knew that when he referred to...his people... he was talking about his mother's people.... The Cherokee.

"I knew there was a lot of trouble being stirred up by some of the younger war chiefs," Matthew said. "Especially, Double-Head and Dragging-Canoe and maybe even Pumpkin-Boy or Standing- Turkey, but I thought old chief Oconostota had them pretty well reigned in."

"At one time, he did," Thadis said. " But Oconostota is getting on in years and the land he, Attakullculla and Savanooka traded to the Transylvania Company at Sycamore Shoals last spring cost him a great deal of prestige among our people. You were there, same as me. You saw how angry Dragging-Canoe was; saw how he publicly berated the old chiefs for the deal he made with Richard Henderson and Nathaniel Hart."

"Well, I don't care much for Dragging-Canoe, but I can sympathize with him on that issue. It still seems like an awfully one-sided deal. Someone played Oconostota for a fool, if you ask me," Matthew said. "Trading all the land between the Kentucky and Tennessee Rivers, millions of acres, for a cabin full of muskets, powder and shot, seemed more like a giveaway than a fair trade."

"Oconostota may be old and feeble but he is far from being a fool. I guess it depends on how you look at it," Thadis said. "I believe all the old chiefs know from hard experience that they cannot win a war against the whites, at least in the long run, whether they are English, French or the colonial settlers. It's something they have known ever since old Attakullculla and six other chiefs traveled

60

to England over forty years ago. They know there is an unending supply of white men to replace any they kill and that if their people are to survive, they must adapt to white ways. The land the chiefs traded off was territory they won from the Shawnee years ago, when the nation was stronger. The last Cherokee/ White war, fifteen years ago, annihilated over half the population of the lower and middle towns. Not enough warriors to defend it against a new Shawnee attack. Better to have white settlers there than relinquish the land to their ancient enemies. Let Boone and the Wataugans wanting to settle there fight the Shawnee for their land."

The old trader grew quiet and pensive, his face, in the reflection of the dying fire, evincing a multitude of sorrows.

Matthew, from past experience knew that his friend was trapped between two colliding worlds. Understanding both but helpless to change either. All Matthew could do was to remain quiet as his friend stirred a big spoon in a cauldron of conflicting emotions.

"You know," Thadis said, at last breaking the silence. "Back around '60, when the English were fighting the French, I had a cousin among the twenty-four white settlers massacred by Ettowee's warriors in a raid at Long Cain Creek, a sweet little girl, only fifteen years old. In the war that followed, I lost cousins, uncles, nieces and aunts as well as my grandfather. I lost friends and family on both sides. No one won. Both sides lost."

"It seems the same, no matter where in the world you go," Matthew said sympathizing with his friends anguish. "In England and Ireland, it's the Catholics and the Protestants killing each other over whose religion is best, or in the Middle East it's the Muslims and Christians slaughtering each other in the name of God or Allah. I guess there will always be those who would force their own beliefs on others or take what is not theirs by force. There never seems to be enough good men to stand up to the oppressors."

"I guess you're right," Thadis said, using a dry twig to stir aimlessly at the glowing coals. "One thing is for sure, times are changing, and the old ways are gone. Only the young braves are filled with enough piss and vinegar to believe if they unite all the tribes together, they can drive all the white men back into the sea."

"I've been told that the Shawnee Chief, Cornstalk and a few others from the Iroquois Confederation have been moving up and down the frontier trying to unite all the southern and northern tribes," Matthew said.

"Heard the same thing myself. Might work too," Thadis replied. "If they could stop fighting among themselves for long enough, but you put a Shawnee and a Cherokee on the same path, blood is gonna soak the ground. They have been at each others throats for hundreds of years. Smoke from a thousand peace pipes ain't gonna change that one whit."

"One thing for sure," Matthew said. "Dragging-Canoe is pushing the whole nation closer and closer to an outright war every day. Two weeks ago, I came across a burned homestead over on the headwaters of the Yadkin. One man, one woman and two young girls, all scalped. I buried them in a single grave."

"Well, things are about to get a whole lot worse," Thadis said, at last shaking off his melancholy mood.

"Someone   has   been kidnapping young Indian
women and girls. All really a dozen or more have come
up missing in the past two weeks."

'"Well, I'll be damn," Matthew said, jumping so
abruptly to his feet that Thadis grabbed for his gun.

Chapter 7

"What do you mean you saw one of the girls being carried off," Thadis said, his voice sounding slightly agitated and little elevated as he slide his oversized knife back into it's buckskin sheath at his side. Mumbling under his breath he placed his rifle back against the tree where seconds ago it had been grabbed up.

After hearing Thadis tell about a number of young Cherokee women and girls being kidnapped, Matthew had jumped up in such fervor that older man was sure they were under attack by some unseen foe. By the time Matthew had gotten the out the words, saying that he'd seen some kind of strange occurrence yesterday on the river, Thadis had been crouched, knife in one hand, gun in the other, his eyes intently searching the darkness.

"Sorry," Matthew said, squatting down on his knees and looking a little sheepishly at his friend. "Didn't mean to spook you. Its just that its something I've been thinking about ever since this past morning, trying to decide what to do about it."

"Tarnation boy. Are you going to tell me what happened or are you waiting to say the words as a eulogy at my funeral when I die of old age."

"I was getting to it, you grumpy old bear," Matthew said, his grin belying the gruffness of his words.

To this Thadis only rolled his eyes and groaned.

Matthew began recounting the previous day's events, trying to accurately describe his strange encounter with the canoes and captive girl. What he could not find a way to put into words was the strange effect the whole thing was having on his mind. He was torn between the need to act, to do something to help the girl and the fear that if he interfered it would only make things worse. He left these things unsaid.

When he finished his tale, Matthew sat back down, all the while watching his friends face for some indication of what he was thinking.

For a while, the old trader sat pondering on the story. He had no doubts about the validity of what he had been told. If Matthew said he'd seen Shawnee warriors dressed like Cherokee, then that's what they were. He trusted the young mans judgment and skills as much as if he'd witnessed the events with his own two eyes. What he was trying to figure was what it all meant, how it tied in with what he already knew.

"You say the Englishman looked like a soldier," Thadis said, at last ending the long silence.

"Not just a soldier...an officer or gentry...someone use to giving orders and having others do their work."

"What about the girl. Did you get a look at her?"

"Couldn't tell much....the way she was tied....appeared to be young...less than twenty. Smallish build. Big eyes... probably pretty. One thing was sure though, she looked frightened as the devil."

"Sounds like you're describing old Gray-Fox-Killer's

granddaughter, "Thadis said. "It don't make no sense though. She was kidnapped, by a group of about a half dozen white men early yesterday morning about fifteen miles up river. The braves from her village tracked them for or five miles east before they finally lost the trail."

"You think they could have circled around, made their way back to the river and the boats," Matthew asked?

"From what you saw yesterday, I don't think it could have been much of anything else. But it ain't the normal way of thinking for an Indian. Their minds just don't follow that kind of a twisting path. They might have tried to cover their trail, make a few switchbacks to throw off any pursuit, but on their own they would never think to disguise their tracks. It takes a white man to come up with this kind of deviousness, which, I guess pretty much explains the Englishman you saw in one of the canoes."

"How did you get involved in all this," Matthew asked?

"Gray-Fox sent a runner, one of his nephews over to my place to bring me back. He needed me to help look for his granddaughter, but also needed someone to read a letter that the warriors found tied to a tree just before they lost the trail."

"A letter," Matthew said, astonishment written across his face. "What kind of a letter?"

"It was supposedly written by the newly established colonial congress, full of big words and fancy phrases, but once you cut through the dross, it's nothing more that glorified ransom demand. It aint the only one either. It seems they've turned up in other places, all saying the same thing. They said that the girls had been taken to

Charles-Town, where they would remain as *guests* of the colonial government, to insure that Cherokees remained neutral in the war with England."

"I believe that's got to be the most idiotic thing I have ever heard of," Matthew said. "Do you believe it's true?"

"Not for one minute," Thadis said, not trying to hide the scorn in his voice. "Any damn fool knows that tactics like that won't work with the Cherokee any more than they would with any other tribe. It won't do anything except incite them to even more hostility against the colonist, set more warriors on the warpath and cause more deaths on both sides of the river."

"It's hard for me to believe that this new congress would sanction such low skullduggery," Matthew said. "I thought the whole idea behind this war was to do away with tyranny, not create new versions of it."

"First off, I ain't so sure all this business is what it's made up to be," Thadis said. "For the most part, my mother's people have long been Tories, remaining loyal to the English Crown. Superintendent Stewart, the king's representative, on an almost daily basis, warns them that they must remain neutral in the impending conflict."

"I saw him at Chota, last winter, presenting his plan to the council of Chiefs," Matthew injected. "He seems like a good man. I believe he has the best interest of the Cherokee in his heart."

"I think he does as well," Thadis said. "But I'm not so sure about the English Parliament. Do you really believe they want any of the tribes to stay out of this war? I don't think so... They learned a hard lesson fighting the French. If the Cherokee chiefs have not sent warriors north to fight the Shawnee, who were allied with the French, that war might have ended differently. No. They might not want it known, but if it comes down to a fracas, the English would come out way ahead of the game if this new Continental Congress had to divide it's efforts, send part of it's army against the Cherokee."

"I remember hearing my Uncle talk about the war with France," Matthew injected. "But at the time I didn't pay much attention because I was young and didn't think it was something I needed to know."

"Well I know, for a fact, because I fought with them. Back then, I was a young, a reckless hellion, just looking for trouble. Found it too. Bad thing was though, after the fighting was over, the folks up along the Ohio River valley turned against us, left us to our own devices, cut us lose to make our way back home, on foot and with no food and very few provisions. Hell of a payback for pulling their behinds out of the fire. We broke up into smaller groups to head south, back to the Carolinas. Some the warriors were so angry over this treatment that they started raiding homesteads, stealing food and horses, as they made their way home through the backwoods of Virginia. Shortly after that, a group of Virginia volunteers attacked ambushed one band of near starving Cherokee warriors, killing twenty-four warriors. To say that the chiefs were outraged by this latest treachery would have been paramount to calling the Atlantic Ocean, a big pond. Eventually this open wound festered to the point that it lead to the massacre of Long Cain Creek where twenty-four white men, women and children were slaughtered, in retaliation, by a bunch of hotheaded braves. After that, an all out Cherokee and white war was inevitable. A War that wiped out half the Cherokee population ended only when the old Chiefs turned over a hundred square miles of territory, all the land between the Wateree and the Santee rivers to the white settlers."

With a dead twig the old trapper absently stirred last few glowing embers in the fire pit. His eyes seemed focused not on the present but on some far distant time in memory.

"No," Thadis said a last. "I do not think my mother's people will any time soon be persuaded to fight for any cause other than their own."

For a time both men sat without speaking. In the quiet of early morning a few birds began to stir in the nearby underbrush, their first tentative calls sounding a lonely herald to the approaching dawn. Stars along the horizon slowly faded as the eastern skyline took on shades of pink and red. Somewhere in the distant woods a gray fox voiced its high pitched shrill bark, advertising his presence to the dawn and any receptive female close enough to hear. His plaintive call aroused no response other than to set of a chorus of owls along the distant river bottom.

Normally the brief few moments of half-light between day and night would have been a time of quiet peaceful contemplation for both men. A time to ponder and plan the day's chores and activities, but this day's sunrise offered no solace, no peace of mind. Instead in the growing light of a new dawn, both men thoughts, though

69

unspoken, were the much the same. No words were necessary for each man understood the implications of those thoughts.... The Cherokee might not be willing to fight for either side, but if they could be goaded into a war with the colonist, it would serve the English cause ever bit as well. The end result, like the rising sun, would paint the horizon with shades of red, paint it with the color of blood.

It was an hour past sunrise. The two men had spent the morning trying to form some plan for averting the impending bloodshed. It seemed a hopeless obstacle. Too many forces had been set into motion. Both men felt as helpless as dried leaves in the path of a whirlwind.

"What do you think they will do with the girls," Matthew asked?

"Hard to say," Thadis said, rubbing his hands through his long gray hair. "Kill 'em, maybe but most likely trade 'em to other Shawnee for slaves as payment for their help. Be more merciful to slit their throats."

At first Matthew had trouble believing that the King of England could condone such brutal atrocities, but then he remember how his own Irish decedents had been treated in much the same manner. And even the experiences of his own life, having to flee London as a criminal.

"One thing is for sure," he said. "They would not be heading to Charles-Town."

"No, Thadis replied, "they won't be staying with the river for too long either."

"What makes you say that?"

"About thirty miles north of here the French Broad

makes a wide westerly turn before flowing into the Little Tannasa and then right into the heart of the Cherokee stronghold. Also the river gets awful rough over near the hot springs area, lots of rocks and white-water."

"You think they'll have to portage around it?"

"Could, but likely they'll abandon the canoes. Strike out overland for Shawnee territory or maybe east toward the Virginia coast."

"You think we got any chance of catching up to 'em."

"Maybe? Problem is one of us needs to go to Chota to try and convince the chiefs to keep a tight hold on all the young braves, then on to Charles-Town or at least over to Davidson's Fort to head off any attack. That only leaves one of us to take on who knows how many Shawnee and English."

"You're the only one with any influence among the chiefs," Matthew said. "The people at Davidson's Fort welcome me, but I don't know a soul down in Charles-Town."

"Trouble is you don't know anything about the country they are heading into."

"Guess I'll learn," Matthew said with a weak grin. "Besides I was getting a little bored hanging around here anyway."

During their conversation, Matthew had been sorting though his packs and gear, taking out the bare minimum of things he might need. Powder...shot... extra flints...a little dried meat. A short, stout Hickory bow and a dozen arrows, that Thadis had helped him make, made and

71

taught him how to use, went into the necessary pile. The rest of his supplies went back into the hollow log where he'd hidden them earlier.

He needed to travel as light as possible. He couldn't hope to catch the boats traveling on foot and sticking to the riverbank. They were much to fast, but like all rivers the French Broad followed a meandering course. Using a piece of charcoal from the fire and the back of the ransom letter, Thadis was busy drawing a map of the river showing landmarks where

Matthew could cut across country, making up time. Plus the canoes could not be used at night for fear of crushing their fragile bark hulls on hidden rocks and logs. By pushing himself hard, traveling when he could at night, Matthew hoped to make up a little more time.

Both men suffered from a compulsive need for action, to be on their way. So after a short discussion of the map and of what Matthew could expect to see in that part of the country, they shook hands and picked up their gear to leave.

"One more thing,' Thadis said as they parted. "Keep your eye on your back-trail. I got an itch between my shoulder blades that says there's trouble brewing close at hand. If it turns out the girl you saw in the canoe is Gray-Fox-Killers granddaughter, all hell is gonna break lose around here. Dragging-Canoe has been trying to talk her grandfather into marrying her off to him for a couple of years now. So far, the old man has left it up to the girl and she ain't having nothing to do with it. If that hothead finds out she's gone, you can bet he's gonna come looking. If he can bring her back unharmed, as a gift to Gray-Fox, then the old man will have no choice but to offer her back in marriage. And if he don't find her, Dragging-Canoe's gonna spill a lot of blood before his vengeance is sated."

With that said, the old trader turned and with a few long ground eating strides, vanished among the gray tree trunks.

With a sigh, Matthew slide the bow on his shoulder into a comfortable position, made sure his knives, arrow quiver and pistol were secure. After checking the powder in the pan of his flintlock rifle, he took it in hand, at a point where it balanced well, then set off in the opposite direction, not running but in a steady ground eating trot, one he could maintain for long hours.

"Rabbits," he mumbled under his breath. "How in the world could two half grown, skinny rabbits have caused such a bloody lot of trouble?"

Chapter 8

Her wrist bound painfully tight by tough leather straps and being led along like an unwilling stray dog was only marginally better than being carried like a sack of potatoes over the shoulder of a bull necked warrior as she'd been for the past few hours. It was all she could do to keep up with the pace set by her captors. Any time she slipped or lagged behind, a hard yank on the straps binding her wrist was a painful reminder of the low esteem with which she was held.

Laurel could tell by the position of the sun that her captors were gradually changing direction, in fact, was making a large circle. She'd felt certain the men who'd captured her would make an arrow straight retreat away from her village. Instead they now seemed determined to return. She knew she couldn't be so lucky and this, of course, proved to be true. Her captors soon met up with another group of warriors.

Then a strange thing happened. One of her abductors took a piece of paper from a leather pouch and attached it to a tree with a leather thong. Then she was handed over to the second group of warriors and promptly led away. These men, however, took great pains to hide their trail.

It took a couple of hours before Laurel was finally able to make any sense of their strange behavior. At what she estimated to be a half a days walk north of her village, they came to a small deep stream that fed into the main river. Concealed in the underbrush along the river were two canoes, unlike any Laurel had ever seen, though she had heard stories told about them. Birch-bark covered, lightweight boats, built for speed, though not suitable for shallower streams of the mountains, the French Broad for the next five or six days walking would be deep and relatively free of rough water.

Laurels hopes dipped to an even deeper level as she realized that if her captors were skilled in handling these canoes, she would have no hope of being rescued by warriors from her village. Then to make things worse, when they reached the boats, they were joined by two more men. The first man was an Englishman, wearing a pompous, haughty expression that bespoke of an inner disdain for anyone of lesser status than his own, which she could tell included everyone present, even his own men. The other man was a tall thin faced Shawnee warrior with a surly disposition and disease pocked face.

The Englishman gave orders to his gruff companion who in turn, translated, then relayed them to the other warriors. Laurel had a fair understanding of the white man's words. She had spent many hours learning form Reverend Hollister, who called himself a missionary, visiting her village to try a *save* " her people. She had never been quite sure what he'd been trying to save them from, but learning the words helped her in dealing with the white traders when they came to her village. Because of this, she understood that she was to be tied into the front of one of the canoes. However, nothing in the man's word had implied that she should be treated such harsh disregard, that she be shoved, jerked and

75

painfully bound in an awkward, uncomfortable manner. Undoubtedly the Shawnee took on those responsibilities as a labor for the love of spite. In their eyes she was female, of no value other than for their pleasure, but worse, she was viewed as having the potential to bare children, male children, who would grow up under the strange irony of being enemies to their mother's own people.

So it was that Laurel, a member of the deer clan, granddaughter of Gray-Fox Killer, as well a very frightened young woman, found herself, gagged and bound to the front of a strange tree-bark covered boat, headed toward an unfamiliar forbidding land and future that seemed dark, fearful and stripped of even the faintest glimmer of hope.

By the time the sun had started to drop into the treetops bordering the western side of the river, Laurel had all but given up hope of rescue from her village. No one there would suspect the method by which she was being carried away. The unrelenting paddle strokes of the Shawnee warriors had already carried the canoes more than a days walk down steam. Even after most of a day spent as a captive, her situation seemed unreal, like a bad dream lingering long past the passing of night, or a mind craze brought on by eating bad mushrooms.

Wish as she might to the contrary, Laurel knew how real and desperate her situation truly was. And try as she might to not let her enemies see any weakness, the burning in her wrists, the agony in her neck and shoulders, along with the pain in her unrelieved bladder, finally won out, released a trickle of tears that flowed down her cheeks, disappearing over the edge of the canoe, mingling without a trace into a river that had once

76

seemed her friend, but now turned tormentor.

Because of the tears in her eyes, Laurel almost missed seeing the man hidden on the riverbank, or rather seeing his eyes, for they were the only things visible in the green tangle of river cane and there for only a brief second before blinking shut..

At first, Laurel thought she might have imagined seeing those strange disembodied eyes. In her desperation, did her mind create what she needed to see? No she told herself as she drifted on by; she knew they had been real, alive, deep green and swirling with a backwash of emotions.

What things lay hidden behind those eyes, she could not comprehend, but she had no doubt they were the eyes of a white man. It seemed strange that such a brief glance could reveal so much emotion, anger, regret, perhaps more than anything else, compassion.

White men had seldom brought anything good to her people and yet strangely, in that brief fleeting glimpse of those disembodied eyes, Laurel found a tiny glimmering spark of hope. In the crushing darkness that threatening to swallow her soul, it was a tiny pinpoint of light, distant, weak and flickering, but enough to focus her mind on and know that she was not alone.

CHAPTER 9

Crouched behind the moss covered trunk of a ancient, fallen hemlock laying halfway up a steep rocky ridge covered with ferns and dog-fennel, Dragging-Canoe watched as a solitary figure, a lone man dressed in buckskins, made his way along the path beside the river. Five other warriors lay concealed in similar shadowy nooks along the ridge, their brown skin and smoked stained deer-hide clothing making them all but invisible against the backdrop of winter dried leaves.

From the way the man moved, in long ground eating strides, his feet making not the least trace of noise as he moved along the trail, and from his gray shaggy hair and beard and the manner of his dress, Dragging-Canoe knew this was the trader who cabined near the *Flat Rock*, the half-blood, Smith.

For a few seconds, he contemplated leading his warriors ahead to set up an ambush and kill the old trader. It would be risky. Smith was not a man to be caught easily unaware. Then there was also the matter of his friend, the **guloque-digotlvsgi, (fixer of guns)** the man known as *Smoke.*

Smith's friend was a dangerous man and likely to be somewhere close. Also, if they should fail to take the old man's scalp and word got back to the old chiefs, it would be big trouble. Smith was well liked among the villages, and a friend to Attakullculla, as well as Nancy Ward, the head of the women's council at Chota.

Ultimately it was the fear of incurring the wrath of one of the ghigau that stayed his hand from ambushing

Smith. The ghigau, or revered women of each village, were responsible for preparing the **black drink** consumed by the warriors to purify their bodies and bring good fortune, before going into battle. He was not willing to risk bringing out bad spirits to cause trouble for him and his warriors over a single gray scalp.

The old chiefs, his father included, were like young children, weak, frightened, like women cowering in their lodges, afraid to bloody the war hatchet against the Unakas, the white intruders. They listened over much to the endless chattering of the Scotsman, Henry Stuart, the so called superintendent assigned by the English King to guide his people. For as many years as he could remember, Dragging-Canoe had listened to the tales told by the old chiefs who'd traveled across the ocean to visit the so called ***Great King*** in a place called England, had endured the rambling of old men like Little Carpenter, who preached that a war against the white man could not be won, that the only path was to make peace, to live as the whites lived.

Dragging-Canoe did not fear, nor did he need this so called 'Great White Father' to set his feet on the right path. As far as he was concerned, one white man trespassing on Cherokee land was one too many. He would gladly bury his war ax in the neck of each and every one, even a half breed whose blood was only partially profaned by white stink. Gladly would he use the razor edged blade at his waist to slice scalps from them all, as he and his braves had already done over the past few days.

At his waist, woven onto a deer-hide leather strap,

were three round blood crusted circles of drying skin with hair attached. Two were long, blonde, females; the other was from a male with shorter red hair.

These were his latest trophies from their most recent raid, markers of his personal kills. The two blond scalps had come from a woman and her young daughter in the first homestead they had attacked. The older woman had screamed and fought until he'd bashed her head in with his war ax. The younger girl, even as he'd mounted her, sprawled across her mother's dead body, had only whimpered and cried until he'd grown bored with her, finally slitting her throat.

The red-haired scalp had been from male settler, leaving his cabin, to milk their bony, half starved cow. He'd been surprised to find an arrow suddenly protruding from his throat. Dragging-Canoe's warriors had cut the cow's throat as well, and then stripped some of the choicer cuts of meat to carry with them.

Dragging-Canoe had restrained his enthusiasm for butchery at the other two homesteads they had raided. A good leader, he had allowed his men to indulge in most of the killing, scalping and raping, it was part of the reason they followed his command so well.

As he watched the old man disappear around a bend in the trail, Dragging-Canoe reached a decision. Smith was traveling with a determination that spoke of some special purpose. He would follow along behind the old trader; find out what had him in such a hurry. There would be other days, other opportunities to offer up the old mans blood as sacrifice to Num Yunu wi. (The Stone Man.)

Chapter 10

After only twenty minutes Matthew had to slow from a hard run to a slow walk in order to let the catch in his side ease up a little. He knew it had been a stupid mistake to start at such an unforgiving pace, therefore when the pain in his side eased off, he set off again, this time at a steady even trot. After a short while, he got his second wind, the steady drip of adrenalin producing an almost trance like state in which his legs seemed to move without conscious thought, allowing him to maintain his pace, all day if necessary.

In places a landscape of giant hemlocks and pines towering over gnarled oak and river birch passed in an endless blur of motion. At others the path became obscure; almost tunnel like, beneath crowding rhododendrons and mountain laurel. Through it all he ran.

In his mind, Matthew knew the odds were stacked against ever catching up with the captured girl. There were just too many miles to cover and the fast moving canoes were already outpacing him by two days . But fate had left him no other course, so he ran and when he grew tired, he still ran and when he grew hungry he ran so more.

All the while he maintained a watchful awareness for any danger that might crop up out of nowhere. He would be of very little help to the girl, or anyone else for that matter, if he ran head on into war party of young braves, out lifting hair and intent on making a name for themselves. One on one, or even two or three, Matthew felt he could handle. If he ran into a hand full at one time however, things might get a little tight.

Even though he tried to keep his mind focused on his surroundings, at times his thoughts drifted back in time, back to his uncle's gun shop on the outskirts of London, back to another time when he'd tried to help young woman in trouble. A time that had ended in tragedy and with blood stains on his hands.

**

Strolling slowly down the cobblestone lane, the arm of a beautiful and exciting young woman intertwined with his own, had Matthew feeling like he had at last grown to be a man. Michelle Marcella was not only lovely, she was charming, intelligent and she had his heart racing like a team run away horses with a bee's nest caught in the trace chains.   It was an experience like nothing he'd ever dreamed could exist.

Oh, he had been flirted with before. His cousins were all girls and they were constantly bringing their friends around the shop. In the past couple of years he'd had more than a few eyelashes batted in his direction. This was different. The girls he'd known in the past were, well... just that...girls, more often than not, giggling and acting silly or childish.

Michelle might be young, but she was mature beyond her years and every bit a woman. Just being seen with her, made him stand taller and walk with more dignity in his step. He did not say much as they walked along, not for lack something to say, but more in fear that his words might come out wrong, making him sound cloddish and uncouth. Besides he enjoyed the sound of her voice. She was not only lovely and charming, she was bright, well educated and had traveled to other countries. By comparison, his life was dull and uneventful.

After a while, she must have realized that she had been dominating the conversation for she suddenly paused as though thinking about what she was about to say and deciding to say something entirely different.

'Forgive me," she said, flashing him a dazzling smile. "I fear that I have again been letting my tendency toward uncontrolled prater get the best of me. My father has a saying. *'A babbling brook is always shallow, but still water runs deep.'* You must think me to be the shallowest of waters."

"I think you are amazing," Matthew said impulsively. "Smart and beautiful." Then fearing he might have offended her, he felt a sudden heated flush of embarrassment begin to creep up his neck and face.

"You're very sweet," she said, gripping his arm a little firmer, seeming pleased rather put off.

"Tell me about yourself," she said.

"There's not much to tell," Matthew said. "My life is pretty much what you've already seen. I spend most of my time working in my uncle's shop."

"You must be very talented. Your uncle trusts you enough to leave you in charge of business while he is away."

"Not much involved in minding the shop," Matthew said. Then on impulse he asked a question that had been worming its way around in his mind. "Who is this man, this *Rafael* fellow, who has been harassing you?"

She suddenly stopped walking, and still holding his arm, brought Matthew to a halt as well.

"*Je peux pas le blairer*," she said, falling back on her native French, a frown casting a dark shadow across her lovely face. Then seeing the confused look on his face she changed back to English. "*I can't stand him*. Rafael Montague is buffoon, a drunkard, a brutish ill-bred oaf who fancies himself a great lover, but in truth he is a dullard, unable to distinguish between love and lust. Like a rutting animal, he has not interest other than his own beastly perversions. I had thought to escape his attentions by coming on this trip, but it seems I have severely underestimated his blind determination."

"He followed you here from France" Matthew asked incredulously?

"Yes. I fear it so. He attends ever showing of our play. Never takes his eyes off me through out the entire performance. Sometimes his gaze, his unrestrained probing of my body with his eyes, is so disconcerting that I must struggle to remember my lines."

"Can't the play promoter or the constables do something about him."

"He pays his money for the tickets and never causes a scene at the plays. The manager says it would be bad for business to turn away a paying customer. The magistrate I spoke to, a lecherous old degenerate in his own right, who spoke directly to my bosom, instead of my face, said that as far as he could tell, the man had committed no crimes in his jurisdiction; therefore he could do nothing to help me."

"Maybe, given time he will grow weary and leave you alone."

"I don't think so. He may be lacking in couth, but he has the tenacity of draft-ox. He will not go away. On several occasions, he has been overheard boasting to his cronies, that if he can not have me, then no one will. But enough talk of this despicable scoundrel, he brings enough misery into my life without dwelling on the matter unnecessarily. Let us enjoy the remainder of our afternoon stroll with no more talk of bad things."

So it was that for the next few moments they walked in undisturbed silence. She seemed to have shaken off her bleak dispirited mood, as though by sheer force of will she driven back the darkness that threatened to eclipse her sunny disposition.

All too soon, they arrived at *The Seven Oaks Inn & Tavern*, a large two story brick building where the Cordovan Performance Company had reserved the entire a second floor of rooms for its actors. The taproom, taking up less than a third of the ground level, had an entrance separate from the Inn, so the more sedate patrons could egress their rooms without mingling with the oft-times less savory-drinking crowd.

"I hope you have no cause to use this," Matthew said, taking the pistol from his waistband and carefully handing it to Michelle when she paused in front of the heavy wooden door leading to the second floor of the Inn. "I promise to have your gun ready, first thing in the morning."

"*T' es un lapin...* you *are a sweetheart*," she said, quickly concealing the gun in the multitude of yellow ruffles of her dress. "Tomorrow," she said then standing on her tiptoes; she kissed him lightly on his cheek. In a swirl of petticoats and yellow silk, she vanished through the doorway leaving Matthew standing dumbfounded, staring, as though in a trance, at the dark lacquered wood of the closing door. If love at first glance truly existed, then surely he must have stumbled unknowingly onto the fountainhead of its source. He was already looking forward to the morning when she would return to his uncle's shop.

It was the sound of a man speaking to him that disrupted his sweet daydream. Words spoken in French. Words he did not understand by anything other than their tenor. The voice was arrogant, sneering, slurred by too much alcohol flowing in veins and emboldened by the man's own swaggering opinion of himself.

Before he turned to look, before the fact that he was being insulted in a foreign tongue had fully settled in, Matthew knew, beyond any shadow of doubt that when he turned, he would be facing Michelle's stalker, Rafael Montague.

"Are you deaf as well a stupid," the snide voice spoke again, this time in words Matthew understood all too well? "I asked if you *avons couche esemble.....slept together...* you ignorant English *la queue.*"

Appearing to be in his early thirties, Montague was a big man with a pox-marked face and dark thick eyebrows shadowing dull gray eyes. He wore expensive knee length black leather boots, a black silk shirt with engraved silver buttons, black trousers and a black silk cape, all fashionably tailored. A heavy gold chain hung around his neck, on the outside of his shirt as if to thumb his nose at the cutpurses and pickpockets.

Despite the scars marring his face, he might have been called ruggedly handsome, had it not been for the brutish, sadistic sneer that seemed to permanently distort his features. Cruelty was not a sometime thing with this man. It was his obsession.

Partially concealed under the cape, Matthew spotted the silver butt-cap of a pistol. A large belt knife protruded from the opposite hip and in his right hand he carried a cane made of polished ivory, embossed with gold and silver inlays. The cane was not an aid for walking, it was a weapon. The bottom of the shaft could be being easily removed, revealing the two foot long razor edge blade concealed inside. Matthew had seen the type before. A gentleman's weapon, usually favored by men of sustenance, men who feared being accosted by ruffians or robbed by thieves. Matthew doubted that Rafael carried the sword cane for reasons of self-protection.

All these things were deduced in less time than it took to turn and face the man. Obviously, a natural born bully, used to having his way, now drunk and spoiling for a fight, Rafael stood less than twenty feet away, his legs spread, braced for battle, his hate filled eyes seeming to boring holes through Matthew body.

Matthew had pitifully little experience in the harsh realities of the world to draw upon, but intuitively he knew how truly dangerous this man really was. And while the brashness of youth left him little room for fear, he, never the less, had no desire for a confrontation if it could be avoided. So despite the insult, he decided to try ignoring the villain. Unfortunately it was not a viable option. Rafael had seen Michelle kiss him. He would not step aside.

"English swill," he mumbled, his words slurring slightly as reached down pulled to a ten inch blade from the sheath at his waist. In the fading light, the razor edged blade seemed to glint with evil intent. "When I've cut away the tongue from your pretty face, and sliced away your *les burnes*.... then we shall see if the *pouffiasse* still wishes to spread her legs for you."

Matthew had heard enough. He could ignore slanders cast upon his own character, but he could no longer bare the vicious insults intended to defame someone as innocent and pure as Michelle Marcella

"What gives a vulgar walking cesspool like you the right to right to impugn the reputation of someone like Michelle," Matthew demanded, trying to heap as much scorn as possible on his words.

"Ah! The little puppy learns to growl," Rafael sneered. Swinging the knife back and forth in a figure 8, he started to advance. "Let us see if the puppy has grown sharp teeth as well."

Realizing his chances of surviving a knife fight...without a weapon...were so slight as to be nonexistent, Matthew desperately cast about for something with which he could defend himself. There was nothing.

The desperation of his search brought forth a wicked smile on the face of his   antagonist.

Before Matthew had time to react further, the door to the Inn swung open, slamming into his left heel, causing him to stumble and almost fall. By the time he'd regained his balance, Michelle was standing behind him, his pistol in her hand, aimed at Rafael. He was no longer advancing.

"J'en peux plus. J'en ai plein le dos," she shouted. "Casse-toi!"

"Mon coeur, is that any way to speak to your most ardent fan, not to mention your beloved cousin, and the man destiny compels you to wed." Rafael said, his tone implying that he truly believed his own words. "And let us not be rude. We should speak in the language of your young barbarian friend, so as to not make him feel more inferior than he already is."

"Have it your way, *cousin,* first off, I am not your darling," Michelle's words were bitter, as though they left a foul taste crossing her lips. However the pistol in her hand never faltered, never shook. "A disgusting mound of offal has the same foul stench, no matter what language is used to describe the smell."

"Such coarseness is unbecoming of a woman of your station," Rafael said. "I fear this uncivilized country is having a bad influence on you. I also see, by the look in your little puppy's eyes that he does not know about our unique relationship, that we are cousins and are to be wed."

"I would rather rot than become your accursed wife," Michelle almost sneered. "Nor shall I ever share the foul pigsty you call a bed. And as to the unfortunate

89

circumstance of our associated parentage, who could possibly boast of a family tree whose fruit sometimes turns foul and rots on the vine. Who would not be shamed by a linage containing perverted swine and deviates?"

"You should be proud of your... our... bloodline. It should be kept pure, untainted by such common filth as this," Rafael growled, using his knife to indicate Matthew.

Matthew started toward the man but Michelle grabbed hold of his shirtsleeve with her free hand.

"No," she pleaded. "This should not involve you. He will only hurt you and I do not want that to happen... Please go while I detain him with your gun."

"You should listen to her... little boy. Run home to *ta mere*...your mother. Leave dealing with a grown man until later, when you have grown some *les coquilles* ...testicles," Rafael said, sheathing his knife with a practiced smoothness, while glaring Matthew with the unconcerned look of disdain he might have bestowed on a passing cockroach.

"Enough," Michelle almost shouted. *"Casse-toi*!...Go away. You're drunk and disgusting. If you do not leave, now, I swear to you I will shoot you in the stomach to watch you die, slow and painful."

"As you wish, *mon amour*," Rafael said, adjusting his cape before turning away. Then, in a blur of motion, he quickly whirled back around, having drawn and aimed his own gun. "But not before I teach this cur a lesson in manners."

For Matthew, the air seemed to jell, turn liquid, clear

90

and syrupy, slowing motion and perception. He saw the hammer on the gun drop. Saw the flash as the powder in the pan ignited under the shower of sparks. Saw a yellow blur of motion, felt a sudden push as Michelle dove her body hard against his side. Saw her head jerked abruptly to the side, blood erupting in a spray of red droplets from the back of her neck.

Someone was screaming a long drawn out " no-o-o-o."

As Michelle crumpled slowly to the cobblestones, a broken flower amid a swirl of crimson splattered yellow, Matthew realized that the scream had erupted from had his own agonized soul.

Matthew fell to his knees, anguish tearing at his heart, tears already flooding his eyes. The lead ball had pierced her neck, severing her spine just above her collarbone. She had been dead before she hit the street.

Matthew gently reached out to touch her face, so suddenly pale, so fragile in death. The dark red stain slowly inching is way into the once gay yellow fabric of her dress seemed an abomination to her spirit, to the radiance that had once emanated from her very being. He could not seem to make his mind function. All could feel was an agonizing sense of loss and emptiness that threatened to consume his soul. How could such tragedy come to pass in the blinking of an eye? How could such happiness as he'd known earlier be so brutally transformed into despair?

The shot had brought a crowd of people rushing from the tavern as well as the Inn. People were shouting.

91

Some stood at a distance gawking, unsure whether to approach or run. Others ran to inform the authorities. Above the chaos, Matthew heard Rafael roar like a wounded beast.

"*Fils de pute*! This is all your fault," Rafael screamed. Dropping the gun from his hand, he jerked away the bottom from his cane, whipping out the two foot length of deadly steel. "I will gut you like the English pig that you are."

With an animal roar, Rafael charged.

Later, Matthew would not be able to remember reaching down to take his pistol from those still warm, small delicate fingers. He would not remember swinging the gun up in what seemed surreal slow motion. He did not remember pulling the trigger or the sudden recoil as the gun discharged. Nor did he see the look of shocked surprise on the face of Rafael Montague, looming above him, driving his wicked blade downward, when the lead ball caught him above his left eye.

What he did remember was the sudden shock, the fiery agony spawned by a two foot length of cold steel passing under his collarbone and out his back, grating savagely against the bones in his shoulder or the slower, more intense pain born when he reached up, wrapped his hand around the ivory handle, and with a grating of metal against bone, withdrew the blade.

His shot had not been soon enough to deter the downward plunge of the blade, but it had been enough to deflect the aim. Fortunately the blade angled away from his heart.

Struggling to his feet, knees weak and rubbery, head spinning, vision blurring, fading, Matthew let the blade fall from his blood soaked fingers. Looking down at the dead girl, then at the man sprawled at her feet, he shuddered, then raising his hands, he stared forlornly at the blood dripping from his fingers He vaguely wondered it was his or Michelle's.

Matthew did not have long to ponder the thought. Darkness, a deep well of oblivion, struggling to draw him into its shadowy embrace, at last won out. He crumpled to the paving stones, his head landing on the hem of a yellow dress worn by a girl he had known for less than one hour. Now dead. Her smile would haunt the shadowy realm of his thoughts, almost daily, for his entire life.

***

Moving at a steady trot along the trail following the river, chasing after two canoes and one captive Cherokee girl, Matthew was filled with self-doubt as well as self-loathing. Raising his one free hand before his face, he stared at absently for a few second, as though expecting to see some trace of red still present there. Sometimes it seemed he could still see the blood, could feel the hot stickiness of it, clinging to his fingers. It seemed a strange twisted irony that Michelle Marcella had traveled to London to perform in a Shakespearean play in which one of the main characters, Duncan, ended up with similar phantom spots of blood on his hands.

He had read *Macbeth,* during his month long recovery, but never wanted to see the play.

Matthew dropped his hand. As shadows began to lengthen across the mountains of the Blue Ridge, he ran.

93

Chapter 11

Dragging-Canoe, along with his warriors, remained hidden until the old trader was well on his way up the river path. His anger churned, boiling just under the surface, like molten lava straining at the walls of a volcanic caldera. Yet even while fighting to control his anger, he never let signs of its show. On the outside his face remained as unmoving as chiseled granite, devoid of emotion, a statue cast of bronze.

After a short while, he stood, motioned for his men to follow. Like a silent precession of brown skinned ghosts, the warriors drifted noiselessly down the rugged mountain side, their passage around the moss encrusted boulders, and through patches of green fiddle-back ferns, creating no more stir than did the breeze that whispered through the tops of the giant hemlocks towering over their heads.

Dragging-Canoe motioned for one of his men to travel ahead, an advance scout and another to fall behind, watching their back trail. He and his men had been carrying out hit and run raids for several months now, traveling as far south the as river the whites call Savanna and north to the lands of the Seneca's. At times they number more than two hundred warriors, but mostly they kept their numbers to a dozen or less. Small raiding parties, attacking single outlying homesteads, then when they were pursued, disappearing into the dark forests where they could scatter, then regroup later.

Simple tactics, yet effective. For the time being

anyway, most of the burned   out cabins and outbuildings were not being rebuilt. And as of yet only a few of his warriors had been lost in those small but quick devastating attacks.

The only area where his efforts failed to stem the flow of white trespassers onto the lands of his people was along the Cumberland River. There, led by the man called *Boone*, the hated bunch called the Wataugans had built several fortified settlements. Like a tick, with its head buried deep in the flesh of an animal, no matter how much he harried the body, the head remained firmly embedded in the flesh of his homeland.

It mattered little to Dragging-Canoe that the land settled by the Wataugans had been legitimately purchased. As far as he was concerned, the deal made by the old chiefs (his father included) with the Transylvania Company was as false as all the other treaties the whites had tried to use to steal their land.

That the muskets carried by his men, as well as the one cradled under his arm, not to mention the powder and lead balls in the deerskin pouch at their side had been part of the payment in that same transaction, given by Nathaniel Hart and Richard Henderson the previous spring, mattered not on whit to Dragging-Canoe.

The words spewed from the tongues of white men, the trinkets they handed out, were like poison, blinding the eyes of the aging chiefs, stealing the wisdom from their minds.

The old chiefs were weak. Women. They had forgotten the feel of the fire burning in their blood, the raging fever brought on by holding the handle of the war-ax in a blood stained hand.

Dragging-Canoe had not forgotten.

Heading south, paralleling the river as the sun had climbed to the highest point of its path across the sky, the band of warriors trailed along behind the old trader, never lagging more than a half mile away. Then abruptly Smith took another path, heading due west leaving the river valley heading into the mountains.

Dragging-Canoe, standing where the trails forked, was trying to decide if he should follow the old man further or continue on to the village a few miles up stream. The trader was obviously heading across the mountains, the most direct route to Chota, or the village a Sycamore Shoals. Undoubtedly, Thadis Smith had business with one or maybe all of the old chiefs, Oconostota, Savanooks maybe even Attakullaculla. (Dragging-Canoe's father.) What that business was, Dragging-Canoe could not guess, on top of which he had other business of his own to attend too.

The war-ax was not the only thing that fueled fire in the blood of Dragging-Canoe. There was also the girl, Laurel, the willowy granddaughter of Gray Fox-Killer. She too, made his blood boil in more ways than one. His passion for this tiny wisp of a girl, not much beyond a child, and less than half his age, had almost grown to the point of being debilitating. The warriors in his band were aware of this failing, but they dared not speak of it out loud.

Tall, handsome, as well as a popular war chief, Dragging Canoe was by no means a stranger to the sleeping furs of the women of his tribe. To gain status or

96

security for their daughters, most Cherokee fathers would have been more than happy to offer their daughters in marriage to a man of his rank. Literally, he could almost have his pick of the eligible women in his tribe . . . save one . . . Laurel.

It was not precisely love that drew him to the young woman. Dragging-Canoe was not a man much moved by such a singular emotion. It was rather a combination of lust, male pride and a need to possess that compelled him to return time after time to Gray Fox's lodge.

Doubly compounding his frustration was the fact that the girl would have nothing to do with him. She was always polite, kept her eyes downcast, as was proper for a woman in the presence of a warrior, but always shook her head, refusing his overtures or the gifts he offered. She had even turned down his offering of a string of ten scalps, a great honor. Her refusal was an affront of the worst kind of humiliation. He'd stormed from her grandfather's lodge in a barely restrained killing rage.

Her grandfather should have beaten the girl for the refusal, should have forced her to marry him, but the old man was weak. Only the fact that no one knew how horribly he'd been shamed by her refusal allowed him to lead his men without disgrace.

In his own mind, Dragging-Canoe refused to admit that he too was weak when it came to the girl. Despite the humiliation he'd endured on his last trip, he was ready to return. He would make one more attempt, but his patience had reached the breaking point. If the old man would not relent, force the girl into marriage, then at some time in the not to distant future, Dragging-

Canoe planned to take matters into his own hands. He would have her . . . one way or another.

Thoughts of the girl overshadowed Dragging-Canoe's desire to follow the old half-breed; instead he led his men off in a different direction. He didn't get far. The warrior he'd sent forward as an advance scout returned, bringing someone with him.

It turned out to be a young Cherokee boy, only a year or so away from being old enough to travel the warpath. Dragging-Canoe had seen him before. He was from the village of Gray-Fox. What he didn't know was he was the same boy, the runner Gray-Fox had sent to bring the old trapper to his village. Thadis Smith being the only person Gray-Fox trusted to read the English words, written on a piece paper that had been found tied to a tree where they'd lost the trail of his granddaughter's captors.

After delivering the note to Thadis, the young man, knowing Dragging-Canoe's passion for Laurel, and seeking to gain the favor, had come looking for the war-chief to inform him of her abduction.

Dragging-Canoe, stone faced as always, listened as the young runner told of Laurel's capture and what the letter posted to the tree had demanded. When the words had finally settled in, they spawned a rage whose heat at last melted away his granite composure.

A coarse, guttural growl rumbled deep within his chest, finally erupting from his throat in an ear-piercing war cry. Dragging-Canoe grabbed the tomahawk from his belt, slinging it with all his might at a massive oak tree beside the trail.. The war-ax bit deep, burring most of the deadly blade in the ancient hardwood.

98

In a dozen long strides, Dragging-Canoe stepped to the tree, then with a mighty heave wrenched the war-ax free, tearing out long strips of the tough bark and wood. Once again he voiced a savage, almost animal, roar of frustration. Then for a few minutes, he stood in absolute stillness.

After a while, he gathered his men close together, giving them instructions. When he'd finished, they spit up like a covey of quail startled by a prowling fox, each warrior headed in a different direction.

Dragging-Canoe himself headed for the village of Gray-Fox to await the arrival of the men his warriors had been sent to bring back. No longer would he listen to the weak voices of the old chiefs. When enough warriors had been gathered, he would attack, not stopping until he'd killed or driven every accursed white trespasser back to the shores of the sea. When the rivers ran red with their blood and the hair cut from their heads was piled higher than the tallest lodge pole, Dragging-Canoe knew that his thirst for vengeance against the white's treachery would not be quenched.

Chapter 12

Dripping wet from walking through the last of a passing thunderstorm, Thadis waited in front of the deerskin flap that served as a door to the council lodge, while the chief's great-great granddaughter went in to announce his arrival. He remembered her name, "Morning Flower."

The lodge was a fairly large structure built of up right logs chinked with leaves and mud, the roof was covered with a mixture of bark and mud woven together with broom straw.

After a short wait, the deerskin was swung aside and he was motioned to enter. It took a minute for his eyes to adjust to the dark interior.

Attakullculla, seated on a rug of woven reeds, rose stiffly to greet his guest.

"Aya alihelisdi nanai hia osda aylvnudvnadegv vhnai atsilvquodi oginali," (I rejoice at the good health of my distinguished friend.) Thadis said, falling easily back into his mother's language as he locked his hand around the wrist of Attakullculla, in greeting.

The aging chief's grip around his own wrist felt as weak as his frail appearance might have suggested. His hair, once raven black, now haloed his wrinkled leathery face in a cloud of white. Sitting beside a small fire, smoking a pipe filled with tobacco, the old chief seemed no more than a shadow of the man he'd once been. Thadis was saddened to see how thin and feeble the once powerful Cherokee leader had become.

For years Attakullculla had been the guiding force, the

coagulating influence, solidifying the various villages into a community. Fortunately his wisdom, experience and a sharp mind were still evident in his dark brown eyes.

Thadis had grave doubts about the future of his mother's people when the old chief eventually reached the end of his journey in this world. With so many hot headed young war-chiefs following their own violent paths, he felt sure only ever worsening tragedies lay ahead for the Cherokee people.

"Welcome, son of my sister's daughter," the old man said, motioning Thadis to sit beside the fire.

The heat from the fire, along with the normal July warmth had the room to the point of being smothering. Accustomed to spending most of his time outdoors, Thadis sat as far from the fire pit as possible without being deemed rude. He did his best to ignore the stifling atmosphere.

Attakullculla passed Thadis the pipe he was smoking.

Thadis reached out for the pipe, again, not wishing to offend his host. Hot smoke in his lungs would only add to the sweltering heat in the lodge. None the less, he took two long draws from the long stemmed, intricately carved pipe. Exhaling the smoke, he handed it back to the old chief.

The smoke, blown from his nose and mouth, joined that of the fire, slowly rising to a small opening in the roof. For a while both men sat in studied silence, watching the dancing flames ghost along the bed of glowing coals.

After what seemed like a small eternity, the old man at last spoke. "I see a great sadness, as always, written in the eyes of *the cub of two peoples*, only today, I see there is an even deeper sorrow in your heart."

Thadis had to smile at least inwardly at the words the old chief had chosen. To most folks he was simply Wolf, or Gray Wolf. Only someone who had lived through as many winters as Attakullculla could refer to him as a young anything

As to the reference that he was troubled by his mixed blood, Thadis started to gather the usual denials in his mind, then he paused. Perhaps the old chief was right; he had always been caught between two worlds. He hid it well…except from the old man.

Attakullculla had always seemed to have a deeper insight into the workings of his mind than Thadis cared to admit. He had always looked deeper into his soul, known more of his troubled inner thoughts than even he was aware of.

"Yes honored one," Thadis said. "My heart is heavy…I fear for the safety of our people."

"That same fear, I have lived with for the better part of my life," the old chief said, the sadness in his own eyes reflected in the flickering firelight.

"What are you planning to do about the army of white soldiers headed this way?" Thadis said, as he studied the old chief's wrinkled, weathered face in the dancing firelight, searching for some sign of what he might be feeling.

For a long while, the old man, lost in though, gazed into the fire, seemingly mesmerized by the sinuous dance of the flames. So much time passed that Thadis was beginning to wonder if the chief had heard his question.

When Attakullculla at last looked up, his eyes seemed no more than dark pools of liquid, reflecting bits of dancing firelight. His face seemed more etched with the passage of time, a map of the sorrows of his people.

"Many years ago," he said, turning away from the fire, locking his gaze on Thadis, "when I was still a young man, seven warriors were chosen to travel across the great ocean, to visit the home of our *great father in England.*"

Thadis listened with out speaking. He had been ten years old at the time, but he remembered it well. It had been forty-six years ago. The warriors leaving by boat to England had been the major topic of conversation for months…until they arrived back home.

The old man took another deep draw on his pipe before continuing, "At that time, I had not become a chief, but I was well respected among the people. I was known then was **Little-Carpenter.** I was given the name because I could build things. Not things like this lodge, but things in the head. I could work out trade agreements and treaties with other tribes or with the English, the French, or the Spanish people who bickered over pieces of our land. So it was decided that I should be one of those chosen to make the journey to visit this King who had promised to protect us from all our enemies. The Cherokee have many ancient and fierce enemies. To offer such a thing, we though this King must be a mighty warrior and were anxious to meet such a man. The

103

journey was arranged by a man who had traveled often among our villages. His name was Sir Alexander Cuming.

It was a hard journey. For two full moons we journeyed across those terrible waters. At first all our people were sick in their bellies. The men on the ships laughed, until Sir Alexander threatened to have them whipped; though I think perhaps it was more because Kettagusta, a fierce war chief, stood nearby with his hand on his war-ax, glaring in their direction.

In England, we were given much wine and food, which was good, but it was a strange place, filled with foul smells and much noise, and many, many white men. I wanted only to return to our homeland, but it took many weeks before we got to see King George. When at last we stood before the great King that we had waited so long to see, we were shocked. This man was not a warrior at all. How, we wondered, could such weak appearing man, command so many. How could this frail man strike such fear into the hearts of so many people that even armed solders kneeled at his feet like slaves.'

Attakullculla paused in his narrative to refill his pipe which he lit with a brand from the fire. After a couple of puffs he again offered it to his guest. This time refusing would not be considered an insult, so Thadis shook his head.

The old chief sat, cradling his pipe in his smoke stained fingers, again working out his thoughts before he spoke.

"England was a strange place, cold and wet. It was a place I would not chose to return to. I saw many things there, some of which I still do not understand after these many years. When we returned home and told people of the strange sights we had seen, many thought we lied. Others said we had been given the black drink and made to dream these things. But what we saw was real."

The chief again drew on his pipe.

Thadis had spent most of his life in the mountains, but he and visited Charles-Town on a few occasions, and his father had traveled to many places before he settled in the Carolina Mountains, marrying into the Cherokee tribe. As a young boy, he and spent many wide-eyed nights listening as his father described, in detail, many of the very same sights seen by Attakullculla and his fiends.

"Many times," Thadis said, "my father would entertain my mother and myself with tales of the things he had seen in other lands. I think my mother often though he made of wild tales to entertain us, but I know he spoke the truth."

"Yes," Attakullculla said looking up and smiling at Thadis, "your father and I spoke often of these things. Like his son, he too worried of what would happen when the white settlers pushed further into our lands."

"He often told my mother that the Cherokee would have to change, adapt to the ways of the white man, or be swept away as leaves before a fierce wind."

"Unfortunately, you father was right. Once I would not have believed it so, but after traveling across the sea, my thoughts have changed. It is said that the white people number more than the stars in the sky. I think maybe this is true."

"Yes," Thadis agreed, "when I travel to Charles-Town for supplies, there are so many people that I find it hard to breath. Never understood why anyone would choose to live in such a manner. I need feel the wind on my face and have the smell of the forest filling my nose. It always makes me feel better when I return to the mountains."

"White men are very strange. I do not understand their thinking either, but I know we must learn to live as they do. This is not a popular belief with many of our warriors, my son among the worst of them."

"Dragging-Canoe's actions have brought much trouble to the tribe."

"My son seeks only his own glory and foolishly races toward the war-trail with no thought of what will happen to the rest of our people. He no longer listens to the words of this feeble old man. Once I could have stopped him. No more. His words heat the blood of our young warriors. He convinces them they can defeat the whites if they unite with the northern tribes, our old enemies."

"He has aroused the wrath of the white settlers, Thadis said, his voice reflecting the fear in his heart. "They will send soldiers to avenge the things he has done."

"Perhaps," the old man said solemnly. "But I think maybe they will be too busy fighting among themselves and with the English, to send an army against us...I think the war they wage with the English will take many years, Attakullculla said. "I do not think the Americans can defeat the army of their own King."

"I hope you are right," Thadis said, slowly shaking his

106

head. Secretly, he feared the old chief would be wrong this time.

"My friend, Matthew says that many people in England are unhappy with King George, that he treats many of them much the same as slaves."

"I have seen this with my own eyes," the old chief said.

Realizing that nothing he said would sway the old man's mind set; he aimed his next question in a different direction.

"Has any word reached you about the raid on Gray-Fox-Killer's village?"

"A runner brought word that his granddaughter had been stolen away by a group of white men, We have received a dozen reports of other girls missing from other villages. I think perhaps a group of bad men are capturing our young women to sell as slaves... This has happened before."

Thadis was immediately concerned about this bit of news. If more than one girl had been captured, there had to be more men involved than the ones Matthew had seen in the canoes. He had no doubts that the boy could take care of himself, even against odds of four or five to one, but from the way things were shaping up, there might be dozens of raiders involved. He wanted to kick himself not realizing the danger sooner. He was suddenly very worried about his young friend.

"This was done by Shawnee warriors, being led by an English officer." Thadis said.

"How do you know this," the old chief asked, his interest suddenly quickened.

"Matthew spotted them traveling down the French Broad River. Gray-Fox-Killer's granddaughter was tied in the front of one of the boat. The canoes were birch-bark over willow frames, not the kind used by our people. He follows them even as we speak."

"Why would the English want to steal our women," Attakullculla asked, a look of confusion adding new lines to his weathered face.

"The English want the Cherokee to fight at their sides in the war the Americans as we did in the war with the French."

"They ask, but we refuse."

"You won't fight for the English, but it would be much the same if you are drawn into a war with the Americans. By stealing our women, making it look like it was done by white men from the settlements, would it not make the young men, like those following Dragging-Canoe, more anxious to take up the war ax?"

The old chief sat quietly, drawing the last bit of smoke from the tobacco in his pipe. His eyes seemed older, his face more lined than it had only a short while earlier.

"If what you say is true; your young friend is in grave danger."

"I will be leaving soon," Thadis said, rising to his feet. "Matthew has a week's head start. I only hope I can catch up before he runs into more trouble than he can handle."

"Your friend is fortunate to have a friend such as

yourself," the old chief said.

"Will you move the village before the soldiers arrive," Thadis asked?

The old chief once again took a long time before he answered. "Once, many years ago, after our last war with the whites, we had two long years when many members of the tribe died from the *sickness that eats away the face;* I was much worried about the fate of our people. To seek answers, I spent two days in a sweat lodge, and then took the black drink that foretells the future. In my dreams, I saw many things, strange visions that I cannot begin to understand. I saw that our people would be divided, beaten, and spread to the reaches of sunset in the west, but in the end, we would once again flourish in our own lands."

"I hope your visions of the future prove true," Thadis said, "but it is the present that worries me."

"Ease your heart, Wolf-Cub. I have already posted scouts, two days run away, on all the trails leading here. If trouble comes, we will know in time to move into the forest."

"As always," Thadis said, bowing his head to Attakullculla, as he prepared to leave, "your wisdom humbles me."

As Thadis headed back to his lean-to, he felt a little better about the safety of the tribe. But he was still worried about Matthew. He planned to leave tomorrow, just as soon as he gathered supplies. It would be the beginning of a long hard journey, one that he had no idea where it would lead…or where it would end.

Chapter 13

Matthew almost missed the rock formation Thadis had said would mark the spot where he should turn away from the river and head overland, or rather over-mountain as it turned out to be.

The river valley, after the sun burned away the morning fog, was one of the most strikingly beautiful places he'd ever seen. Hugh river birch and hemlocks towered over his head, silent, primeval sentinels shadowing his footsteps. It was a wilderness untamed, yet tranquil enough to make him almost forget the desperation of his journey.

The steep mountainsides, covered higher up with hemlock and pine, then lower down, giving way to chestnut, oaks and river birch, sloped almost to the rivers edge.

Cardinals and wood thrush called to each other another as they flitted from perch to perch among the underbrush. Tiny streaks of red or brown, flashing briefly across a canvas of dappled sunlight. Their songs, echoing unnaturally loud along the river, were accompanied by the sound of a limb from a fallen tree slapping the water as it repeatedly snagged in the current, freed itself only to be snagged again.

Higher up the mountain, perched in the very top of a giant white-pine, a raven, its black feathers, no more than iridescent dot against a background of green blue, voices it's deep, raucous call. Further down the slope a tom turkey gobbled its own deep throated warbling call,

110

advertising his presence to any nearby hens.

Under different circumstances, Matthew might have considered going up the ridge, using the wing-bone call Thadis had helped him make to try calling the gobbler close enough to kill with his bow.

"Not today," he mumbled under his breath.

Already he had let his mind be distracted by his surroundings enough to cause him to almost miss his landmark, a large outcrop of granite, a rock face that had been undermined and shaped by sand and water where the river made a sharp turn against the mountain side.

Thadis had said to look for two long protruding pieces of stone that resembled the mouth of an alligator.

He did manage to spot the formation . . .barely. If you turned just right, squinted your eyes; it was possible to see what might be said to resemble a giant pair of jaws. Never having seen an alligator though, he would have to take the old man's word on the resemblance. This was the spot where he needed to turn away from the river, going overland.

Thadis had said it would be a long hard climb up the steep rocky mountain, then down the opposite side, but it would save a full hard day of walking along the rivers edge.

According to the old trader, at that point the river started making a long thirty or forty mile loop from its northern direction to head almost due west and eventually flowing into the Little Tanassee River. By going over the mountain, then heading northwest for a

111

few miles, he could again pick up the river and cut off more than a day's journey.

Thadis had also said that somewhere not far beyond that point the group of warriors would have to abandon the canoes or portage them around ten miles of water too rocky and rough for the thin skin of birch-bark covered canoes.

Matthew's only fear was that they might strike out overland and abandon their canoes somewhere up-stream.

With no way of knowing for sure, Matthew was .left with no choice but to climb.

Making his way upward, moving around ancient fallen tree trunks and moss covered boulders, all the while trying to keep an eye, and an ear, open for the angry buzz of a timber-rattler, Matthew chewed on a tough piece of dried venison. Probably tougher and with less favor than one of his moccasins, the jerky did little to pacify his hunger.

As he moved up the mountain and away, off to his right, concealed in a stand of chestnut tress, the old Tom turkey continued his insistent gobbling.

In his mind, Matthew could only daydream about having the old gobbler skewered on a slowly tuning hickory spit, roasting over a fire. He could almost smell the tantalizing aroma; almost hear the sizzling crackle as fat, dripping from its slowly browning skin, fell among the red hot bed of embers.

Further up the steep slope, the noise of the lonesome gobbler slowly faded away, and along with it, the imagined feast in Matthew's mind, leaving him with only the bland taste of smoked jerky.

"Oh well," Matthew, grumbled to himself as he grabbed hold of a sourwood sapling to help lever himself over a rough spot. The stringy piece of jerky, he was doing his best to chew, might not be the worst thing he'd ever eaten, but it was a close race. At least, he thought ruefully, it causes a lot less trouble than trying to eat a couple of skinny rabbits.

*

The trip across the mountain proved to be uneventful. No rattlesnakes buzzed from underneath the countless rocks he stepped around and no ill tempered bears blocked his path, even though he'd seen claw marks several trees, and a set of huge tracks when he'd passed through a fern covered gap when cresting the mountain. In fact, had it not been for the arduous climb and his urgent need for haste, Matthew might have enjoyed the trip.

Trouble was not destined to cast its dark, ominous shadow across his path until much later that same day.

Matthew figured there was five warriors and two young boys or maybe women on the trail somewhere ahead. He'd come across their tracks earlier, but until they had crossed a low swampy area, they had been too faint to determine a lot about their nature. In the damp spongy soil, he could read them better.

One single track, one of the smaller ones, had been made in a spot so wet that it was still filling with water. Matthew figured they couldn't be more than half a hour ahead.

The pleasantness he'd enjoyed during most of the day was whipped away like dry leaves before a cold winter wind.   The forest ahead remained unchanged, yet somehow seemed cooler, darker, almost forbidding, as though unknown dangers lurked among the shadowy boles.

Matthew felt a quick chill pass down his spine. The long, sweat dampened, hair hanging down across his neck seemed suddenly cold and wet, as if dark cloud had passed across the face of the sun, stealing away its warmth.

Stepping of the trail used by the passing band of warriors, Matthew stopped. Puling back the frizzen on his rifle, he checked the powder in the flash pan. Then taking the bow from his back, he placed the lower limb between his legs. Using one ankle and the calf of his other leg, he bent the tapered wood while carefully working the woven sinew string into the notch carved at each end.

After the bow was strung to his satisfaction, he wrapped his fingers around the string then drew it back, testing its feel. Satisfied, he continued along, paralleling the trail but staying a good bow-shot away.

Under the floppy leather hat slouched low on his head, intense green eyes searched the landscape ahead. Instinctively, with each step, his foot paused just inches above the ground, then slowly eased down, feeling through each worn mocassin for any dry twigs or limbs that might crack, betraying his presence.

The Indians were even closer than Matthew had first believed. He'd been slipping quietly along the edge of a dense stand of sycamores, following the rolling landscape, when he smelled wood-smoke. He could also detect the damp musty smell that told him he was growing close to the river once more.

Immediately, he crouched low as his eyes intently scanned the dense timber ahead. There was no visible sign of smoke, but he was confident of what his nose had told him. Somewhere ahead someone was preparing food over a fire built dry pine. Pine would burn hot, give off little smoke, but the burning rosin gave off an unmistakable smell.

Crouching even lower, almost crawling, Matthew inched his way forward among a green tangle of underbrush covering the crest of a low hill. Reaching the top, he carefully moved aside a few weeds and vines. This allowed him to see the river. The Indians were in a small clearing fifty yards from the water's edge. At a glance, he saw that in was not the same group he'd been trying to overtake.

Two young Cherokee women moved about the fire, preparing a meal. Their ankles were bound by short lengths of braided leather, allowing them to move about with slow shuffling steps. Running would have been impossible.

Four Shawnee warriors sat roughly encircling the girls, performing various tasks. Two braves kept their eyes trained on the girls, while one brave, used strips fresh intestine to bind flint arrowheads to hand full of wooden shafts. The other worked at repairing a torn moccasin.

By the way the group had been moving, Matthew figured they had been in a hurry. Now they had made camp with a couple of hours daylight left. This could only mean that they were waiting for someone.

These observations had no more than crossed his mind when a more troubling though began to worm its way into his head. There had been five sets of tracks, not counting the smaller tracks of the girls. One warrior was still unaccounted for.

Matthew lay perfectly still. A sudden crawling sensation between his shoulder-blades and an inner voice, an instinct often developed by those who spend their lives in close proximity to danger, told him that he'd made a deadly mistake. Moving his eyes only, Matthew tried to scan the area around him. Nothing. Ever so slowly he began inching his way back down the hill. Once out of sight of the camp, he stood and began walking away.

He'd gone less than a few feet when a slight blur of movement caught his attention. The fifth Shawnee warrior suddenly materialized less than thirty yards away on the ridge to his right. The brave already had his gun aimed and was squeezing the trigger.

Lunging to one side, Matthew saw the small puff of white smoke as the guns hammer fell, driving the flint in jaws across the hardened frizzen, driving it back in a shower of sparks, igniting the powder in the flash pan.

Even as the muscles in his legs flexed, Matthew knew it would not be enough. His mightiest efforts could not

116

push him out of the destructive path of the on-coming bullet, so the impact came as no surprise. The intensity of its strike did.

Once during a storm, shortly after he'd first gone to sea, Matthew's ribs had been cracked when a free swinging yard arm had knocked him off his feet. The .58 diameter lead ball tearing across those same ribs was infinitely more painful.

Only one thing saved Matthew's life...Neglect

Had the Shawnee warrior been using a bow, his arrow would probably found its intended mark, the center of Matthew's chest. Instead the warrior's ancient smooth bore musket had long-fired. Powder fouling or moisture from a previous shot had collected in the guns bore. The brave had undoubtedly pushed his shot and charge into the guns bore without swabbing it out, pushing the fouling deep into the tiny flash hole.

The Shawnee, like all the other Indian tribes Matthew had encountered during his travels through the southern mountains were notoriously poor at maintaining their firearms. It was a strange phenomenon. A brave would take meticulous care of his bow, arrows, and even his bowstring, taking care to keep them dry and well protected . Yet the cheap trade-musket, for which he had traded countless furs and deer-hides, was apt to be neglected, in ill repair and usually rusty.

Matthew had encountered dozens of similar cases, where a little cleaning and oiling had returned firearm to working condition. His work had been welcomed among the various tribes. Usually, after entering a village he

117

would be swamped with fouled or broken guns.

Matthew would never have believed a miss-firing gun could have saved his life. And in truth, at that very moment, because of the searing agony in his side, he wasn't so sure it had. He didn't have time to dwell on the pain. The warrior, who had wounded him, had pulled his war ax and was rapidly closing the distance between them.

Chapter 14

A slight frown formed, then just a quickly vanished, on the face Richard Caswell as he glanced up from the task of grooming the large black horse, which stood like an ebony statue in front of the riding stables. His dark eyes quickly appraised the group of five men strung out in single file, approaching the barn from the direction of the main manor house.

He already knew who they were and what they wanted. It was the mark of any good politician to know, ahead of time, what was on the minds of people he was purported to lead. His aides had informed him of the group's arrival in the Capitol earlier that morning.

Determined to finish his work before meeting with the men, he went back to running the currycomb across the horse's shoulder and rump. Carefully he worked out the tangles and removed any burs from the animals hide. He could feel the tense muscles, under the horse's sweat dampened hair begin to relax as he continued the long gentle strokes.

Earlier, he'd ridden the animal hard, putting him through his daily hour of exercise. The animal deserved to be rewarded. It had been and enjoyable ride for both horse and rider. A rare treat. Something his new position and hectic schedule had, for the most part, precluded.

His colleagues, as well as his staff, constantly fumed over his determination to care for his own horse. They argued vocally that it was unbecoming for the new governor to be performing such menial labor. There were slaves and hired stable hands for such jobs.

He repeatedly turned a deaf ear to their protests. Grooming his horse was something he enjoyed doing, nor did he have any intention of stopping. And what the hell, he wasn't the governor yet, at least not officially.

Of course, his newly established office might as well have been official. The Provincial Council had been more than happy to delegate over the whole bubbling caldron of problems that went along with establishing a new state in a new country. Throw in the war with England on one front and war with the Cherokee on the other side and you had the perfect recipe for disaster. At times, he wondered at his own sanity for accepting an oath, which entailed such overwhelming responsibilities.

Not that had really had much choice in the matter. It had been pretty much thrust in his lap. After all, he was 'the hero of *Moore's Creek Bridge*. He almost laughed out loud at the absurdity of the thought. He was a simple man, a farmer, and could no way think of himself as being a hero of any shape or description. All he had done was what had to be done. He'd led men into battle, fought and triumphed. But in truth he was only saddened by what had transpired on that day, by the futility of this war and all wars, saddened by the knowledge that the men they fought had once been considered friends and neighbors.

His personal feeling not withstanding, Richard fully

understood that there would be more battles on the horizon. The war with England would be long and bloody and paid for with countless sacrificed lives. Unfortunately, it was a sad but necessary fact if this fledgling country was to accomplish what the Provincial Congress had set out to do.

No doubt, the price of freedom would be paid, most dearly. Richard knew he would soon be faced with the grievous task of sending men off to war. Men among who some would return wounded or crippled, while countless others would not return at all.

Finished with the currying, Richard unfastened the bridle from around the horse's head, then with friendly slap on the rump, sent the big steed galloping across the green grass carpeting the pasture.

The men waited patiently at the gate that joined the white picket fence to the tack room side of the barn.

It was a different war, though one just as inevitable, just as disturbing, that brought this delegation of strangers to his home, to his barnyard...on this particular morning.

"Good morning, gentleman," Richard greeted the men with a warm smile. Switching, the bridle and the currycomb to his left hand, he wiped his hand on the tail of his white cotton shirt before extending it to the closest man. These were frontiersmen. Men whose hands were roughened by the handles of plows and axes, not pampered town dwellers who would take offence at the smell of horse or honest sweat.

"I'm Richard Caswell," Richard continued. "What

121

brings you gentlemen here on such a glorious morning.?"

"Edward Mills," the first man said by way of introduction, shaking Richards hand with his own huge callused paw.

The man's grip was every bit as bear-like as his appearance would suggest. Richard was over six foot tall. This man seemed to tower over him by at least half a foot. The man's voice had the deep, slow rumbling quality of boulders being shifted around by a small earthquake. Yet despite the young mans formidable size and fierce looks there seemed to be an underlying gentleness about him. And there was no cruelty visible in the piercing blue eyes that gazed out from under a shaggy mane of shoulder length blond hair.

What his eyes did reveal, however, was a not too well hidden sense of loss. At some point, not too distant, this giant of a man had suffered some tragedy that had tore at the heart and withered his soul. It was a look Richard had seen all too often of late.

"This is Jessie and Mitch Osteen, the young man said, introducing two standing next in line, obviously brothers.

"Jimmy Martin."

"James Capps."

Richard shook hands with each man in turn, and while he already knew the purpose of their visit, he felt it was only polite to give them a chance to voice their petition.

After a short period of uncomfortable throat clearing and nervous feet shuffling, it was one of the Osteen brothers who at last spoke   up.

122

"Your Honor," the brother named Mitch said. "We've each come here on behalf of our friends and neighbors to request your help in protecting our families from the Cherokee who've been raiding up and down the whole the frontier. Ain't a man here among us hasn't lost friends or family to murdering renegades.

My own niece and her daughter were raped and murdered less than two weeks ago over along the Yadkin River. Her husband, Daniel, had gone over to Davidson's Fort for supplies. When he got back, he found 'em there on the floor of their cabin. Raped and scalped. He buried 'em, then burned the cabin, he'd worked for a year to build. So far he's not spoken a word to anyone. Now he just sets there on Jessie's porch staring at nothing."

Reliving his losses had them nearly at the point of tears. Richard waited without speaking while he worked to regain his composure.

'Jimmy, here, from up Hickory Nut Gorge, lost a brother. Ambushed while walking to his barn to milk the cow. James lost a first cousin up near Sugarloaf Mountain.

Edward here, found his twelve year old son burned at the stake, less than a quarter of a mile from their cabin. He returned from Morgantown to find his wife murdered a scalped, his son missing... found him a few hours later, still tied to a tree. He was still alive...barely. The murderous bastard's didn't stick around to make sure the fire did its job. He died in his father's arms as he carried him home."

123

"He was a good boy, my Michel," said Edward Mills, his voice cracking. "He didn't deserve to die like that. Nobody deserves to die like that." The shaggy, heartbroken, young giant had to turn his back to the rest of the men for a few minutes as his huge shoulders shook in silent grief. Every man there was acutely aware that each of his companions had similar heartache. In silence they respected his grief.

"A terrible tragedy," Richard said after sufficient time had passed, his voice low, his heart truly saddened by the suffering these men had endured. "I can't begin to express my sorrow at your losses. Even as a stranger to you, it affects me most severely, therefore I am sure that I cannot even begin to grasp the depth of sorrow you must feel at losing loved ones. You can rest assured; I will do anything within my power to come to your assistance."

"Thank you, your Honor," said Edward Mill, his voice still shaky.

"Gentlemen," Richard said, trying to dispel a little of the gloomy atmosphere. "If you don't mind, let us dispense with all this pontificating. Titles just don't fit me. You can call me Richard, or *Governor* if you must, but, the fact is we are all men, cut from the same fabric. Our goals should be and are the same....to make this country a better and safer place for our families and friends."

Richard waited quietly amid a flurry awkward thanks and hastily expressed opinions as to what course of action each man though would work best to stem the hostilities along the frontier.

Actually what the men wanted, the plan they had

devised was not a bad one. In fact it was a fairly close match to the one he had already implemented. A plan he'd set into action several days ago.

Unfortunately, at the moment he was not a liberty to reveal the details of those plans, or at least not to men of whom he was not a hundred percent certain of their political affiliation. There were Tories, loyal to England to be found everywhere. As the battle he'd so recently fought, near his own home, could attest.

Fifteen days ago, a courier had arrived at Richards's office with a dispatch from General Washington. The sealed envelope contained a letter describing a British scheme to enlist the aid of all the Indian tribes from New England all the way south to Florida, in the war with the colonies.

It was Washington's contention that if the tribes joined with the English forces, it would be all but impossible for the, already outnumbered, colonial forces to win in a war against Great Britain.

Washington was urging the Governors of Virginia, North and South Carolina and Georgia to muster volunteer forces to subdue the hostile tribes. In particular, the Cherokee, who were for the most part, Tories, know for their past support for their *father*, King George.

Richard had already sent his on dispatch rider with a letter authorizing General Griffith Rutherford to begin gathering volunteers and preparing for a march against the Middle and Valley towns of the Cherokee. He'd received word from Georgia that Colonel Samuel Jack and 200 Georgians were already on the march toward the villages that lay between the Chattahoochee and the Tugaloo Rivers. Colonel Andrew Williamson had gathered 1100 South Carolinians and was preparing to invade the lower villages along the Seneca River basin.

So far, no word had arrived from the Governor of Virginia, but Patrick Henry was a good man, as well as a close friend. Richard had no doubt that he would do what was necessary to fulfill General Washington's proposal.

Richard's own orders, to General Rutherford, had been to assemble a force of men at Davidson's Fort. There, he was to organize and move his force in secrecy, using less traveled trails into the heart of Cherokee territory, to strike the villages before the Indians had time to scatter into the forest.

His orders had also made it clear that it was not the intent of this raid to commit wholesale slaughter, but rather to subdue, to destroy the villages and food sources.

Richard was no fool. There would be fighting, of course. He knew the Cherokee warriors would resist and he expected his men to have to defend themselves, but he also wanted to avoid unnecessary deaths, epically those of women and children.

The Cherokee lived mostly by farming, augmented with hunting and a little trading with the whites. It was General Washington's belief, and Richard concurred, that once their villages and farms were destroyed, their people scattered, it would take years for the Cherokee to rebuild their strength, there-by giving the colonial forces the time they so desperately needed to deal with the

126

Red-Coat army.

Richard would very much have liked to reveal the workings of General Washington's plan to the men standing so solemnly before him, to offer some succor to their trouble minds, if such a thing were possible. Considering the overwhelming heartache these men had endured, Richard doubted much of anything could bring them peace of mind.

It was not that Richard found anything untrustworthy about these men. Quite the opposite, they seemed to be honest and forthright, men who lived by their word. But the success of all their impending attacks hinged primarily on surprise. If word of the raid leaked, his men would be bogged down by a continuous assault of hit and run ambushes. A style of fighting in which Indians were more schooled than his men would be.

'Gentlemen," Richard said, shifting his gaze from man to man, letting his eyes momentarily lock, unwavering with those of each man. "There are things that, unfortunately, for the time being, I cannot reveal to you, but suffice to say, your concerns are being dealt with, even as we speak. My sincere regret is that it did not come in time to prevent the suffering inflicted your families and yourselves."

Richard was once more hit with a full-side of questions and speculations, to which he listened and did his best to answer as fully as was possible under the constants of his office.

After a time, the delegation at last seemed satisfied and ready to leave. They turned and began moving single file through the gate by the barn. The last man to leave was Edward Mills, the young giant who's son had been burned at the stake. He stopped and turned back toward Richard.

"Everyone says it was Dragging-Canoe and his band of followers, what's doing the raping and murdering and that he was the one responsible for what was done to my Michael."

Again Richard was caught up in the man's piercing gaze. His pain filled eyes still held no trace of cruelty, but their blue/ green depths were lit with an inner fire. In that fire, Richard saw was not a need for revenge, but rather a desire for simple justice.

For an instant, Richard was almost tempted to tell the anguished young man that he should go to Davidson's Fort, where he could join the volunteers gathering to attack the Cherokee.

"Yes," Richard said instead at the last second not willing to risk even this small breech of security. "My scouts inform me that Dragging-Canoe is one of several responsible for the attacks on the homesteads. There are others. The Raven, Double-Head, Pumpkin-Boy. However, Dragging-Canoe is by far the most vocal in making threats. His hatred for the white-man is legendary."

"They say he's planning to attack the settlers along the Cumberland River," Mills said. "My sister and her husband live there in a small cabin at the end of Carter's Valley, near the mouth of Holston River."

"I have not received specific information about where these attacks might occur," Richard said truthfully. "For sure, there is no love-loss between Dragging-Canoe and the Wataugans, even thought it was his own father who traded all that land to the Transylvania Company. He's been shaking his war ax in their direction for more than a year now. Given the current state of things, an attack now would not surprise me."

"That's where I'm headed," Mills said, the conviction in his voice leaving no doubt about his intent.

"I wish you the best of luck," Richard said, his words heartfelt. Reaching out, he again shook the man's bearish hand.

When the men had at last vanished around the back of the barn, Richard walked slowly into the tack room. It smelled of leather and oil, of hay and sweat. Simple things. Reminders of simpler times.

Placing the grooming tools on the shelf, Richard then hung the bridle on empty wooden peg, one of a dozen driven into a massive oak beam for holding harness. The tools put back in place, Richard let out a long troubled sigh.

From the way things were stacking up, it was going to be a long-long four years.

Chapter 15

The Shawnee warrior, gripping a wickedly curved knife in one hand, his recently emptied musket in the other, was closing too fast for Matthew, who was still on his knees trying to bring his own rifle into action. Frantically, he grabbed at the pistol tucked into his belt.

The warrior's face was distorted with rage, his teeth bared in a animal like snarl as he leaped, diving the last few feet in Matthews direction. Like and oversize tawny mountain loin, the warrior flew through the air, intent on not giving his enemy time to regain his footing or the opportunity to bring his weapons to bear.

Matthew pushed the pistol forward, thumbing the hammer and squeezing the trigger in one motion. The gun bucked in his hand.

Before the smoke from his shot obscured his vision, Matthew saw the face of the warrior distort even further as the round lead ball struck him just above his left eye.

His attacker died in mid-air, but momentum of his charge carried his body forward, a lifeless missile, once more knocking Matthew off his feet. He had to kick and squirm, digging his heels in the soft soil and vines, in order to pull out from under the dead man's weight. This frenzied movement renewed the spasms of fiery agony where the bullet had gouged a path across his ribcage.

Matthew could only grit his teeth and struggle shakily to his feet. The remaining warriors would not be long in arriving. Grabbing a hand full of buckskin war-shirt, he struggled to drag the dead man a few yards off the trail. If he had to make a hasty retreat, the last thing he needed was another obstacle to avoid.

Inching his way back to the crest of the little hill, Matthew carefully peered through the wiry tangle of vines and leaves. Only two men remained guarding the captive girls, which meant the other braves were out searching for whoever fired the shots.

Matthew waited in silent pain, carefully scanning the gray tree trunks and the scattered underbrush for any sign of movement. He could feel hot sticky blood, slowly trickling down his side. Patience grew to agony. He had just about decided to move when he spotted a flicker of motion, a hand moving.

The warrior was moving in his direction, always staying behind trees trunks or thick brush. Matthew had spotted the slightest of movements, a couple of dark fingers parting the green bushes a hundred yards down the hill.

Easing back behind the cover of vines, Matthew took the bow from over his shoulder and knocked an arrow. These, he placed off to one side. Then, worming his way back to his observation point, he again searched for the warrior. Knowing where the man had been made finding him easier the second time.

Matthew slowly slid his gun through the opening in the vines. Looking down the sights, he waited. When he at last saw a tiny flicker of movement it took only a slight adjustment shift of his aim. His finger tightened on the trigger and the rifle recoiled against his shoulder.

Again his vision was blocked by a cloud of gray-black smoke Then Matthew saw the wounded man stagger to one side then fall to the ground, his legs twitching spastically a few times before he at last lay still.

Without hesitation, Matthew dropped his rifle, then sliding backward, picking up the bow, he rose quickly to his knees. As he had suspected the second Shawnee warrior was stalking up the hill behind him.

A look of surprise crossed the man's face as Matthew rose up out of a patch of dog fennel and ferns, holding a bow a full draw. His arrow caught the warrior in the throat just below the chin. The startled warrior never had the chance to cock the hammer on the ancient trade musket he carried. For an instant the man could only stare blankly, as though trying to understand how the wooden shaft had come to suddenly sprout from his neck. Reaching up as though to touch the offending object, the strength suddenly left his body and he fell face first to the ground.

Matthew quickly, but carefully, reloaded both his guns. Then tucking the pistol in his belt, and slinging the bow back across his shoulder, he walked over to the dead warrior who lay face down in the weeds. With a quick snap, he broke off the blood stained metal arrow tip protruding from the man's neck, dropping it into his pouch. He'd hammered out the metal tips himself, a time consuming task, plus the metal was hard to come by. They worked better than the stone heads used by the Indians. Later he could reattach the head to another shaft, but for now he had at least two more Shawnee warriors to worry about.

Inching his way back up the hill, he again studied the

campsite. The two girls were now tied, back to back, in the middle of the small clearing, seemingly abandoned. Of the two remaining warriors, there was nothing to be seen. From all appearances they had fled, leaving the girls to their own devices.

In the back of his mind Matthew could almost hear old Thadis snort. "Boy, it'd take a damn fool to fall fer any set up like that."

These men were not about to surrender their captives without a fight. He had no doubt the warriors were still close by, more than likely watching the girls from some concealed shadow or nook, just waiting for some green-horn fool to prance in and try cutting them loose... a damn fool indeed..... And yet that was exactly what Matthew planned to do.

Quickly he made his way back to each of the two dead Shawnees. Not wanting to waste time trying to wrestle their limp bodies, Matthew used his knife to cut away their shot pouches and powder horns. Then picking up their muskets, he started at a painful trot down the hill.

When he reached the trail running parallel with the river, he stopped and scanned about until he spotted the place he needed, a huge fallen chestnut tree, laying fifteen feet off the trail, overgrown with underbrush.

Careful to leave no sign of his passage, no tracks, no broken-down weeds, he moved behind the fallen tree. There he stashed his bow, his rifle and light pack, along with the guns and gear he'd commandeered. Then picking up one of the muskets, the one he knew was empty, Matthew used his own powder horn to prime the

133

flash pan. He didn't put a powder charge or ball down the bore.

He needed a deception, a trick to lure the remaining Shawnees away from the girls long enough to allow him to cut their bonds. He had no idea if what he had in mind would work. On the surface is seemed utter madness, but at the moment he could think of no other way.

Taking the empty musket, Matthew moved back to the trail. There, he trotted away, making certain his tracks were visible, even dragging his feet in places where pine needles blanketed the trail. After a quarter of a mile, he started placing his feet carefully until all sign of his passage disappeared. Then easing off the path, he made his way carefully back to his chosen hiding place.

This time, moving in the direction of the camp, he paid careful attention to any place where a man might lay in ambush. He expected the men to be concealed on the riverside of the clearing in positions where no one could approach unseen from the rear, but this was an assumption. Taking any thing for granted in this part of the country could get you killed quicker than a hawk swooping down to snatch a chipmunk off a log.

Approaching the camp, Matthew could feel the hair on the back of his neck begin to rise.   Suddenly overwhelmed with doubt, chastising himself for walking into an obvious trap...with and unloaded gun... he was beginning to feel like 'a damn fool.'

For a moment the temptation to turn around and hightailed it back down the trail, to leave all this trouble behind, was overwhelming. But he couldn't and didn't. He'd set the course, hauled the anchors. Now he had no choice but to follow the wind.

Matthew was banking on the hope that the hidden Shawnee warriors would not risk a shot at him until he was well within the limited accuracy range of their smooth bore muskets. If either one of them had gotten hold of a gun with a rifled barrel, the extended range and accuracy it would afford, would put him in big trouble. It was possible. A warrior could have picked up one after a raid on a homestead, or even traded for one for that matter. At the moment it was something he didn't want to dwell on.

From the edge of the clearing, Matthew spotted several places, dark shadows, hidden crannies, where an enemy could lay in ambush. The two girls, tied back to back in the center of the campsite, saw his approach. Wild eyed and frantic, they tried to wiggle out of their bindings. Undoubtedly they were as frightened of any white man as they were of their captives. Matthew ignored them, instead keeping his eyes moving, constantly searching the woods for any slight movement. He saw none.

The woods around the camp seemed unnaturally quiet. No birds called. No crickets chirped from under pieces of wood or bark, no grasshoppers buzzed in the tall grass. It seemed as if the world waited in tense suspense.

Matthew could feel drops of sweat slowly inching down his back and sides, some stinging painfully as they found their way into his wounds. His pulse raced, pounding like a hundred hammers striking a single anvil behind his eyes. His time was running out.

Raising the musket to his shoulder, Matthew pulled back the heavy hammer holding the flint. Then pointing

135

the worn smoothbore gun at the most likely hiding spot, he pulled the trigger. The powder in the pan flashed and, as he had expected, the gun didn't fire. Frantically, he re-primed the flash pan, closed the frizzen and again aimed the gun and pulled the trigger. Once more there was a flash when the shower of sparks from the flint ignited the priming powder, but no following explosion of the gun firing.

With a loud yelp, Matthew dropped the gun. Then, in a stumbling panic he fled, running wildly away, as fast as he could make his feet pound the ground. In the back of his mind, he prayed that his wild scheme would work. For an instant, he feared it hadn't. Then from behind, the air was rent by a chorus of shrill war cries. The temptation of gaining revenge, against an apparently unarmed enemy, had proved too much to resist.

Rounding a bend in the trail at a dead run, Matthew glanced back just in time to see both warriors bounding across the clearing. They seemed to be in a footrace, competing for the chance to sink a war-ax in his skull. He didn't plan on sticking around to give them the chance. No longer concerning himself with the pain in his side, he ran.

Nearing the spot where he stashed his gun and gear, Matthew slowed. When he reached his hiding spot, he slipped quietly behind the fallen chestnut, picked up his rifle, cocked the hammer, then squatted down among the ferns. He didn't have long to wait.

The two Shawnee were running fast, but not incautiously. Their dark eyes constantly scanned the trail ahead, as well as both sides of the trail. They stopped directly in front of his hiding place. Matthew dared not

136

draw a single breath.

One warrior spoke several words that Matthew could not understand. The other one only grunted, pointing his gun at the trail ahead, then, suddenly both men took off a dead run once more.

When they had moved a hundred yards down the trail, Matthew drew in a desperate gulp of fresh air. His hands were shaking as he lowered the hammer on his rifle. Likely, he could have killed at least one of the men before they passed out of range. But Matthew could not bring himself to shoot any man in the back, even ones intent on hunting him down.

Grabbing up his gear and the remaining musket, Matthew set off at a trot toward the camp. It wouldn't take long for the two experienced Shawnee warriors to unravel his frail deception. He needed to hurry.

At the perimeter of the camp, Matthew paused long enough to pick up the musket he dropped earlier. Waking to the center of the clearing, he placed the two muskets, the shot pouches and powder horns, at the side the bound girls. Taking out his belt knife, he knelt down and carefully cut the leather straps from around the girls ankles. Then leaning in closer, he sliced the bindings around their wrist.

The girls quickly scrambled a few feet to either side, then sat looking fearfully through owlish, large brown eyes at the wild looking, blood stained apparition standing before them.

"Take the guns," he said, pointing at the muskets. "Take 'em and skedaddle   out of here.... Run."

The girls only looked bewildered, even more frightened.

Matthew knew only a slight spattering of the Cherokee language.

. Words or phrases he'd picked up here and there in his travels and trading among the villages. Now he wracked his brain for the right words, but they seemed as elusive as foxfire in a fog filled swamp.

He smacked his forehead with the palm of his hand as if it might somehow jar the words from his memory. Amazingly, it must have worked.

"Atogiyasdi utsatina," he almost shouted in frustration, the words suddenly erupting in his mind. "Run, damn it. Run."

Chapter 16

Mesquites and gnats, God, how he hated them. Like a pestilence come to life from the pages of the Old Testament, one of the seven curses called down upon the ancient Egyptians, they swarmed around his head, got in his eyes and buzzed in his ears, searching for any exposed bit of flesh. They had transformed his life into a living, itching torment. No matter how many he slapped, how many he swatted, for each one squashed into bloody pulp between his fingers, a hundred more arrived to take its place.

For more than two weeks now, since the weather had grown warmer, it had been the same each night. With the arrival of darkness, their riverside camp became a battleground. It was a war he was losing on drop of blood at a time.

What made this situation even more unbearable was the fact that his four companions, Shawnee braves, did not seem bothered, in the least, by this stinging, biting horde.

Perhaps it was the horrid smell from their unwashed bodies that kept the insects at bay. To the best of his knowledge, not once, in the six weeks since he'd been in their company, had a single one affected to bath.

Sitting on a rock in font of the small cooking fire, he felt the oppressive weight of the night settle across his shoulders as he watched the glowing coals slowly fade from bright orange to dull red. His face was expressionless. Inwardly he seethed at his own sad state of affairs. For the past month he had endured the most horrid of living conditions, tolerated the intolerable, put up with things of which no gentleman of refinement, much less an officer of distinction in the greatest army in the world should be subjected to.

God how he hated them...the mesquites, as well as the Indians.

At the moment, Colonel Thomas Hayward hated just about everything involved with the current sorry state of his life, the Indians, these bloody rebellious colonials, and the fact that his family fortune and status had not been sufficient to preclude him from being involved in this undisciplined war. These so call Americans had no respect for the traditional rules of warfare. They fought, without organization, without discipline, every bit as savagely as their Indian counterparts. He hated being here, especially in the darkness, surrounded by men he did not trust. Men he was sure would slit his throat, without a thought, if they felt it suited their needs.

Had his father not squandered away most of his wealth on a long line countless mistresses... most no more than common street harlots... as well as prolonged periods of drunken debauchery...then he would not be trapped here in this god forsaken wilderness with this lot of unwashed savages.

Never once, even during his worst bouts of depression, did it cross Colonel Thomas Hayward's mind to lay any blame for his miserable plight at his own feet. An over-bloated sense of self-esteem added to a bottomless well of snobbish superiority prevented any such unwelcome fruit from developing on the tree of his self worth.

The fact that greed was by far more to blame for the current state of his circumstances than his sense of duty, was undoubtedly a rotting apple growing on the back side of that tree, far from his line of vision.

And as if he didn't already have problems enough, there was the girl, their latest captive. This one was different. Somehow her presence had him feeling ill at ease, even more tense and irritable than normal. He wasn't exactly sure why and this fact bothered him. Sometimes she would look at him with those big round, liquid eyes, as if she could see what was going on inside his mind. As if she was passing judgment on his actions.

The other girls had not caused him even a passing moment's concern. To him they were no more than chattel, property to be disposed of as he saw fit and a means of securing his financial future.

Originally he had been assigned to a post in Detroit, attached as a strategic advisor to the office of Henry Hamilton, the British governor of the Northwest Territory.

Hamilton had devised a plan to enlist the aid of all the Indian tribes to help fight against the colonial forces, up and down the eastern seaboard. To his way of thinking, with the aid of the Indians, it would be possible to crush the bulk of the American fighting force in a pincer movement.

Hamilton was a fool, he thought ruefully as he sat on his rock, his eyes focused on the gradually fading embers of the fire. It was a plan with no possibility of success. The northern tribes, who had sided with the

French, only a few years ago, were still resentful, distrusting of the English, of whom they'd fought and lost.

While on the other hand, the southern tribes, primarily the Cherokee had always remained loyal to the crown, but had been so decimated in the last major war with the colonials that the older chiefs were determined to remain neutral. Attakullculla and Oconostota had staunchly refused to even acknowledge his proposal. Undoubtedly, this had been at the urging of John Stewart, the Scotsman assigned as superintendent to the Cherokees by the King.

Grudgingly, he had to admit that Stewart took his job to heart, wholeheartedly embracing his assignment as guardian to the Cherokee people. For years he'd worked unflaggingly to steer them in directions best suited to their own needs. The man truly cared for his wards.

He'd been told that Stewart, suffering from bad health, had returned to Charles Town, leaving his deputies, Alexander Cameron and John McDonald, in charge. He'd thought, in the old mans absence; it might be possible drive a wedge in the old chiefs stubborn indisposition. Undoubtedly, he underestimated the old Superintendents lingering influence.

The only positive upshot of his visit to the village of Chota, had been his discovery that Dragging-Canoe, the notorious, renegade war chief was, according to rumor, once again off, visiting the village of a young maiden, over whom he'd become enamored to the point of distraction.

The information at first had seemed inconsequential, worth less than the crock of rum for which it had been

142

traded. And yet that same little seed of information had taken root and sprouted into the tree of his present course of action. A plan that, from all appearances, was causing significant agitation between the tribes and the settlers.

With the aid of a dozen Shawnee warriors, he systematically begun kidnapping young Cherokee women, making the crimes appear as if it were the work of the Americans. It was a brilliantly simple scheme.

Knowing full well that it would have exactly the opposite affect, he'd even left letters stating that the girls were being held hostage in Charles-Town, insurance that the Cherokee remain neutral war with England. He'd seen first hand, the effects of his manipulations. Burned homesteads and brutally scalped and charred bodies.

He viewed these scenes dispassionately, neither saddened nor happy over the deaths, only pleased at the success of his work. After all be damned, he'd been given a job. He would see it done.

His orders had been explicit...seek out and enlist the aid of the major chiefs in each tribe. And if their disinclination was too staunch, then he was to do whatever was with in his power to ferment unrest, or outright war between the frontiersmen and the tribes. He would be given virtually unlimited power over his own actions, answering only to the governor...and of course the King.

By no means happy with this new assignment, he had protested the orders, but Governor Hamilton had not relented. His contentions were that an agent was needed to travel among the villages, swaying them toward the British cause. He was also to move in secrecy among the American, essaying their strengths and weakness.

Realizing further objections would be useless, even detrimental to his career, Colonel Hayward, with grave reservations, acquiesced to the governor's commands. After all, what choice did he have? Officers unwilling to follow orders didn't remain long in the service the King.

Thomas Hayward may well have been pompous and arrogant, even egotistical and self-serving, but the fact that he was now deep in the wilderness, surrounded by a band of hostile savages, committing overt acts of sabotage against other savages, was testament to his courage...if not his common sense. But then greed...as so often happens...obscures rational thought under its dark and shadowy veil.

To his credit it must be said that selling these Cherokee women into slavery was not in his plan from the start. In fact it turned out to be the solution to a very real problem. What do you do with a dozen kidnapped women? Kill them? Lock them in cages or turn them over to the Shawnee warriors who'd help abduct them? No, he was not a complete barbarian.

He'd made arrangements to sell the girls to a profit minded slave trader who saw the benefit of delivering a cargo of black slaves to the markets in Virginia, then picking up a load red ones for the return voyage.

Female slaves, especially attractive ones, were always sought after, a commodity in high demand in most Spanish and Middle Eastern ports around the world. Twice now, he'd delivered his cargo, a dozen shackled girls, to a lonely stretch of beach where, under the cover

144

of darkness, a row-boat manned by armed sailors waited to ferry girls to a slave ship anchored beyond the break waters.

In payment, one of the men, a short, gruff, Portuguese sailor with a shaved head, a hand full of gold rings in his each ear, and a wicked toothy grin, tossed him a canvas sack filled with silver coins. Each girl fetched the price of 50 pounds sterling. So far he'd collected almost 15,000 pounds, a handsome sum for a few months work.

He hadn't bother to count the money, confident that the slaver would not try cheating him. He would be expecting another delivery of girls, next month. It was much to lucrative an arrangement to risk losing over a few missing coins

The really great thing about this arrangement was that it was all profit. His expenses as well as those of his Shawnee mercenaries were paid from the coffers of the British Army. The Indians worked cheap. A few inexpensive trade muskets, shot, powder, a little silver, but mostly a number of crocks of cheapest rum available, kept them happy, at least until the hangovers arrived.

More than anything else, it was the promise of more liquor, more of that river of liquid fire on which they could enter the world of spirit dreams that kept the warriors under his limited control.

And, until recently, everything had been going along just as he planned. Then had come the swarms of tormenting misquotes and the troublesome girl.

The insects, he could only curse, swat, and cruse some

more. About the girl, he wasn't sure what course of action to take. She was the young woman over whom Dragging-Canoe had become so enamored.

It had been a risky business, sending his Shawnee deep into Cherokee country after a specific girl. An act, sure to drive the already hotheaded war chief in to a killing frenzy. Governor Hamilton would be proud.

He had taken ever precaution, planted every deception, even gone so far as to bring in two fast moving northern canoes to insure a speedy escape. The one thing he had not planned on was the girl herself.

Perhaps, he thought to himself as the last of the embers faded and the darkness settled in, he might not sell her to the slaver after all.

One thing was for certain and it didn't take a military strategist to figure it out. The English were not going to win this war. At least not by fighting the way they were trained. The Americans used hit and run tactics learned from fighting Indians. They fired their rifles from behind trees and haystacks, doing devastating damage, then running away to regroup.

No, this war was unpopular with the people of England, who were unhappy at fighting with their friends and families and King George's Army was already stretched far to thin from fighting too many other wars. He was on the losing team. A team whose leaders looked poorly on underlings who lost their battles.

If he lived through this war and England did loose, he would likely be transferred to some god-forsaken spot in some obscure country where his chances of promotion would be nil.

For all these reasons, Colonel Thomas Hayward worked diligently at his plan, at his future.

If things went well, he would have enough money to leave the army, to live as his birthright dictated, to live the life of a gentleman. In that new capacity, he would need a house-slave to clean and attend his needs. So why not this pretty little, dark eyed Indian maiden.

In the dark of night, on the banks of an insect infested river, deep in a savage wilderness, a smile...the first one in month...crossed his face.

Chapter 17

Despite all his urging for the two girls to flee, they continued to cringe fearfully on the ground at his feet. From the fear they exhibited, Matthew wondered if he might not have sprouted horns, a forked tail and had lighting bolts shooting from glowing red eyes.

"Hanigi. Ulisdi. Awidvdi digaque." (You go. Hurry. Carry guns.) Matthew said, trying to soften his words in order to calm the girls. Pointing at the guns, he then moved his hand toward the west, indicating that they should run in that direction.

The older of the two, a girl of maybe seventeen or eighteen, at last seemed to understand what he was trying to communicate. Scrambling on her hands and knees, she scooped up the two cumbersome flintlock muskets and shot pouches. Then rising to her feet, she looked once at Matthew, briefly locking her eyes with his. What she saw there must have assuaged her fear. Turning away, she gripped the arm of the younger girl and together they hurried away.

Before the two girls reached the edge of the clearing, the younger one broke away and ran back to the campsite. Matthew was afraid she might still be too frightened to think rationally. His fears dissolved when the girl stopped to pick up a canvas sack, obviously containing food, then hurried back to the other girl. Then like a pair of frightened deer, they ran in the direction he'd pointed.

148

He felt sure the girls were more than capable of making their way home...that is providing they were not followed. If the Shawnee warriors picked up their trail, it would only be a matter of time before they were captured again.

Studying the trail down which he'd come, Matthew looked for any sign of the two warriors. He saw nothing, which didn't reassure him in the least. An unseen enemy was a far greater threat than a visible one.

His hastily laid out deception would not fool them overly long. He had no doubt the two Shawnee braves would be returning soon...with blood in their eyes, seeking revenge for the deaths of their friends. They might even now be creeping up on the campsite, in much the same manner as he had done, sighting down a rifle barrel at his chest.

No doubt they'd be madder than a nest of angry hornets at discovering the escape of the captives they'd worked so hard to obtain. Throw that fact on their already raging anger and you'd have ignited a short fuse to huge powder keg. An explosion was inevitable. He was depending on it.

As to his own safety, Matthew was confident that he could drift away into the forest, leaving no sign of his passage. The two Shawnee would not be able track him. What worried him, however was the two girls. He doubted they possessed the necessary woodcraft to escape undetected. He would have to create some kind of a diversion.

Walking toward the center of the campsite, Matthew

could here a querulous voice deep in the recess of his mind. The voice of Thadis Smith, sounding as if he were right there, admonishing the actions he was contemplating. "Boy, don't be a damn fool. Them Shawnee don't give a rip about fighting fair. If you ain't gonna skedaddle outta here, then find yourself a hidie hole over there among them rocks. Put a ball in the first one of them rascals to show himself. Even the odds, then take care of the last one, come what may."

"Probably, good advice, "Matthew grumbled to himself, hobbling to a stop in front of a small fire that still burned in a circle of rocks. With each step, with each breath, his side throbbed painfully.

A grouse and a squirrel were skewered on a hickory sticks and suspended over the coals. Ignored in all the frantic activity, they were burned black as charcoal on the bottom sides. The topsides, however, showed some possibility. Hell, the ravenous hunger in his belly would have made a cooked moccasin look good.

Reaching toward the stick that held the overcooked meal, he pulled up short at the sharp pain in his side.

Cautiously with the fingertips of his left hand, he explored the ragged wound across his ribs. It hurt like all hell, but at least the bleeding had stopped. His buckskin shirt was stiff with dried blood. Ragged pieces of the leather were stuck to bloody gash along his side. He didn't dare try pulling it free for fear of starting the bleeding once more.

Soon he would have to take time to find fresh water where he could clean the bullet wound and gather enough spider-web to cover it. Cold water would stop the bleeding and the spider web would help seal the wound.   Another trick he'd learned from Thadis Smith.

Taking out his knife, he half cut half sawed away the top portion of the grouse. Disregarding the pain in his side as well as the heat from the dripping grease, he tore at the bird with his teeth. It was overcooked, dry and unseasoned. He couldn't remember ever having tasted anything quiet as delicious. Quickly he gulped down anything not to hard to chew and swallow.

He would have started in on the squirrel, but after dropping the grouse bones, he looked up to see a Shawnee warriors standing in the trail staring at him. Matthew threw up his hand and waved.

Apparently, thinking he had completely fled the area, his sudden appearance and strange behavior was apparently a total shock to the returning warriors. For a brief instant they seemed unsure what to do. A very brief instant. Amid a chorus of guttural howls and shrill war cries, the two angry braves charged directly toward him.

Matthew, returned his knife to its sheath, grabbed his gun, then bracing himself for the pain he knew was to come, headed in the opposite direction from the one the girls had taken...at a dead run.

He was having second thoughts about his plan; maybe Thadis had the right idea after. Shoot first, work out the details later, but it was too late now.

Matthew had always been a strong runner, had always loved to run.   Right now his life depended that skill. Desperately, he hoped there was enough strength left in his tired and battered body to keep ahead two very angry Shawnee warriors. Thinking of the wicked scalping

151

knives and the deadly war axes, the pair no doubt carried proved to be more than sufficient incentive to keep his legs moving...fast.

For the first quarter of a mile, the warriors closed a little on the hundred plus yards gap that separated them and Matthew. Fortunately the trail twisted and turned around trees and boulders, making it impossible for his pursuers to use their guns. His side ached horribly, but he knew he couldn't let up the pressure.

He was depending on pride of the two warriors to keep them hot on his trail. The further he could draw them away from the girls, the better their chances were of escaping. He would stay just far enough ahead to keep the warriors in pursuit. After a few miles, he would give it all he had, gain enough lead, then slip off the trail at a convenient spot. If he couldn't shake off his pursuers, he might even fire a shot over their head to give them a little 'caution'. He wanted to avoid any further bloodshed if possible.

It was a plan that might have worked....... that is if fate, in the form of a small protruding hemlock root, had not intervened.

The terrain had grown steadily rougher. Matthew had just rounded a curve where the trail swerved around a massive, moss covered tree when he felt his foot suddenly snag on a root. Desperately he tried to keep his balance, but momentum sent him hurtling face first toward ground, his shoulder scraping painfully across another gnarled root, his elbows digging into the rocky trail.

Matthew felt his rifle go flying from his fingers, sailing into the near-by patch of weeds. Then with a dull thud, his head smacked against a flat rock.

The world spun wildly, tilting at an odd angle before slowly sliding toward a sea of black. With ever once of strength he could muster, he fought at the encroaching darkness.

Slowly drawing himself up on his knees, Matthew looked back down the trail. His vision was blurred, the trail, the trees all appeared double.

The two warriors, side by side, were almost on top of him. Then his vision cleared somewhat, causing the two men suddenly merged into a single warrior. The second Shawnee, having fallen behind, showed up about seventy-five yards back.

The first warrior, having seen his enemy stumble and fall, let out an eager war cry, pulled out his war ax and charged wildly forward.

Matthew tried to reach for the pistol tucked behind his belt, but discovered that his right arm had become entangled in his bowstring and quiver strap. Frantically, with his left hand, he managed to draw the gun. Thumbing back the hammer, he squeezed the trigger.

The hammer on the little pistol flew forward driving the flint, in a shower of sparks, against the frizzen, but there was no flash or following explosion. Somehow in falling, he'd lost the priming charge out of the flash-pan.

Dropping the gun, Matthew fumbled around for any available weapon. He had his own knife and tomahawk, but tangled as he was, he doubted being able to use them.

153

The warrior, realizing his advantage, lunged forward, swinging his own ax down in a mighty arc.

Matthew dived forward, trying to get under and beyond the fall of the deadly blade, all the while bringing up the only weapon he could think to use, a steel tipped arrow. He felt his shoulder go numb as the tough hickory handle of the ax landed. Fortunately only the very edge of the blade dug into the flesh of his back, cutting a half inch deep gouge across his shoulder blade.

Hunched over, staggering backward, the Shawnee let go of his ax handle then straightening up, a look of confusion crossed his face as he stared at the arrow protruding from his chest. Drunkenly, he staggered a few feet off the trail, slowly sunk to his knees, then fell face forward into a patch honeysuckle vines.

Matthew didn't waste any time contemplating just how lucky he'd been. His shoulder throbbed like someone had dropped a tree across it. His right arm and fingers were numb, hanging uselessly at his side.

Reaching down, using his good hand, he grabbed the pistol he'd so recently dropped. Awkwardly he thumbed back the frizzen on the little gun, cradling it in the crook of his arm. With trembling fingers he gripped the powder horn hanging at his side. Pulling the plug from the end of the horn with his teeth, he shook way too much powder into the priming pan causing it not to close properly. Quickly he shook out the excess and once more closed the frizzen.

Seeing his partner stagger and fall had caused the remaining warrior to pull up about fifty yards away. He seemed unsure of whether to continue his attack or back away. Deciding to do neither, he instead swung up his

154

musket, sighting down the barrel at Matthew.

It was a long shot, much too far for the short barreled pistol, but seeing he had no other choice, Matthew squeezed the trigger, then dropped flat on the trail.

A shower of hemlock bark buffeted Matthew as the large musket ball tore a gash in the tree a few inches above and behind where his head had just been.

His own hasty shot missed its mark, instead striking stock of warrior's musket, then careening to the side, in the process, driving several long splinters of wood into the man's arm. With a scream of pain, the remaining Shawnee flung down the damaged weapon. Then cradling his wounded arm in the other, he paused long enough to glare hatefully in Matthews' direction, then turned and ran.

Matthew rose to his feet, staggered and spread his legs wide in defiance of a world that threatened to turn black once again. After a time, his head stopped its wild gyrations. Feeling began to return to his wounded arm, bringing with it a fiery agony.

"Thadis, old buddy" he mumbled under his breath. "Next time, I'll listen to your advice."

Moving slowly, trying to drive back the swirling fog in his head, Matthew began gathering up his scattered possessions. With relief, he found his rife was undamaged. After assuring himself of its working condition, he loaded the pistol and wiped both guns down with an oily rag from his pouch. Only then did he turn his attention to his battered body. He needed water to clean, his wounds. Wearily, on trembling legs,

155

Matthew trudged in the direction of the river.

"Hell of a diversion… yes sirree," he mumbled between each painful step

Chapter 18

General Griffith Rutherford sat on a moss-covered boulder situated at the crest of a steep wooded ridge, studying the details of a hand drawn map spread across his knees, as he conferred with one of his three buckskin clad scouts. Unfortunately the map was proving less than reliable.

The rain from the previous night had turned to fog by early morning. Now, at midday, the sun had burned away the last of it, leaving the day hot and steamy.

His detachments, a group of about twenty-five hundred men, were strung out for more than a mile down the steep wooded slope. Looking in their direction he could see them, sitting or standing in small clusters, waiting for his orders to move. He could sense their impatience and restlessness. He too, suffered from the same affliction.

The scout, a tall and tough looking, redheaded Scotsman, by the name Jamie McConnell, stood with his leather hat rolled up in his hand, a flintlock rifle resting easily in the cook of his arm. He scratched idly at his equally red beard, as he tried to explain the lay of the land over the next few miles.

"General," he said, pausing to spit out a stream of tobacco juice, then wiping his mouth on his sleeve. "Ain't nothing down the center of the next valley but a tangle of laurel and ivy."

"You couldn't find a trail, of any kind, passing through it," the general asked?

"Oh, there be trails a plenty," McConnell replied. "Trouble is they ain't fit fer nothing bigger than bloody coon, and a wee one, at that."

"Then what do you suggest," Rutherford asked, a bit more tersely than was prudent with a man like McConnell. After all, the man was here of his own accord. He could simply walk away. As could any man here.

"Sorry," the General said after a short, uncomfortable silence. "I fear my patience has grown a little ragged these last few days."

Their present location put them more than fifty miles away from their destination. Three days and they'd covered less than twenty miles as the crow flies.

The problems incumbent with moving a large force of men across steep, often thickly timbered mountain terrain was decidedly more troublesome than he had anticipated. These men were not soldiers. They were volunteers, frontiersmen, familiar with travel in the mountains. Any single man could have made the journey of twenty miles in a single day. Yet, clumped together, they had been reduced to a third of that.

He was doing his best to not to let his irritation at the slow progress in this campaign against the Cherokee show.

To be successful, any assault launched against the villages along the French Broad River and the Holston Rivers would by necessity, need to be a surprise. If the

158

Indians got word of the attack, they would gather their possessions and simply vanish into the forests. It would take years to roust them out. For all these reasons it was imperative that his army move in secrecy.

So far they had confined their movements to little used, often twisting and winding roads and trails. This of itself had slowed their progress to a snails pace.

"General," the scout said, his feathers unruffled, obviously having taken no offence at his commanders comments. "I can't figure any way around it, 'cept to skirt this ridge and try again in the next valley."

"How long of a delay?"

"Bout five miles. It'll take most of today to move the men through there."

For a short time the General sat quietly, mulling over his options. At the moment they seemed woefully limited.

He had hoped, once he got the campaign under way to leave the bulk of his troubles behind. The problems he'd encountered at Davidson's Fort over the previous two weeks had for a while seemed insurmountable.

Putting together, organizing and arranging for supplies for an all volunteer force of this size had been a major undertaking. Keeping the lid on their plans had been monumental.

In small groups, he'd taken the new recruits to the side, told them of his plans, then swore them to secrecy. Fervently, he hoped it had been enough, but in truth, he wasn't sure how much success they'd had with that

159

aspect of this campaign. They might, after all, end up chasing after an elusive will-o-wisp.

Running his hand through his hair, trying to shake of the mental fatigue, the General turned his attention back to the scout.

"Can you locate Morgan and McCall," the General asked, refereeing to his other two scouts

"Aye, they should be coming in any time now, providing they've not run into a passel of trouble."

"Is there any place up ahead where we can camp?"

"There is a spot. Not far ahead. Relatively flat, in the head of a little cove. A small stream, good water. It'll be tight sleeping quarters, but the men can spread out and make do."

"Good. As soon as we get there, I want you and the other scouts to move forward. Find me a decent trail out of these infernal thickets. Scout ahead as far as the river valley, if you have to."

"Yes sir," McConnell said, ejecting another steam of tobacco juice. "Once we reach the river, we'll be in territory I've tromped over afore. We won't have no more trouble after that."

When McConnell trotted off to start the men in the direction the camp site, General Rutherford stood, folded the worthless map and tucked it in his pouch. Before donning his hat, he once again used his fingers to brush back his brown hair. It had grown over-long and shaggy. He should have had it trimmed before departing on this campaign. He just simply hadn't had time. Ruefully he thought, by the time this journey was over, he'd be lucky if it hadn't all turned gray.

160

Chapter 19

Wet, chilled and trembling, Matthew awoke feeling disorientated and unsure of where he was or how he'd gotten there. It was a feeling that quickly turned into cold paralyzing fear. Fear that came in two very different directions.

First there had been the sound of voices near by. Shawnee voices, speaking a language, he could not understand, but by their tone, left no doubt that the speakers were angry and frustrated. He also heard a few distant words spoken in English, but they were muffled and indistinct.

The speakers had been close enough to rouse him from the state of near unconsciousness in which his wounds and fatigue had locked him for most of the night.

By habit he never opened his eyes, instead he remained still, listening intently to any sounds near by, trying to access his surroundings. For this reason, he was dreadfully aware of the weight of a very large snake stretched out across both his legs. He had felt the snake's body flinch ever so slightly at the sound of the voices.

It was all he could do, not to panic, to continue to lay motionless. His mind kept dredging up images of six foot long timber rattler he'd barely missed stepping on a few weeks earlier.

Cautiously, he opened one eye then the other. He was surrounded by a miniature forest of green stems that ended just above his head in a canopy of broad green leaves. Each leaf sagged with the weight of dozens of clinging drops of water. Beyond the leafy surroundings, river fog, thick enough to cut with a knife, turned the world fuzzy and white. That explained why he had not been spotted by the passing warriors.

Very slowly Matthew lifted his head, trying not to make the slightest twitch in his legs. When at last he could glimpse at the black and white stripped back of the snake, he let out the long breath he'd been holding in.

Gently, Matthew shook his leg. The big, nonpoisonous, king snake lifted its pointed indigo head, turned its eyes to stare disdainfully at him before leisurely crawling off into the weeds.

With a sigh, Matthew lowered his head back to the ground. At least, one of his problems had not been as serious as he'd feared. He still had to contend with of a new batch of Shawnee, not to mention the fact that lifting his head had sent spasms of pain shooting down his neck and shoulder.

Just before dark, after the previous days running battle, he'd staggered to the edge of the river intent on bathing and dressing his wounds. With cold river water he'd bathed the bullet wound on his side, the packed moss over it. It was shallow. He could feel the rib was broken, but not shattered. Gritting his teeth, he had carefully worked the broken ends back together. By the time he'd finished his breath was coming in short gasps and sweat ran in streams off his body.

162

The war ax wound across his shoulder blade had proved near impossible to treat. No matter how he turned, he couldn't manage to reach the jagged cut. In the end he'd had to settle for scooping up water in the palm of his hand and pouring it over his shoulder. After about ten minutes the icy water had at last stopped the bleeding. He'd tried to fashion a bandage of sorts to cover the wound. It kept slipping off. Giving up on the idea, he used short pieces of fringe from his shirt to repair the two torn places. Rinsing away as much of the blood as possible, with a great deal of pain, he pulled the damp buckskin back down over his head and shoulders.

By the time he'd finished, his hands were shaking and his head was spinning wildly. Weak and dizzy, he'd started away from the river, intent on finding a sheltered place to spend the night. He needed to build a small fire to dry his shirt and warm his body.

He only moved a few yards from the waters edge, when his foot tangled in a vine. Face first he landed in a thick patch of fennel weeds, the breath knocked out of him.

Rolling over on his side, he lay for a few minutes fighting to catch his breath. When at last, he tried to sit up, the pain in his side and shoulder proved more than his battered body could endure. His mind fled from the pain, swallowed down that long, dark spiraling maw of unconsciousness.

Sometime during the night Matthew's mind drifted from a state of unconsciousness into a fitful dream filled sleep. Trapped in a twisted nightmarish dreamscape, he was constantly tormented by the black cloaked, hooded figure. The face, glaring hatefully from under a hood, shifted from the distorted image of Rafael Montague to the blood smeared face of Michelle Marcella.

In his nightmare, Matthew was bound hand and foot, even thought he could not see the bindings, and was unable to defend himself from the dark figure that continually thrust the broken end of a wicked sword cane into his back and side.

Waking up, cold and wet, in the midst of his enemies, even sharing his bed of an overly friendly reptile, had been preferable to the terrible night he'd just spent.

Even so, lying there on his back in a wet, dripping patch of weeds, Matthew knew, beyond any doubt, that he was in trouble. He needed to find shelter, to build a fire, warm him and dry his clothing. He also needed a couple of days rest and some decent food to build back his strength. It was the very same course of action he'd started the previous evening before he had collapsed.

Now time was working against him. The fog would soon burn off, leaving him exposed to any watchful eyes. Matthew wanted to be hidden away in some sheltered spot, well before that happened.

Unfortunately, lady-luck must have been stumbling around blindly in the fog as well. For on this wet, dripping morning, if she'd cast even a tiny tidbit of good fortune in his direction, it had been a complete miss.

After gathering up his spilled gear and checking the priming of both guns, he had just started toward the trees when once again; there came the sound of voices. This time he had no trouble telling from which direction they originated. The voices had originated from up stream, somewhere close to the rivers edge. Fog had a strange effect on sound, so he wasn't sure of the distance. It might have been a hundred yards, maybe less. Either way, it was too close for comfort.

On hands and knees, Matthew cautiously crawled through the weeds toward the riverbank, doing his best to keep a careful eye pealed for any more unwelcome visitors. The way his luck had been turning out, he would not have been the least surprised to run up on a whole den of snakes, or failing that, to have a nest of angry bees fall from a limb and land on his head. Fortunately, he encountered neither in the few yards to the river.

In a slight bend in the river, the current had uprooted of a large sycamore tree, leaving a cluster of roots standing upright at the bank. Peeping around the tangled mass of dirt and roots, Matthew could see no more than a dozen yards in any direction.

Suddenly, from somewhere up stream, a gunshot, followed by a couple of muffled shouts, shattered the quiet uneasiness of the morning. Then the fog seemed to grow heavier, settling in like a wet blanket over the river valley.

Once he though he heard the sound of something slap the water. Quietly, he strained to hear any other out of place sounds. Nothing. The sound of the river, an age old conflict of water against stone in it's a never ending quest to return to the sea, was interrupted only by the occasional calls of unseen birds. Their lonesome calls sounding muffled, lost in the mist of a primal forest canopy.

Time seemed suspended, the world shrunken, reduced to no more than a misty sphere less than a bow shot across. A half hour passed with no change in the eerie view. Then almost as if materializing out of thin air, a canoe appeared in the middle of the river.

The river current created air movement, occasionally expanding his field of vision by a few yards. During one of these brief moments, the forest seemed to almost take a deep sigh, drawing back the mist for a hundred yards. A single boat appeared phantom like, cutting through an almost indistinguishable line of mist and water.

Matthew had no doubt the canoe was one of the two he'd seen a few days earlier. Now the craft lay deep in the water, weighted down by two warriors, one in the front and one in the rear. Between them sat three girls. To his surprise, instead of moving with the current, the canoe was angling stiffly across the river, the warriors pulling hard on their wooden paddles to fight the current.

The canoe had no more than touched its bow against a sand bar running out from the opposite bank, when the second canoe, loaded identical came into view. It too followed the same course.

From out of the woods on the opposite shore two warriors walked out onto the sandbar. Without preamble, the pair waded waist deep into the water where they began roughly hauling the trussed and gagged girls out of the boats. By the time they had the first boat unloaded, the second one had arrived to deliver its captive cargo.

A third warrior, a surly, stout looking fellow, wearing a green cotton shirt and deer hide leggings and breech cloth strolled out of woods and began roughly checking the bindings around the ankles and necks of the six girls. Then, like cattle, the three men led the girls off into the trees. The four men in the boats had to paddle furiously against the current to move the canoes back across the river. Obviously, there were more passengers waiting to be ferried.

Concealed in the mist and underbrush, Matthew had no fear of being seen. He was, however, beginning to wonder what kind of strange mess he'd gotten himself into. He'd set out with the intent of freeing a single girl. Now that number had increased. At least six captive girls on the far bank. How many Shawnee warriors were in this group was anybody's guess.

To the best Matthew could tell, Gray Fox Killer's granddaughter had not been in either of the canoes. Of course, she may have already been taken across, or still might be on this side. Nor had he seen any sign of the man he suspected to be a British officer.

And for the moment, it seemed, he would find out no more. The fog, having revealed only tantalizing tidbits of information, suddenly seeming to conspire against him, once more drawing a misty curtain across his view.

Resting his back against the rough bark of the downed sycamore, Matthew pondered what course of action he should follow. What he was up against, seemed more than a little overwhelming. Judging from what he'd seen, he guessed there had to be at least ten, maybe a dozen warriors in this group, at least one white man and a whole gaggle of captive girls. At that moment he was in a lot of pain from his wounds, he was bone tired,

167

weak from blood loss, cold and hungry and in truth, he had no idea what the hell to do next.

More than anything else, right now, Matthew was wishing that Thadis was here. The old trader would know exactly what to do, would not even hesitate, would plunge ahead and it would turn out right.

Not for the first time, Matthew found himself envying the calm self reliance, the unfaltering self sufficiency with which his friend seem to handle even the worst of situations. He might boast, brag and sashay around in the old mans presence, but when you came right down to it, Matthew's experiences with life, didn't amount to two drops in a bucket, when compared to the working knowledge Thadis had gained from a life in the wilderness. God, how he wished the old trader was here now.

Lost in thought, weak with pain, Matthew almost missed seeing the two empty canoes go silently drifting past. Like misty apparitions, the fog shrouded boats floated by. Empty, deliberately set adrift with their paddles still propped against the willow framework, the boats turned pell-mell at the current's whim.

Abandonment of the canoes could only mean one thing. The Shawnees and their English leader were, for what ever reason, taking their captives away from the river, striking out overland. Setting the canoes adrift left no doubt; they didn't plan to return.

The only bright spot Matthew could envision on an otherwise gloomy horizon was that a group of this size would not be hard to follow.

Chapter 20

"Crush these and rub them on the bug bites," Laurel said, taking a hand full of leaves from the inside of her deer-hide dress. Reaching out, she handed a assortment to the Englishman sitting beside the small cook fire where she worked.

In the mixture were needles from a balsam fir, leaves of the dogwood, figwort and elm trees. She'd collected the leaves as they traveled through the forest during the day.

She would rather use Pennyroyal. The juice from the leaves, the stems, even the tiny blue flowers, by themselves, would have worked as itch reliever, as well as a bug-be gone, but she had passed none of the flowers in their travels.

Back in her village, she had a supply of the dried flower in her medicine bag, along with a number of other useful bits of dried bark, leaves and roots. All the things her grandfather had taught her to keep handy for treating illnesses and injuries.

Thinking about her village, about her grandfather, about all the things she'd loved and now gone from her life, made her heart ache. She fought to keep the tears from welling up in her eyes.

There were other things that, when combined, would work almost as well. Gathering the necessary ingredients had not been an easy task, bound as she was, neck and ankles, by thick leather straps leading to the girls in front of and behind her. Each time she had passed a bush, she would grab a few leaves, secreting them into her dress.

"They will help keep the *sgoyi* away," she continued.

Seeing that he did not grasp her meaning, she reached her hand up to pantomime slapping away an invisible mosquito. Then to reinforce her words, she took one of the leaves, crushed it between her fingers and rubbed in on her arm.

Her face remained emotionless, but secretly, she took a small measure of satisfaction from the startled look her words had wrought on the man's face. In the two weeks since she'd been captured, she had not let on that she could, to any degree, understand, much less speak fairly well of the words of the English..

Her actions were, by no means, derived from a sense of misplaced sympathy. It was simply a matter of choosing the lesser of two evils. For several days now, she had watched him claw and scratch until his arms and face were a mass of bloody whelps and scabs. Given her choice, she would have let the misquotes and gnats suck out every drop of blood from his body.

All too well, she understood that this man, Colonel Hayward, planned to sell her, as well as the other girls, as slaves. This information, she had managed to piece together from bits of conversation, overheard between Hayward and the big, cruel warrior who went by the name of Big Neck.

Big Neck was the war-chief of the group of Shawnee who had captured her and the only member the raiding party who understood the orders given by the

Englishman. He was also contemptuous, at times, openly scornfully of Hayward's authority.

The war-chief and the Englishman looked upon her with the same thoughts. She could sense the lust in both men, as their eyes followed her every movement, when going about her morning and evening chores. Even during days of endless walking, she was seldom out of sight of one man or the other.

Only two things kept either man from acting on his passions. For the Colonel, it was a twisted sense of honor, a strange moral dilemma for a man who'd turned to selling other human beings for profit.

With Big Neck, it was much simpler matter. His lust had, for the time being, not overpowered his fear of losing his promised payment of rum.

It was a tenuous path she traveled; one misstep on that narrow ledge would plunge her into treacherous and deadly waters. Her hopes of escaping seemed to diminish with each passing day, so baring some unknown miracle, she faced two unsavory fates.

As much as she hated the Englishman, Laurel realized that should anything befall him, should he grow ill from the mosquito sickness, or in some other way, become of no use to the warriors, it be only a short time until Big Neck had his way with her. She fostered no doubt that when he grew tired of using her like a rutting bull, he would simply slit her throat, leaving her to drown in a pool of her own blood.

So far, she had been lucky. Some of the other girls had not been so fortunate. Ten other girls and young women had been being held at a spot a couple of miles upstream from where they had left the river, guarded by four warriors. On the first night of her arrival Laurel had noticed that two girls, each of about thirteen summers, were withdrawn and frightened, refusing to raise their heads or meet anyone's eye. Both had bruised faces and bloodstains on their thighs.

From whispered snatches of conversation with the other girls, Laurel had learned that each night during the Colonels absence, these same two girls would be led off into the woods by two of the warriors. Later, the two men would return and the remaining two would leave. From what she could gather, this had gone on for over a week.

The two young girls were absolutely terrified, refusing to even be comforted by the older girls. Laurel was sure the girls had been beaten and warned that they would have their throats cut in the middle of the night if they did not remain silent.

They had spent a full day at this encampment. It was during this layover that Laurel learned that all was not well in the camp of her enemies.

Another group of warriors, due to arrive with more captives, had yet to appear. At sun up of the second day, a lone, wounded brave straggled into camp with a tale of being set upon by a group of frontiersman. Their captives had escaped and the other warriors had been killed.

Big Neck had been furious, berating the wounded man as a coward and raving in general frustration. When his anger had subsided, he ordered part of his men across river to search for any sign of where the girls had gone.

In less than a day the warriors had returned to camp, empty handed. Of the girls, no trace could be found. They had vanished into the forest, taking great pains to cover their trail. The searchers had discovered the bodies of the dead warriors, but only the footprints of a single attacker.

At this news, Big Neck went berserk. With a yell, he began kicking and shouting at the wounded brave. Then seeming to regain his composure, he turned and started walking away, only to abruptly turn, raise his rifle, and shoot the wounded man in the chest. With a wave of his hand, he ordered his men to drag the body to the river and toss it in.

During the brutalizing of the wounded man, the colonel had stood up to intervene, but not soon enough. After the shooting he said something to Big Neck, which Laurel could not overhear. For a few brief seconds the two men stood glaring at one another. Laurel began to fear Big Neck might turn his weapons on the Englishman.

During this brief moment of conflict she began to realize the irony of how tenuously her life was tied to a man who planned to sell her into slavery.

She watched the unfolding drama in silent horror. The brutal killing had taken place so quickly; she could only gasp in astonishment. She wasn't, however, given more than a brief few minutes to contemplate the sad, unnecessary waste of human life. Orders were given to move the captives. All the girls, with her at the rear, were being roughly forced toward the two canoes tied at the riverbank.

173

A week had passed without interruption since the day they had crossed the river then headed north-east on foot.

For a time, thinking about the unknown man who'd fought to free the two girls had given her a small degree of hope. She couldn't help wondering who the stranger might be or why a white man would, single handedly, risk his life trying to help them. Her thoughts kept drifting back to the man she'd seen days earlier, crouched in the concealment of a patch of river cane. It seemed inconceivable; they could be one and the same. Also in the past week there had been no further sign of the man.

All these thoughts passed through Laurel's mind as she reached across the fire to give medicine, aid and comfort, to a man she hated, a man who, at least for the time was her protector.

Reaching out a whelped, scratched raw hand, the Colonel accepted the proffered treatment.

"Thank you," he said. Taking the leaves, he began to do as she had instructed.

His words had been simple; his eyes, however had spoken volumes. Laurel saw a confusing welter of emotions written there, not the least of which was anger, perhaps at her, she could not tell, mixed with an undercurrent of lust and perhaps a slight twinge of guilt.

"Where do you take us," Laurel asked, looking away from his gaze as she reached down to rotate a spit holding several chunks of venison?

Just before dark, one of the Shawnee scouts had returned, a small doe slung across his shoulders.

174

Unceremoniously, he dropped the carcass in front of the captive girls. Knowing what was expected; they had skinned and prepared the meat for cooking without being told.

Looking up from her task, Laurel again made eye contact with the Englishman.

"If you behave, you'll be taken to a place that is by far more civilized than this accursed wilderness," the Colonel said at last.

"This is our *ovwenvsv,* our home," Laurel said flatly. "You may find it, as you say, 'accursed'. For us, it is the place we choose to live." Her words, not so much what she said, but the fact that she had spoken in English, once more seemed to make him uncomfortable.

'In time you will learn better,' he said sharply. "Your eyes will be opened to a new, a better world. You will see things you could never imagine. In time you will be happy. You will be grateful for what I'm doing for you."

"I was happy before... before your men *gvnosgisv* me," she said.

"I am not concerned with what does or does not make you happy," he snapped back. "Your only concern need be in doing what you are told, in not causing trouble, keeping your mouth shut and just maybe you'll live long enough to develop a little respect for your superiors. Otherwise, you might end up as part of the payment due to Big Neck and his men."

Realizing she'd probably pushed her luck beyond what was wise, Laurel decided to say no more. Keeping

175

her eyes downcast, she focused her attention on the fire and cooking their evening meal. She couldn't understand why her words, along with a harmless offer of help, had so disturbed the man. Across the fire he sat in sullen silence, rubbing the crushed leaves on his arms and face. When at last he did look in her direction, his eyes still flashed with pent up anger.

Laurel decided that this man too, traveled a narrow treacherous path, a trail with steep cliffs on either side and littered with pitfalls. She preyed to the Great Spirit that he didn't stumble and fall too soon.

Chapter 21

Normally in late spring/early summer the village of Chota was a scene of bustling, purposeful activity. The first harvest of corn and beans were ripening; squash, cucumbers and tomatoes needed to be weeded, and if the weather turned dry, it would be necessary to carry water from the river keep the potato plants from shriveling under the intense summer sun. Potatoes stored in straw lined pits dug into the ground and corn and beans dried in wooden cribs were essential for the survival of the tribe in the hungry months of winter.

Fortunately rainfall had been plentiful; gardens were in good shape, the vines and stalks green and verdant. The village should have been in a state of busy bliss. Unfortunately, it was not.

For the past three days Chota had been in a state of confused uproar. Women moved about their chores with hurried steps, their anxiety obvious in the worried, serious expressions they wore and the way their eyes continually moved, watching over the smaller children as though they feared the ground itself might open, swallowing them whole.

Men, old and young, sat around in groups ranging from two to two dozen, speaking in angry, sometimes overly loud and boasting voices, a sure sign of how dire the situation had become.

Rumors of war, of impending attacks by army of white settlers, hung like a dark ominous cloud over not just this village but also the entire Cherokee territory.

Only the small children seemed to take no notice of the brooding mood of their elders, taking all the gloomy mumbling talk, of war and death, in stride. Like children everywhere, the young Cherokee were blissfully innocent of the memories of hunger and pain, the devastation that inevitably follows in the wake of any war.

Even the young boys, shooting arrows at make believe animals or kicking around balls made of rolled up deer hide, were not old enough to remember the hunger pains in their empty bellies. Nor had they seen the slow lingering deaths brought on by wounds and infections, the inevitable result of war. So they too sat in groups, imitating the adult men, bragging about what bravery they would exhibit, if war did come.

The women, however, remembered all too well the tragedies of war. For as always it had been their lot to deal with the disasters resulting from the battles of their men. It was they who must tend the wounds and listen to the cries of hungry children.

The teenage girls, trained by their mothers, and well inaugurated with their fears, helped watch over the younger children, who in turn played with their corn-shuck dolls or carved animals.

Thadis had been in the village for almost a week. The first few days had been spent in a futile attempt to convince Attakullculla to move his people deeper into the wilderness.

On the fourth day, Dragging-Canoe had returned from an unsuccessful attempt to find the captors of Gray-Fox Killer's granddaughter, the young woman over whom he had become so besotted.

In a surly mood, having found no trace of the young woman, or her captors, the angry war chief instead, focused his ire on his long standing enemies, the settlements along the Cumberland River valley.

Immediately, Dragging-Canoe launched into an attempt to arouse the younger warriors into a state of frenzy, goading them into following him on an impending attack against the settlements along the Cumberland.

Loudly he bragged of the many white scalps he planned to add to his war hoop, of the glory and status he and his followers would surely gain. No surprisingly, many of the young men had fallen prey to his words.

Attakullculla as well as Henry Stuart, the present English superintendent, tried in vain, to reason with the angry war-chief, to defer him from any action against the settlers.

In return, the now furious, Dragging-Canoe threatened Stuart's life, warning him that if he wished to live, he should leave the Cherokee lands at once.

Overhearing these threats and fearing Dragging-Canoe might follow through on his threats, Chief Oconostota had advised the superintendent to leave. Stuart having no other option, reluctantly departed.

Dragging-Canoe turned his fury against his father, publicly berating the old man for the deal he'd struck with the hated Transylvania Company.

Thadis, standing near the old chief's side, had been forced to bite his tongue. The taste in his mouth was like eating green persimmons, bitter at having to stand in impotent rage while a respected old friend was maligned, It was all he could do to keep from drawing the big knife sheathed at his waist. But to do so, to have to another man defend his name would have brought dishonor and shame upon Attakullculla.

Thadis could only glare angrily at Dragging-Canoe for his vicious attempt to humiliate his own aging father. Oh, but how he wished for the boisterous troublemaker to insult him personally, to give him a reason for a challenge to an open fight.

Dragging-Canoe, however, was much to cunning to fall into such a trap. He would wait until another time, when the advantage of numbers, or surprise was more decisively in his favor.

Because most of the village, as well the older chiefs were opposed to his planned attack, Dragging-Canoe and his band new recruits left Chota at the first pale light of the following dawn. There had been none of the normal ceremony and pomp usually associated with a departing war party.

Rumors circulating among the women, said that Dragging-Canoe planned to attack the settlements along Island Flats on the Holston River on July 20th. At the same time, the Raven and Abram, two other like minded chiefs and cronies of Dragging-Canoe, were to attack Carter's valley as well the homesteads along the Nolichuky River.

An hour after Dragging-Canoes departure, Nancy Ward,

great niece of Attakullculla, head of the women's council at Chota, came to visit the lean-to that Thadis kept near the trader's yard.

Like Thadis, Nancy Ward, was of mixed blood. She had also lost her husband, Kingfisher in a war with the Creeks many years ago. She had never remarried. It was only one of many things the two shared in common, not the least of which was a mutual desire to see their people safe and prosperous.

"Greeting and good health," she said, with a warm smile as she paused in front of the shelter where he sat. "May the sun touch the face of the Wolf-Who-Never-Howls, honored brother to the wolf clan and husband to my uncle's daughter, for many years to come."

Thadis looked up from where he was seated on a deerskin spread over a cushion of dried pine needles. In his lap were two trimmed pieces of deer-hide, a bone needle, leather punch and a couple of lengths of sinew. He was making a somewhat futile attempt at repairing the worn bottoms of his spare pair of moccasins. Looking up from his task, a smile slowly etched it way across the craggy weathered lines of his face.

"Days of warm sunshine and good health would be wonderful thing, honored Ghigau," Thadis replied in a gruff voice, belied by his warm smile. "Right now I'd settle for a little nimbler set of fingers."

"Even an old wolf like you needs a good woman to care for him," she said. Her voice reflected the same tone of authority she might have used in ruling over the women's council. Reaching down she took the moccasins and the

181

other items from his hands. With astonishing speed she began attaching the new bottoms on the old moccasins. The dexterity of her fingers did not in the least diminish her ability to scold him as she worked.

"You should take a new wife," she said, glancing down at him over her work with a stern look of disapproval, one she normally reserved for willful young boys who refused to obey the dictates their elders. "There are many eligible women in the village, anyone of which would make a good a wife for you."

It was a years old argument between them. Thadis was use to it, would not in fact, have felt normal without hearing it repeated at least once during his stay.

Nancy Ward was a practical sort of woman, who viewed the world on a matter-of-fact basis. From her point of view, no man, left to his own devices, was capable of taking care of himself.

Thadis had tried for many years to find a way to make his cousin understand that he had been in love once, that the loss of that love had been far too devastating to ever think of trying again. He suspected she was well aware of this fact and simply choose to ignore it. After all, the woman he had loved, married and buried had been one of her life long friends.

For Nancy Ward love mattered and personal needs mattered. She was a loving caring person but always, in matters of life, practically came first. This was one of the reasons she had risen so quickly as leader of the tribe, why she now headed the women's council.

"Where have you been these past few days," Thadis asked? "I've expected to see you every day since I arrived."

"The council has had many problems to discuss and deal with these past few days. As Ghigau, I must preside over all these meetings."

"Do you ever long for those days when responsibility was not such a burden?"

"Why, Thadis Smith," she said sharply, "would I waste my time longing for what can not be? Better to look toward what is possible than what is not."

"No need to get your feathers all ruffled, honored Ghigau," Thadis soothed. "I was only concerned for your happiness."

"Happiness," she said gruffly? "You men, as always, let your heads be by ruled by matters of the heart, matters of pride and vanity, over matters of need or common sense."

"What's put you in such a sour mood," Thadis asked? Realizing his friend was either more despondent over matters than he had thought, or that something else had occurred, something he was unaware of.

For the first time, her fingers stopped working a repairing his moccasins. Her eyes took on a haunted, desperate look he had never seen before.

"Two runners from the village of Keowee, arrived only minutes before I came here," she said at last. "They now speak with Attakullculla in his lodge. Both men were near exhaustion, from the grueling three day journey over steep mountains. The news they carried is an ill wind for our people."

Her voice had developed a tremor as tears began to well up in the corners of her dark brown eyes. Wisely, Thadis

183

did not speak, instead opting to sit quietly until she regained her composure.

"It seems as though your fears of an attack by the whites has come to pass. The runners bring news of an attack by group of soldiers out of Savannah. Villages have been destroyed along the Chattahoochee River, forcing all the survivors to abandon their homes, scattering into the mountains and forests. Another, even larger army, marches form Charleston against the Lower Towns. Already the people flee the towns along the Seneca and Toogaloo rivers."

This time the tears overflowed.

"These troubles have not yet reached Chota," Thadis said, aware of the hollowness of his words, that they held not the ring of truth.

"Troubles enough," Nancy said, regaining some of the rock-edge quality in her voice. "Young women are being stolen from near by villages and Dragging-Canoe, defying the council as well as the chiefs, is luring away many of our warriors."

"As much as I dislike Dragging-Canoe," Thadis said, "right now he is needed here, to help defend the women and children, or to lead them to safety if necessary."

"Dragging-Canoe, as always," she said, making no effort to keep the scorn from her voice, "thinks only of increasing his glory, of adding more scalps to his war hoop. No, he is better off gone. Even as aged and feeble as my uncle is, we are better off under his guidance."

"You are right about that," Thadis said. "I only meant how pitifully few warriors there are to defend the village if an attack does come. And Attakullculla refuses to abandon

Chota."

"My uncle realizes that to abandon Chota now, to leave our crops not harvested, would bring about a slower more painful and lingering death by starvation in the months to come."

"You don't know that for a fact," Thadis almost growled in frustration. "There are always other ways."

"Your eyes, Old-Wolf, have seen much of those bad times. Do you forget the sound of children crying, their bellies swollen for lack of food? Have you forgotten the sadness of finding old men and women frozen in their lodges, too weak from hunger to gather firewood?"

"No one ever forgets such things," Thadis said in an angry whisper. His eyes seemed to turn inward, lost in unwelcome memories of the past.

"No," Nancy said her voice also low, but now filled with compassion. "Those were the terrible times, filled with painful memories that we long to forget but which always seem to creep back into thoughts when you close your eyes at night. They are also things we could not change then, no matter how hard we all tried. Things that can easily come to pass again."

"I know all of what you say is true," Thadis grumbled. "I'm just angry because I cannot think of a solution to these problems. I have wracked my brain for answers. It seems they are as elusive as a trap wise fox?"

"I too have worried greatly over what path we should travel. The only answer with any hope of success would have me betray my own people."

For the moment Thadis was speechless. Betrayal. It was impossible. No one, in his mind, had ever cared more for the welfare of their people more than Nancy Ward. He had no doubts that she would willingly offer up her own lifeblood, if she thought the sacrifice would make things better for their people.

"Betrayal," Thadis asked, the arch of his shaggy eyebrows lending emphasis to the question?

Obviously upset by what she had in mind, it took an uneasy few moments for the Ghigau to piece together her thoughts. Thadis, wisely, remained silent.

"Dragging-Canoe plans to start an attack against the settlements along the Cumberland River Valley on the day after the full moon."

Thadis did some quick mental calculations. From what she said the attack was due to take place around the twentieth of July, less than a week away

"If he succeeds or even if he fails it will fuel grater hatred from the white men living there. But if they were warned of the attack, beforehand, perhaps if they were told that Dragging-Canoe's actions are against the will of the tribe, they will realize that we wish to live in peace."

Thadis sat quietly, mulling over her words. She was right about one thing; it would be a betrayal of some of the men of her tribe. And yet those same men had chosen a path that would ultimately put the entire tribe in jeopardy

"It might work," Thadis said after some thought. "How would you get word to the settlers?"

"Even in these strained times, a half dozen white traders still maintain trading yards at the far end of the village," she said. "Of them, I think Williams, Thomas and Fawling

186

can be trusted."

"Yes," Thadis said. "They are good men. I had planned to stop by and speak with them, before I left."

"If I told them of Dragging-Canoe's plans, and they moved quickly, the settlements on the Cumberland could be warned before the attack." Speaking these words caused her voice to quaver and tears to well up in her eyes.

"Perhaps, it would be better if you didn't tell them," Thadis said.

"What do you mean?"

"Only that it would be better for you not to be the one to speak the words. I think it should be me."

"Dragging-Canoe already hates you," she said. "If he ever found out, he would surely try to kill you."

"Yes," Thadis said, a vicious grin working its way across his face. Drawing his oversized knife, he used the back of the blade to scratch his chin before returning it to the sheath at his waist. "He might even wish to dance with the blades, but it will be his dance of death."

"You are a hard, stubborn man, Thadis Smith, but your heart is good," she said, handing him back the repaired moccasins "The next time, just ask me to fix them for you instead of pretending you couldn't."

With a smile the Ghigau turned and walked back toward her uncle's lodge. As she waked away Thadis, couldn't help smiling. Using his callused fingers like a comb he worked back the thick gray hair away from his eyes. Silently, he wondered how she had known he'd been faking.

Ten minutes later, Thadis was hunkered down beside the fire pit, located in the center of several lodges at the south end of the village, drinking coffee from a metal cup while conferring with the three men they had decided could be trusted to carry the warning to the settlers.

These men, seasoned frontiersman, spoke very little, but listened intently. When Thadis finished his speech, Rawlings, the oldest of the trio, looked solemnly at Thadis, then declared that they all he had 'kin" and friends living in or around the Great Island settlements and Carter's Valley. The other two men nodded in agreement. All three men, having agreed to the request, quietly departed the village within the hour.

Later that morning, after saying goodbye to Attakullculla and Nancy Ward and gathering his few belongings, Thadis too left the village of Chota. His intent was to visit as many villages as he could, especially those along the French Broad River. He would, at least, warn them of the possibility of an impending attack, before heading in search of Matthew.

For a couple of days now, he'd been plagued with an uncomfortable feeling that something was wrong with the boy. He didn't know what that trouble was, couldn't put a finger on his uneasiness. Maybe it was a sixth sense, some hidden intuition. Whatever, the worrisome, nagging deep gut feeling left him with the certainty that Matthew was in trouble, a notion he couldn't he seem to shake.

Thadis had long ago learned to trust his instinct when it came to such matters. He had no doubts about the boys ability to take care of himself, but he might have run into more trouble than any single man, even one as tough as

Matthew, could handle.

As he moved along the wooded trail, Thadis had to resist the urge to let his footsteps move faster than was prudent. This was no time to throw caution to the wind. Even with Dragging-Canoe purportedly off in another direction, which he didn't fully trust, there were always countless possibilities of danger lurking among the shadowy trees.

Two days later, when Thadis at last reached his first destination, his fears for Matthew's safety were validated. Like Chota, the village of Etowah was in an uproar. A large crowd was gathered around two young, haggard looking, girls.

Finally spotting Gray-Fox-Killer, Thadis worked his way through the excited crowd to the old mans side. A first he had thought one of the girls might have been the old man's missing granddaughter, somehow returned, but getting closer look, he realized both these girls were younger than Laurel. He could have also deduced the same fact by the sadness written on Gray-Fox-Killer's face.

The old man, after spotting his old friend, put his hand on Thaïs's shoulder, leading him away from the crowd where they could talk.

"The girls are not from our village," Gray-Fox-Killer said. "They come from a village to the west. They were captured by five Shawnee warriors, dressed and painted like Cherokee. Then they were carried far to the north. They escaped. Ours was the first town they came to."

"How did they manage to escape," Thadis asked, though he was already beginning to   suspicion the answer.

189

"The oldest girl said they had been camped for a day, from what she could understand, they waited to meet with another group of warriors bringing more girls. Both girls say a crazy, lone white man attacked the warriors, luring them away. None of them ever returned. But the white man ran back into the camp, cutting their bindings with his knife. Then giving them guns and food, he told them to run." Gray-Fox- Killer paused to look into the eyes of his friend before continuing. "I fear that this man might have been your young friend."

"You may be right," Thadis said. "He followed the river north looking for your granddaughter."

"She was carried off by men wearing boots," the old man said, his voice breaking with sadness. Our hunters lost the trail shortly after they discovered the paper with the white man's words."

"It don't make much sense to me either," Thadis said. "But Matthew spotted two northern canoes, paddled by Shawnee warriors going down river. In the canoes there was also an Englishman and a single girl who fit the description of your granddaughter."

Thadis saw a spark of hope ignite in the old man's eyes, but then it faded just as quickly.

"The girls say this white man was badly wounded, barely able to stand, his buckskins much bloodied, and torn. They do not know if he still lives. From where they were hiding, they heard shots fired that evening and again the next morning."

Thadis felt a stab of all too familiar pain tearing at his heart, but fought it back. He had no way of knowing if Matthew was alive or dead, wounded or even if it was him at all. Until he learned different, he chose to believe

190

he was alive. Either way, he damn well intended to find out.

"Can you send runners to the other villages nearby," Thadis asked? "Warn them that an army of white soldiers may be headed this way. Already, many towns have been destroyed from the Long Cane Creek country to the Chattahoochee."

"Why," asked the old man, his eyes taking on an even deeper look of sadness?

"I think Dragging-Canoe and some of the other war chiefs have pushed things a little bit too far."

"He has always been a fool thinking he can defeat the whites. They are not better fighters, but their numbers are endless. We must learn to live in peace with them or we will be destroyed." the old man almost spit out the words. "I do not blame my granddaughter for casting aside his proposals of marriage."

Thadis fully understood how Gray-Fox-Killer felt. And while the old man had never looked upon him as anything other than a friend and a Cherokee, he once again felt the rift created by the mixed blood that flowed in his veins. He too realized that if his mother's people were to survive, it would only be through peace.

An hour later, after gathering a few supplies, Thadis headed down river. This time, even despite his need for caution, he hurried.

Chapter 22

A small, straggling beam of sunlight, filtering it's way down through a thick green canopy of pine needles, ended its long journey from the sun against Matthew's right eyelid. Slowly, painfully, he forced his eyes open. The angle of the shadows, cast by the drooping boughs of the huge white pine where he'd taken shelter, told him it was mid-morning.

He didn't have to do much thinking to realize what kind of serious trouble he was in. The chills and pain spasms raging through his stiff body made it eminently clear just how unfit his condition was.

He'd spent a day, a night and part of the next morning under the sheltering concealment of the ancient pine. Or at least that was what he believed. He wasn't sure, for time had seemed to grow meaningless as he passed trough periodic states of fitful fevered sleep or unconsciousness.

Rising to his feet, his body was racked with lightning-bolts of pain. The wound along his side was stiff and sore. The broken rib under the bullet gouge still hurt when he breathed in too deeply, but otherwise seemed to be healing. It was the hatchet wound below his shoulder blade that had him worried. He could not see the wound, but by straining his arm down the neck of his buckskin shirt, he could barely touch it with his fingertips. It was swollen and painful. He could feel the fever, like a fiery hot spider web radiating away from the wound. His fingers came away wet, sticky with fresh blood where his movement had opened the wound once again.

After drying his hands on the layer of pine-needles where he'd slept, Matthew began gathering his gear, preparing leave the sanctuary of the pine. He had recovered a little of his strength, but not enough. His legs trembled like a newborn fawn and his head swooned. For a few minutes he had to lean on his rifle to keep from falling

"Just a damn fool," he mumbled under his breath, frustrated at his own weakness,

Matthew angrily forced himself to stand, while silently berating himself for getting involved in this mess in the first place.

"Just who appointed you to save the world," he mumbled sourly under his breath. "Who said you had to be the one to save a bunch of women. Women you know absolutely nothing about. Or fight a bunch of Shawnee warriors you know way too much about."

Of course, deep down inside, Matthew knew his disgruntled muttering didn't really amount to a drop of spit in the ocean. When he left the shelter of the pine, it would be to follow the trail of the raiding party and the captured girls despite all his self-abasement, he'd never been one to give up on anything he'd made a commitment too. And even in his troubled dreams of the previous night, he was plagued by a pair of large brown eyes, looking into his, and pleading for help.

Before leaving the concealment of the pine Matthew

193

carefully studied the surrounding area, looking for anything out of place. He felt sure all the Shawnee warriors had gone, but he wanted to be positive. He knew for a fact that at least two braves had remained behind, searching for him, or for the two girls, after the raiding party had crossed the river.

He'd been taking his time, carefully crawling through a patch of wild geraniums, watching, waiting, trying to make sure he was alone. At the edge of the weeds, Matthew paused studying the woods around him.

Across the clearing, a gray squirrel, perched in the upper limbs of an old oak chattered noisily at some unseen disturbance. Matthew dropped to his belly and waited. It might have been no more than a fox or a deer that had the squirrel upset, but some sixth sense, a crawling sensation on the nape of his neck, kept him still.

After an hour, weary and hurting, Matthew was ready to give up his vigil, thinking maybe the whole thing had been just a case of jumpy nerves. He was about to stand up when a buckskin clad Indian suddenly seemed almost to materialize between two tree trunks. He waved his arm and moved forward.

From the concealing shadows of an outcrop of rocks to the left, another Indian stepped into view. The two men spoke briefly, too low for Matthew to overhear, and then they trotted away toward the river.

Even after the pair had departed, he had waited another hour before moving out of the weed patch and heading up the side of the mountain. He needed a sheltered spot where he could recover from his wounds. The pine been the best he could find.

Right now, making his way toward the river, even with a full day and nights rest, Matthew didn't feel much recovered. He hoped walking would help loosen up his stiff, sore muscles.

At the river, Matthew made a bundle, wrapping his guns, powder, bow, arrows and other gear in his buckskins. Holding this above his head, he waded into the icy cold water. At mid stream, the water grew too deep, forcing him to swim a few yards until his feet once more touched bottom. Fighting the current left him weak and shaking with fatigue.

On the opposite shore, Matthew unrolled his bundle on a dry rock. Then taking his buckskins, he washed out as much blood as he could. Placing them on another rock to dry in the warm sun, he slipped back into the river.

The cold water seemed to drain a little of the fiery pain out of his shoulder. For a while the water washing over him carried away a reddish tint, but eventually the cold water stopped the bleeding.

Climbing out of the water, Matthew stood, warming in the midday sun. The cold water had awakened his hunger, making his stomach growl. Slinging his shot pouch and belt knife over his shoulder, but otherwise naked, he took his rifle and moved along the shore looking for something to eat.

Down steam a hundred yards, he found a high water pool, now almost dry. Around its edges cattails grew in clusters. Kneeling down, Matthew pulled up several of the taller plants. Attached to each stalk was plump root, looking much like a bleached white potato.

195

Taking a half dozen of these *swamp potatoes* back to the river, Matthew washed away the mud and sand. Using his knife, he peeled two of the roots. The other four he put in his pouch. Tonight would wrap them in leaves and bury them under his campfire to bake. He chewed on one as pulled on his buckskins. The other he would eat as walked.

An hour before making camp for the night, Matthew spotted another of natures gifts from the forest, a bright yellowish-orange mushroom, growing a few feet above the ground, on the trunk of an ancient oak tree.

Thadis called the fungus, *Chicken of the forest,* because the tender outer edges could be sliced into thin strips and eaten, tasting remarkably like chicken.

Later that evening, camped beside a small steam, Matthew roasted the thin strips on a green hickory stick suspended over a small smokeless fire built of dry wood. After eating one of the cattail roots and a few strips of mushroom, then taking a long drink from the stream, he felt a slight bit better. Had it not been for the fiery pain in his back and shoulder, it might have been a peaceful evening.

Leaning against the base of a hemlock, watching the small fire slowly turn into a bed of glowing coals, Matthew pondered what the future held. Right now his chances seemed pretty dismal. How was a wounded man, barely able to fend for himself, suppose to rescue a bunch of women, little alone fight off who knew how many angry Shawnee warriors. It was a fool's errand.

These thoughts tumbled through his mind as he drifted off to sleep.

**

Picking up the trail of the raiding party had been easy. He felt confident it wouldn't take long to overtake the group. Whether his strength would last and what he would do when that time came was another matter.

It took four days to catch up with his quarry. The sign left by a dozen girls tied together was easy enough to follow. By the sixth day he had even seen the girl from the canoe on a couple of occasions.

She seemed to have been put in charge of the other captives. Each evening she went, in the company of a guard, to a nearby stream to bring back water for cooking.

Hidden among the shadows of a near by thicket, Matthew watched as she kneeled to fill a skin container with water. Her guard, a stocky, sour looking man, seemed bored by his task, but dutifully kept his eyes trained on the surrounding area. When they had gone, Matthew slipped away to find a place to spend the night.

By this time, his entire body was once more raging with fever. Several times in the past days he had been forced stop and lay on his back in small cold streams. Once he'd even stood for half an hour under a small waterfall. It helped, temporarily, but always the fever returned.

Between fitful patches of sleep Matthew passed the night under an overhanging rock ledge. He'd racked his brain for some workable plan to free the girls, but so far he'd come up with nothing.

As the stars began to fade in the east, Matthew stood up, and then silently moved into the darkness. On a hunch, he ghosted back to hiding spot where he watched the girl the previous evening.

Just after first light, as he'd hoped, the girl and her guard returned to the same spot for more water. Again he lay still until they had departed. The rough outline of a plan was beginning take shape in his mind. It was a desperate long shot, with very little hope of success, but it was all he could come up with.

When Matthew stood up to make his way back into the forest, his knees were shaking and his hands trembled. He had to stand still for a few minutes, until his head stopped spinning. When at last he moved away, his footsteps were faltering.

.

Chapter 23

Being held captive for almost a moon , forced to walk from daylight to dark and treated no better than an animal, had all but crushed any hope Laurel might have of returning to her village or of ever seeing her grandfather again. Her neck and wrists were chaffed from the leather straps binding her to the other captives. She tried not to think about it, to be strong, at least in front of the other girls for they looked up to her, depended on her for protection. A task she had not sought, nor had any idea how to accomplish.

Sometimes late at night, when no one was awake to notice, tears burned her eyes and dampened her cheeks, but always, by first light, all traces of her fear and homesickness had been purposefully hidden away.

She had thought endlessly of ways to escape, but her captors were ruthlessly efficient. Each night after she and the other girls finished preparing the meal and eating what meager portion was left for them, they were bound securely, ankle and wrist. Left in this uncomfortable manner they clustered together to get what sleep they could on the bare ground until dawn when it was time to repeat the cycle once again.

To Laurel, as with the other girls, being used to the freedom they had known in their secluded mountain villages, this confinement was a living nightmare. Sometimes at night, when the discomfort in her wrist and ankles became too unbearable she would pass the endless hours remembering that past.

She had come to realize how simple and peaceful her life had been. There had always been lots of hard work, but also a simple happiness she'd taken for granted. But these were not her thoughts on this night. Tonight she could only think about a white round stone.

At first she'd though its appearance was a trick of her imagination, but after three mornings in a row, the same identical stone, an oblong piece of white quarts, worn smooth by sand and water on some river bottom, had turned up in three different streams, near where they had stopped to camp for the night.

She had first noticed the stone one morning when she went to the steam to get water. The rock was unusual, out of place for the small brook, and oddly, she had not noticed it on the previous evening when she'd kneeled down at the same spot.

At the time it had simply seemed odd. With all the other problems she had to worry about. The thought quickly faded from her mind until the next morning.

After a full day's walk, covering twenty to twenty grueling miles, and another restless night, she had gone to another stream for water. There was the same stone, lying in the shallow water at her feet.

Quickly she looked around to be sure her guard had not noticed her staring at the rock. Fortunately he was busy watching the surrounding forest. Only when she'd filled her skin bag and rose to leave did he look her way.

One the third morning, at another stream, there was the white stone resting in the shallow water. Positively, it had not been there the previous evening. Someone was trailing them. Watching. Whoever this person was had to know where she went to get water each evening and somehow placed the stone there each night.

Immediately her thoughts went to the stranger she had seen the riverbank the first day of her capture. She also remembered the angry turmoil in the camp on the morning they had left the river. From what she could gather they were supposed to meet up with another group of men. Before they arrived, someone, supposedly a single man, had freed two girls, managed to kill four warriors and wounded another.

Big-Neck had been furious. An argument had almost turned into a fight between him and Colonel Hayward. She had been more than a little surprised when the angry war-chief had backed down.

Laurel knew beyond any doubt that the Englishman would not stand a chance in a fight against the brutal Shawnee leader. Later however, she came to understand that it was the promised payment of guns, shot and powder, and rum that kept Big-Neck from acting on his murderous impulses.

After they had crossed the river, Big-Neck had ordered two men to return to the other shore and wait in ambush for the man, but after two days, having found no sign of the man, the pair had rejoined the main party.

Now, lying on her side, watching the first streaks of

light began to stain the eastern horizon, with shades of purple and gold, Laurel wondered about the unknown man who dared dog the heels of a war-party of this size. He had to be either very good, or very lucky, to stay so close and yet remain unseen. And yet even this thought was depressing. Obviously he was alone. What could a single man do against such uneven odds, and what was the purpose of signaling her that he was out there.

Her thoughts were interrupted, when her usual guard rudely tossed the empty water skin at her head. Reaching down, he untied the strap binding her wrist behind her back

Sitting up, she began rubbing her wrist to help restore circulation. With an impatient grunt, her guard kicked her leg with his mocassined foot. Hurrying to untie her ankles, Laurel grabbed the water skin and started toward the stream.

Kneeling on the bank on a small patch of carpet like moss, Laurel searched the stream bed. The white stone was just in the edge of the water, a few inches deep. On top of it was something she had never seen before. It was an arrowhead, but not made of stone like her people used. This tip was made from metal. She could tell from the gleaming edges that it had been polished to a razor edge.

Without hesitating, she reached down with the skin to let it fill, while underneath, her fingers wrapped around the arrow tip. When the skin had filled, she lifted it out of the water and rose to her feet, concealing the small blade in her palm. By the time she returned to the camp, it was hidden within the folds of her buckskin dress.

All day, Laurel though about the concealed blade. It

would be dangerous. She would have to escape alone. Sometime during the day she would have to secret it in the back of her clothing where she could reach it when her hands were tied behind her back.

She hated the thought of leaving the rest of the girls, but there was no way they could all escape. Maybe together, she and this unknown stranger could find a way to free them. For the first time in many days Laurel dared to let a tiny flickering of hope rekindle in her heart.

Chapter 24

Matthew's hands were trembling. His strength was all
but gone. The fever raging in his body had every muscle
feeling stiff and painful. The wound in his shoulder had
worsened over the past couple of days, to the point that
even laying on his back in a cold steam of water no
longer offered even a small degree temporary relief. Not
only was he beginning to have serious doubts about his
ability to keep up with raiding party, he was beginning
to wonder if he would live through the ordeal.

Hidden inside a windfall of moss covered spruce logs,
located half way up a steep ridge, he watched the camp
down below slowly stir to life. Following their normal
routine, the girl from the canoe, the one Thadis had
called Laurel, had been led away to the small stream
near where they'd made camp the evening before. A few
minutes later the pair had returned. Matthew was
relieved to see that nothing seeming amiss. Silently he
prayed she had found the arrowhead he'd placed on top
of the white stone.

He'd thought about leaving a knife. But even his
smallest one would have been hard for the girl to
conceal. Then he remembered the arrowhead, the one
he'd recovered from the broken arrow he had used to kill
the Shawnee warrior a few days earlier. He'd spent an
hour with a smooth piece of stone honing it to a razor
edge, then half the night slipping down the steam to

place it and the white stone where he hoped she would find it.

He had no way of knowing if the girl had even noticed the white stone had carefully placed in the water the past couple of nights. It was a long shot, the only idea he could come up with to try gaining her attention. He prayed it had, for he was out of options and quickly running out of time. His time.

He'd done everything he could to make sure she would find he arrowhead. The rest was up to her. If she did manage to hide the blade away, she could use it to cut her bindings during the night. The risky part would be when she attempted to slip away. If she was caught, it wouldn't take long to figure out she'd had help. He was in no position to make a quick get away and he sure would not be able to put up much of a fight.

Resting his cheek on one of the logs, he watched the movement as the group prepared to break camp. The cool dampness of the moss offered some small degree of relief from the throbbing ache in is head.

Letting his forehead ease down against the log, Matthew closed his eyes. He only intended on resting them for a second or two......... just for a while....

A half hour later, he was startled awake when a chipmunk, scurrying along one of the logs, ran across his fingers. At first he was disoriented, couldn't remember where he was even why he was there. Then the fog swirling in his mind faded, only to be replaced by anger at his own half-witted lapse in vigilance.

Quickly scanning the camp below, Matthew realized it

205

was now deserted.

"Damn green fool," he berated himself under his breath. He would have kicked his own behind, if he could have reached it and if he'd had the strength, which he didn't. "Good way to get yourself killed."

Knowing self-reproach would gain him absolutely nothing, he instead focused his attention the woods around the camp. He would like to have known if anyone had been left behind to lay an ambush, but his own slip-up had had precluded that possibility.

Cautiously his eyes probed the shadows, scrutinizing any hiding place he could spot. Nothing seemed amiss. Still he waited a good hour before starting down the ridge.

Making his way a hundred yards past the empty campsite, Matthew paused at the edge of the small stream. The white stone was there on the bottom. The arrowhead was gone. He felt a wave of relief as well as sharp stab of anxiety. He'd set out to help the girl, but now he'd placed her in very real danger. But it was done. Now, all he could do was keep as close as possible and wait for whatever fate held in store.

Chapter 25

The warrior assigned to guard girls, the dour, brutish man the girls had come to refer to, at least among themselves, as Corn-Tooth, stirred in his sleep, rolling from his back onto his side. On her knees, ready to slip quietly out of the camp, Laurel froze, not daring to twitch even an eyelid, or draw a breath.

Each night, the big, sour faced guard slept near the girls, a braided leather strap tied around his wrist, running to the straps binding all the girls together. It hadn't taken long.... a few hard kicks and a rough slap or two.... for the girls to realize that Corn-Tooth did not like having his sleep disturbed. He was also her guard each morning when she went about her usual duties.

Laurel loathed the man. Not only for the physical cruelty had he inflicted on the girls, but also for the way his pig-like eyes violated each and every one of them.

Even when they were led into the woods each morning to deal with their bodily needs, he gave them no privacy. His eyes and yellow toothed leering grin... hence the name... always drifted up and down the body of whichever girl he had presently chosen to torment. His actions and crude gestures made it clear what their fate would be, given his own wants.

Fortunately, so far, fear of their leader, Big-Neck and of Colonel Hayward, their employer, had kept the girls

207

safe from further molestations. But as the days passed that fear seemed to diminish by degrees.

After what seemed an unending eternity, Corn-Tooth began to snore lightly once more. Laurel let out the breath she'd been holding. Looking down, she saw the large round eyes of Corn-Flower looking up at her. The girl, really not much more than a child, had been one of the last to be brought into the group. She and another girl named Willow had been treated brutally before joining with the main raiding party.

For a while, Laurel feared the girl might try to get up and follow her. It would have only ended in both of them getting caught.

She hated the thoughts of leaving the other the girls behind, but her chances of escaping the camp undetected were slim at best. Trying to take someone else along would have only gotten them all caught. Her hope was that with the help of whoever was out there in the dark, she could somehow manage to free the others. If he wouldn't help, she would do it alone, somehow.

Almost as if sensing what Laurel had been thinking, the girl gave her a weak smile, then closed her eyes and lay her head quietly back on the ground.

Tears streaming down her cheek, Laurel slipped quietly among the shadows, disappearing into the night without a sound. Acting purely on a hunch, she headed toward the stream which lay about a hundred yards south of the camp. The spot where that evening she filled her water skin seemed to be the common thread binding her to the stranger who was trying to help her.

Beside the shallow stream, she stood still, listening to the sounds of the night, the sounds of crickets and other night creatures. The croaking of the tree frogs told her that it would be raining before daylight. From the direction of the camp there was no sound of alarm or pursuit.

For a brief second she dared to hope that she might have escaped, unnoticed. Then a big rough hand seemed to appear out of the darkness clamping tightly over her mouth. She almost screamed, but the though occurred to her that it might be the man trying to help her.

The thought quickly vanished as the stout fingers began to tighten over her mouth and nose, effectively blocking off her breathing. Another hand began roughly tearing at her clothing.

Frantically, she fought and twisted until she was able to turn her head far enough to see her attacker. What she saw was the sneering yellow-toothed grin of Corn-Tooth.   Obviously, he had been aware of her escape all along, had only feigned sleep to allow her to get far enough away that it would not be overheard by the rest of the camp. Then he would either kill her, or beat her until she was too frightened to say anything.

The big warrior was brutally strong. Laurel fought like a wildcat, kicking and squirming, but she might as well have been sticking at a stone mountain.   Using the arrowhead, which she'd kept in her hand, she swung awkwardly, raking the blade Corn-Tooth's ugly face. The shallow cut she managed to inflict only served to enrage her attacker. Temporarily he gave up trying to get his hand under her dress, and instead used his big fist to club her in the side of the head.

Stunned, her knees buckling, Laurel almost lost

consciousness. Only Corn-Tooth's unrelenting grip around her head, kept her limp body from dropping to the ground. Weakly she tried to bit at the hand over her mouth, but another fist to the head drove any remaining thoughts of fight from her body.

Taking his hand from her mouth, Corn-Tooth unceremoniously dropped her to the ground, then falling to his knees he pushed her dress up over her hips. Using his knees, he pried her legs apart.

Laurel could only gasp for breath, dizzy, sick beyond any hope of resistance.

Sensing his victim's weakness, Corn-Tooth rose up on his knees, awkwardly fumbling with his breechcloth. A triumphant wolfish growl rumbled deep in his throat as a feral toothy grin parted the blood smeared features of his wounded face. He'd waited long to have this girl and now he would. Then he would slit her throat and leave her body for crows to feast on.

Through the swirling chaos in her mind, Laurel was vaguely aware of sudden swooshing sound passing a few feet above her. It preceded another sound, a dull thud, almost like the sound of a pumpkin being dropped against a rock. The big warrior, looming over her, suddenly stiffened, then jerked backwards.

Fighting back the darkness threatening to consume her, Laurel managed to force open her eyes. Silhouetted against a thin layer of clouds and illuminated by a fading moon, she saw an arrow protruding from Corn-Tooth's chest just at the base of his neck, a look of pained bafflement etched its way across his hateful face. His savage grin was gone, replaced by a grimace of pure agony. He looked as thought he wanted to scream, but

210

his throat, having become a fiery torment, had ceased to do his bidding all together.

Slowly raising one arm, Corn-Tooth reached toward the arrow, almost as though disbelieving its existence, as if running his trembling fingers across this strange new apparition sprouting from his body might make it somehow disappear.

Before his fingers ever touched the wooden shaft, the strength fled from his body, his arms dropped limply back to his side as his eyes began to take on a glassy sheen. With a last single gurgling breath, the big warrior slowly toppled to one side, crashing like a giant tree uprooted by the wind, his weight pinning Laurel's right leg solidly against the ground.

Disoriented, eyes blurry with pain and tears, Laurel managed to wiggle and push her leg out from under the dead warrior. Rising to her feet she glanced nervously back in the direction of the camp. Amazingly, no sounds of alarm or pursuit disturbed the night. Even the crickets and tree frogs continued their nightly chorus, paying scant attention as death stalked the forest floor below.

Squinting, Laurel studied the shadowy darkness for any sign of her rescuer. She saw nothing; the night had grown darker, as the clouds bunched tighter, obscuring the already fading moon. A stray, pinhead sized raindrop found her cheek. From the darkness ahead, she thought she heard a slight rustling of leaves, and what sounded like a groan.

Heading toward the sound, Laurel felt her way along the dark trail, pausing each thin mocassined foot just

211

above the ground to feel for any betraying sticks or twigs. She heard the man before she ever saw him.

He was on his knees, leaving heavily on a short stout bow. As Laurel drew near, he mumbled, almost groaned, something barely audible. She didn't hear the words clear enough to understand. Leaning closer, she was appalled by the feel of heat radiating from his body. This was not the normal heat of exertion. The man kneeling on the ground before her was filled with the raging fire of fever. Her nostrils also picked up the faint, sweet sick smell of festering flesh. Her heart sank.

From past experience, Laurel knew that corruption from such wounds would eventually seep into the blood, spreading poison through out the entire body. Death almost always followed.

Among her people it was called *hia gasvsdi vhnai ayohuhisdi,* the smell of death.

Again the stranger uttered a few weak, barely audible words. His breathing was ragged, rasping as if every breath came at a dear cost.

"The arrow," he mumbled across swollen cracked lips. "Get the arrow."

Not pausing to question his reasons, Laurel hurried back to Corn-Tooth's body. Placing her foot on the dead man's chest, she pulled hard on the wooden shaft. The arrow moved only slightly then stopped. Using both hands, she yanked with all her strength. The arrow came free with a wet slurping sound, the metal arrowhead glinting slightly in the darkness.

Looking at the dripping arrow, Laurel suddenly understood the need for its recovery. Her people used arrow tips of shaped stone. The metal tip would have been a dead giveaway that the man who helped her escape was a white man.

Hurrying back, Laurel found the man on his feet...barely. From the way he looked, it was doubtful he would remain there long. Slipping the arrow into the quiver on his back, she bent down to picked up his rifle from where it lay on the ground, then taking the bow out of his hand, she slung it over her shoulder.

After taking only a few of steps the man staggered, nearly falling to his knees. Using her free arm, Laurel reached around his waist to give him a little added support. He was a big man, broad shouldered and heavy, even in his poor condition.   Standing upright, her shoulder lacked inches reaching under his arm

As he lowered his arm down on her shoulder with grunt of pain, Laurel was once again appalled at the fierce heat radiating from his body.

"Thanks," he managed in a hushed croak.

Without replying, Laurel started forward, her steps taking them slowly into the darkness and away from the camp of their enemies.

As they waded into an ocean of shadows, Laurel felt a half dozen raindrops splatter against her head and shoulders. Silently she offered up a prayer of thanks. Moving the way they were, a half grown Cherokee boy could have followed their trail. Rainwater would wash

213

away any sign of their passage. It would also give the man beside her some relief from his tormenting heat.

Moving as silently as possible, more by feel than sight, through the deepening darkness, Laurel tried to sort out what needed to be done. The night offered few optimistic answers. She had no illusions about not being pursued. She was well aware that the war chief, Big-Neck, as well as Colonel Hayward, each had their own plans for her future. She had seen the way each one had looked at her when they thought no one else could see. It was the same look she'd seen in the eyes of Dragging-Canoe.

She tried to put these thoughts from her mind, instead concentrating on moving away from her abductors, on helping this stranger who'd risk his life to free her. Right now, what she desperately needed was to find a dry place, somewhere hidden from pursuit, where she could treat his wounds.

In her heart, Laurel feared it would be too late.

Chapter 26

Matthew had only very vague recollections of the journey away from the Shawnee encampment on that rainy, miserable night. He did however remember having used his bow to stop a big Shawnee guard from harming the girl. He also had memories of leaning on the girl's small shoulder as they struggled through the wet dripping forest, trying to put as much distance as possible between themselves and the Shawnee. There would be pursuit at first light.

Rain had been their saving grace. Weak, barely able to stand, he'd been in no condition to travel in a manner that would leave no sign of his passage. Fortunately the steady downpour had washed away any of their passing.

At one point during the night, she had been forced to leave him alone, leaning against the trunk of a huge pine tree, while she searched for better shelter. Shivering, alone in the darkness, his clothing soaking wet as rainwater dripping from his hat, he'd moved between periods of restless dream haunted sleep and dark unconsciousness.

Matthew had no recollection of leaving the dripping shelter of the pine tree, yet sometime during the night, the girl had returned and gotten him to move.

A few hours later, he remembered momentarily waking, painfully opening his eyes to see a world surrounded in dense fog. He was lying under an overhanging rock ledge extending back about twenty feet. A small stream of water, more than the rainfall could account for fell from the face of the rock ledge.

Dry, wind blown leaves and pine needles had been raked into a pile. He was lying naked in the middle of this leafy bed. More leaves had been piled over him for warmth. He spotted his buckskins, draped over a large boulder to dry at the back of the overhang. His gun, bow and other gear were also stacked near by. There was no sign of the girl.

Trying to rise to his knees, Matthew was suddenly overcome by dizziness. He wanted to check the powder in his powder horn, to make sure it was dry. He also needed to check the loads in his gun and pistol. If they were wet, the weapons would be rendered useless until he could dry them out and reload them.

For a minute Matthew felt that he might black out, each pounding beat of his heart sent waves of pain raging through his head. His back and shoulder felt as though someone had covered him with burning coals. What little strength he'd recovered from resting was rapidly fading away.

Lowering himself back down among the leaves set the muscles in his arms to trembling, using up what remaining strength he had and sending him tumbling endlessly into a world of fragmented visions and tortured dreams, and yet a place seemingly more real than the one his mind had just fled.

At the same time Matthew fought with the demons in his mind, Laurel was fighting her own battle... with time and exhaustion. Time was running out for the man. She knew very well how fortunate they had been to stumble across the dry overhanging rock face. She had half dragged, half carried him for three or four miles southward, away from the camp. After that, he could barely stand, much less travel any further. She'd been forced to leave him under the shelter of an ancient pine tree while she went ahead alone. It could only have been the answer to her prayers that less than an hour later she'd found herself standing under the dry overhang.

Heading back toward the old pine tree and the wounded man, she uttered a prayer of thanks, plus several more for the safety of the man who had come to her aid. She feared he might not be alive when she got there...Miraculously, he was, but it seemed, just barely.

By the time she'd gotten him under the shelter, his lips were blue and his skin as pale as the underside of a mushroom. He shook continuously as fever and chills alternately racked his body. She hadn't dared try building a fire, knowing it would have been a beacon in the night to anyone looking for them. Instead, she had raked all the available leaves and pine needles into a pile at the rear of the overhang. Dirty and crumbing, the leaves made a poor bed, but at least offered some degree of warmth.

By the time she got the man onto the nest of leaves, and then removed his soaking buckskins, draping them over a rock to dry, he was   asleep or unconscious.

In the darkness she could do little to help him. All she could offer was the warmth of her body. Removing her own wet clothing, she crawled into the leaves, wrapping her arms around his shaking body. Through the last hours of darkness she laid as close as possible, feeling the beating of his heart and the shaking of his body.

Dawn came slowly, their hiding place shrouded in a thick layer of fog. When enough light filtered its way under the overhang, Laurel, dressed in her still damp cloths and carefully began examining his wounds.

What appeared to be a bullet wound along his side was raw and ugly, but seemed to be healing. The cut under his right shoulder blade, from its looks, made by knife or tomahawk was a different matter. Angry red streaks of blood fever spread in long fingers away from the wound. While the gash itself seemed to be knitting back together, it was inflamed and seeping yellow poisonous ooze.

Looking closely, she saw something dark protruding from the lower side of the wound. Gently reaching out a finger, she touched it, trying to figure out what it could be. Bending even closer she suddenly realized that it was a tattered piece of leather, likely a piece of his buckskin shirt that had been driven into the wound by the force of the blow. It was little wonder the wound had festered and was poisoning his body.

Pinching the material between two fingers, she gently tugged. The material didn't budge because the flesh had begun to heal around it. All she got from her effort was low painful groan rumbling deep in the man's chest.

Laurel realized the wound would have to be reopened, cleaned and allowed to drain, if there was to be any hope for the man's survival. She would like to have had some rum or ale to give him to numb him to the pain. It was the only good purpose she'd ever discovered for the white man's favored drink.

Among her people, the drink had made men lose all sense of dignity. Once hopelessly locked in its intoxicating grip, she had seen warriors trade everything they owned, even their wives, for one more drink.

Rummaging through the man's processions, she found two knives. A large one, stuck in a belt sheath and a smaller one with a curved, hooked blade. The small blade, she felt sure was used to trim the cloth patches around the round lead bullets when loading his guns. Both were razor edged. She also found a flint and steel for making a fire.

Gathering together all the dry sticks, bits of bark and a hand full of dry leaves. Using the big knife, she scraped a small handful of paper-thin shavings into her palm. It took several tries to with the flint, but eventually she had a small fire burning in the dry tender. Dropping it among the dry leaves, she gently blew on it until the flames caught up. Soon she had a small but hot fire burning.

With any luck, any smoke would be invisible in the fog. Taking the big knife, she went out in search of more wood. She needed pinewood with rosin it, something that would burn hot. She also needed a short length of green sapling to place between his teeth and some fresh green moss.

It only took minutes to gather what she needed. When she returned her little fire had burned down to mostly coals. Carefully she placed a couple of pine knots over the coals, which began to burn quickly. She then slid the blade of the big knife into the coals.

Her hands were trembling as she walked back then kneeled beside the wounded man. He appeared to be unconscious. She hoped that he was.

Placing the green sourwood stick between his teeth, she tied a strip of material cut from her dress to each end, the bound it around his head. Picking up the small knife, she had to grit her teeth to force her hand to stop shaking.

In what seemed an eternity, but was in reality only a matter of minutes, Laurel had the wound reopened and the scrap of buckskin removed. Blood poured freely from the cut. For a time she let it bleed, let it wash the pus and corruption away. Then she began to walk back and forth to the small steam of water falling from the rock ledge, filling her cupped hands with cold water and emptying them into the wound.

After a while the cold water began to stop the bleeding, so Laurel tried to prepare herself for the second part of what she had to do. By this time the handle of the big knife was to hot for her to handle. She had to wrap more material torn from her dress to warp the handle. The blade was dull red.

Carefully she closed the edges of the wound, and then laid the flat of the hot blade across it. The man groaned and jerked spastically, but then lay still. At first she feared he might have died, but after a few drawn out seconds his chest began to rise and fall again. She had sealed the four inch long cut all but at the very bottom. This she left alone to give the wound a place to drain.

Soaking the moss she'd gathered in cold water, she placed it over the wound, then selecting two clean flat stones from the pool of water; she used them to weight down the moss. When she removed the stick from his mouth, he'd bitten so hard, she had to pry it off his teeth. Surveying her work, Laurel was far from satisfied, but for the time being, it was all she could do. She still had a lot of work to do, plants to gather for medicine and food of some type. She had ideas of what she needed; the problem was where to find it.

Once again she looked at the mans pinched face. Beneath the growth of reddish blond hair and beard, his skin was as pale as the fog outside the overhang. She would rather not leave him alone, but had no other option.

Picking up the big knife, she cooled it the rest of the way in the little pool, then she walked away, vanishing into the fog.

Chapter 27

Delirious, fighting for his life against the poisons flowing through his veins, ravaging his body, Matthew's subconscious mind also fought battles of its own against ghostly adversaries, or long dead foes. At other times, his mind seemed to wonder aimlessly lost along a befuddling maze of trails and roads, beginning and ending in the depths of his fevered imagination.

The demons he fought, enemies reincarnated, were spawned in the dark pit of his misplaced sense of guilt. For this reason, it would never be possible that he should overcome them. To win required ending some portion of his self-inflicted punishment, to attain self-forgiveness. In his mind, forgiveness was something he did not deserve.

Once more, in a place of darkness and shadows, he fought the phantom of Raphael Radcliff. Again he felt the vicious bite of the man's wicked little cane sword. Over and over the blade bit into his back and shoulder, it's point grating against his shoulder blade, sending spasms of fiery agony shooting through his body. He wanted to cry out, but found that somehow his jaws were locked shut.

Then abruptly, the scene changed. The dark shrouded figure of Raphael Radcliff faded to mist, carried away by a whipping sea wind, leaving Matthew somehow alone, standing on the bow of the *Midnight-Marry,* droplets of icy cold sea water stinging his face. Around him the sea churned and frothed. Angry clouds of the approaching storm dropped down, uniting with the swelling sea to form an unbroken wall of wind, water and fog.

Looking about, Matthew realized that he was alone, on a ghost ship, silent, save the creaking groan of rigging ropes, straining against ragged, gale tortured sails. Gone was the easy banter of mates, the bustling of hum of activity as men prepared to hear the shouted orders, the call to do battle with an angry sea. Gone...all the things that had once seemed familiar, a comforting part of the life he had, for a short while, lived.

Huge waves pounded against the lapped boards along the ship's bow with such fury, it seemed as though Poseidon, had arisen form his throne and was using his trident to rip the hull asunder.

Caught up in the thrall of this new dreamscape, Matthew could only stare helplessly into the face of the approaching squall. His feet seemed rooted in place, his arms made of lead. The rational part of his mind screamed, protesting that what he saw was not real, was not as it had been in his past. But his eyes and his heart, perceived the approaching horror as real...so it became real.

The year and a half spent aboard the *Midnight*, when he'd first left England had been a harsh but not unhappy time. Many of the men aboard had known and respected his father. Not that it made anything easier for Matthew. By their roughshod, hard-bitten code, any man, regardless of his background, had to earn the respect of his mates.

Working on board a ship hauling iron from Spain up the English Channel, Matthew had eventually managed to carve a niche among those brine-toughened seafarers. It was an arduous college to which he had enrolled. A school callused hands and hard labor. You toughened up quick, carried your load, or were dumped without preamble in the nearest port to find your own way home. After a few months and several fights, most of which he lost, but none he backed away from, the men's reference to him changed from you...boy to Laddie and eventually Matt. In time, even the saltiest hard-cases had come to accept him a one of their own.

Now watching the dark swell of the angry sea grow higher with each passing wave, Matthew longed for the company of even one of those salty men from his past life. Somewhere in the depths of his subconscious, a thought suddenly wormed its way into his mind. Perhaps he was already ghost, like this phantom ship. Perhaps this *was* his damnation, his punishment, to spend eternity alone, facing the horrors of a reoccurring death.

Like a statue of lifeless marble, helpless to do anything but observe, Matthew watched as a huge wave lifted the already floundering ship like so much useless flotsam, then dropped in into the ensuing trough.

The next wave washed over the ships rails with the force of a rock landslide. Matthew felt the breath knocked from his body as he was suddenly enveloped in spinning, rolling avalanche of foaming, churning water.

His lungs burning, with no idea which direction was up, Matthew struggled against the icy cold water until his body could no longer bare the strain. Opening his mouth, he felt the rush of icy salt-water. His lungs screamed... then from the murky depths a hand reached out, took hold of his arm and pulled him upward.

In the shifting, swirling wash of defused light, Matthew turned to stare into the face of Michelle Marcella. The water lifted her radiant blond hair, flowing it around her head like a golden halo. Her eyes were filled with a deep sadness as she looked at him.

Frightened, Matthew, at first resisted the insistent tug of her hand and tried desperately to pull away, but she held him fast, her grip seeming as hard as iron. At last, resigned to whatever fate befell him, he let himself be drawn upward.

As they moved toward the now visible surface, Matthew once again looked into the beautiful face of a girl he once loved, dead so many years past. The sadness in her eyes melted away, replaced by a warm smile. Just as his head broke through the surface of the choppy sea, the phantom Michelle Marcella dissolved like sea-foam torn apart, dancing away on the waves.

Matthew wanted to scream, No! To plead with her, beg her not to leave him alone, but all that erupted from his pained throat was a spew of seawater.

**

Gasping for breath, Matthew tried weakly to rise to his knees, but small hand pressed firmly against the small of his back.

"Howatsu, nihi ase nasginigesvna advnvsdi,"she said in Cherokee.

Then to Matthew's surprise, she said the words again, this time in English. "Please, you must not move."

Turning his head slightly, Matthew tried to make his eyes focus on the source of the voice. The very lovely face of a girl, with large round eyes and dark black hair, slowly swam into view. He was sure he had seen those same eyes from somewhere before, but at the moment he just couldn't seem to remember where.

"Please," the girls' voice implored once again. "You must try not to move. Your wounds will need time to heal. You have lost much blood. If you thrash about, they will start to bleed again."

Confused, disoriented and weak, Matthew dropped back down into the pile of leaves that had grown damp from his own sweat.

Desperately, he tried to make some sense of his surroundings. Illusion and reality, for a time still seemed intertwined as one, but ever so slowly the groping tendrils of each world unwound from one another, fading like smoke, into their own separate realms.

At first glance, Matthew realized that his surroundings had changed drastically since his last conscious memory. In the semi-darkness a small fire burned. The opening along the entire face of the overhang had been screened with a layer of brush, spruce and pine limbs. Sunlight filtered in only through scattered openings. Someone had worked hard to conceal their location.

The girl...yes he remembered her now...the one form the canoe... was on her knees by his side. She had been using a smooth round stone against a larger flat one to crush some kind of green leaves into a pulp, when his movement interrupted her.   She moved to his side.

"Please lay still," she whispered.

He needed no further urging.

Laying face down in the mound of leaves, Matthew was vaguely aware of the soothing cool sensation as she gently spread the wet paste across the wound on his shoulder, then she did the same for the bullet crease across his ribs.

The smell of food cooking over the fire filled his nostrils, set his stomach to growling. It seemed like months since he'd eaten, yet right then, he wasn't sure if he had the strength to open his mouth. Lulled by the girl's gentle ministering touch, Matthew slowly closed his eyes.

This time it was the healthy pull of sleep that claimed his mind. And while his rest was troubled by dreams, they did not have the severe haunting quality of what he had previously experienced.

Chapter 28

The Shawnee raiding party, their captives, as well as their leader, were only six days away from their destination, a small hidden cove on the secluded sea coast of Virginia. It was at this little known location, the juncture of the James River and the Chesapeake Bay, that Colonel Hayward was to deliver his final cargo of human flesh.

Captain Edward Taggard, owner of the slave-ship, *Wandering -Wind* was scheduled to anchor off shore on the night of July 25th. Upon spotting a signal fire on the beach, the Captain was to bring two keelboats to haul back his new merchandise...and of course, to deliver payment in the form in gold coins. He was also to deliver several barrels of rum and wine, along with various other items in payment for the girls.

Then hopefully the Colonel thought, he could pay off his barbarous workers for their services and send the on their way. Maybe, if he was lucky, they would drown in the cheap rot-gut and if not at least he would be rid of their company. Either way, it would not be soon enough as far as he was concerned. Life in this God-forsaken wilderness, among uncivilized, bloodthirsty savages, had been at best, a living hell. Then things got worse.

For almost a week now, ever since the infernal Cherokee girl had somehow managed to escape, he had grown progressively more   agitated. With each passing day his sense of impending danger heightened, as his nerves grew ever more tattered. He was rapidly losing what little tenuous control he had once exercised over the band of Shawnee mercenaries. The girl's disappearance was not the central focus of all his current troubles, but her escape had certainly been the catalyst in its development.

On discovering the girls escape, not to mention the death of one of his warriors, Big-Neck had, for a time, gone as berserk as a hornet stung bull, kicking, stomping and demolishing anything in his path. Later on, when due to the previous night's rain and a thick morning fog, no sign of the girl or her rescuer could be found, the big Shawnee warrior had grown even more sullen and insolent than usual. And as always, Big-Neck's mood was reflected in the actions of his men.

The Colonel had even taken to sleeping with his flintlock pistol concealed under the foals of his coat. His sword, when not strapped to his side, was never more than an arms length from his right hand. He wasn't foolish enough to believe either gesture was anything more than show of false bravado. In truth, neither weapon would do him much good in the event the remaining Shawnee did decide to betray him, it just bolstered his waning confidence.

In the past he hadn't experienced any major problems in controlling his Shawnee followers. He had always paid them well in shot, powder, drink and even silver, if they chose. Without exception the Indians always took the bulk of their payment in the form of alcohol, either wine, ale or rum. His primary trouble had been getting them back to business after an extended period of drunken debauchery. All that had changed on this trip.

Not only had the Shawnee lost a half dozen of their number to an unknown, and seemingly invisible enemy, two days ago they had narrowly missed running head on into a large body of armed frontiersmen. The well-organized group of men, led by a man of obvious military background, were traveling at a determined pace in a southwesterly direction.

Hidden from sight, deep in the shadows of rhododendron thicket on top of a steep ridge, the Colonel and several of the Shawnee braves had watched the men file through the valley below.   He realized almost immediately that the men were Virginia militia, most likely in route to the Cherokee territory, obviously planning an attack on the Overhill Towns and villages along the North Carolina/Virginia border. And while he was pleased to see some of his scheming and work reaching fruition, the presence of so many armed whites had thrown the Shawnee into an angry panic. Some argued to leave this part of the country immediately, take the captives and head back to their own land. There they could sell the girls as slaves.

The Colonel had neither the time nor the inclination to explain to a group of un-washed savages that this group of men poised no threat to Big-Neck or his men. He seriously doubted if any single one these uncouth men had the mental capacity to comprehend their part in what was occurring around them on a large scale.

The Americans would expend vital time and supplies on attacking of the Cherokee. It would take months,

230

maybe even years to rout them out of their mountain stronghold, giving the British army time to organize, time to reinforce their numbers. And, if nothing else, it would give the willful Cherokee chiefs no choice other than allying themselves with their rightful English sovereigns.

God, but how he hated them all... The Indians, like their white counterparts, those ungrateful colonials, committing mass acts of treason by virtue of refusing to obey the king's commands. In his mind, all Indians were base, mindless savages, sub-human with no understanding of the privileges incumbent to rank or birthright. Their lack of respect for their social superiors (him) was infuriating, as well as rankling. When this trip was over, he planned to return to Canada, report to Governor Hamilton that his mission had been successful, and, hopefully-hopefully, never have to set foot in this vile country again.

In a way he was glad the girl had escaped. Her presence would have been a constant reminder of a hateful time he would rather forget. Not to mention the fact that she would have presented an entire host of problems when he returned to Canada. Yes it avoided a number of embarrassing questions from his superior officers.

The girls escape should have ended a point of contention between himself and Big-Neck. The Colonel was well aware that the Shawnee war-chief had plans of his own involving the Laurel.

What a fool he'd been. He had to have been suffering from a case of fever, or delirium from the constant harassment of insects, or the vile half-cooked food that had been their everyday fare, for even a moment's time spent believing a girl of such low birth could have been a suitable companion for someone like himself.

Once again, in the typical snobbish fashion of English aristocrats, Colonel Thomas Hayward arrogantly transferred any blame, even for his own base emotions, for his secret need for love, to someone or thing else and again he used his sojourn in the American wilderness as his whipping boy.

Eventually the warriors calmed down. Later that evening as camp was being set up; Big-Neck held an impromptu meeting with his men, away from the camp, and away from the Colonel's prying ears.

Eventually they decided that there was no profit, or rum, to be had by leaving when they were this close. Eventually they returned to the camp, quietly going about business as usual. The next morning they were once more headed toward the coast

Like steel, drawn to a loadstone, with each step the Colonel could feel himself nearing the end of his journey. In his mind, it could only be deemed as nothing less than a journey away from *the gates of hell....*

Chapter 29

Among the Cherokee there were a great many "old adages" dealing with a person actions, be it whether they had acted with wisdom or in a foolish manner. One saying in particular kept going through Laurel's mind as she made her way back to the overhang shelter. It went something like . . . "only a foolish man sticks his hand in a nest of angry bees."

Well, she certainly wasn't a man, and she hoped she hadn't been foolish when she *had* stuck her hand in a nest of bees. Honey bees. She had come away with a several smarting stings, but also four large chunks of dripping honeycomb. She'd made a torch of small green cedar limbs. The smoke had helped to calm the bees, although handling burning branches had done nothing to calm her nerves as she hung precariously from a limb twenty feet off the ground.

Finding a bee tree was not a difficult task, you began by capturing a dozen honeybees from nearby wild flowers. She'd used a hollow reed with a piece of wood for a stopper to hold the angry bees. Walking through the woods, she had released bees, one at a time at different locations. An agitated bee, released from captivity, invariable flies in a straight line to its hive. By observing these various flight paths, she could roughly calculate the tree's location.

The trouble was most hives were located in spots too inaccessible to reach or in hollow trees with openings too small to get into. She had located three different trees before finding one she could get into, and even it had been dangerous, but she had need of both the honey and the beeswax.

As a young girl, her grandfather had taught her about the many healing qualities of honey. It helped to quickly rebuild strength after a sickness. Today she planned to boil some sassafras roots to make tea, then use the honey to sweeten it. The beeswax, she planned to melt. As it began to cool, she would pour it over the man's wounds. It would make an effective bandage, keeping the dirt and bugs away.

After three days, Laurel was beginning to feel that the man might live after all. For a time she'd had grave doubt about his survival. Fortunately he seemed to have a strong spirit, one that wanted to continue residing in his body.

The sticky honey wrapped in two large Catawba leaves, carried in one hand, Laurel made her way back, through sun dappled forest and bight sunny meadows, occasionally stopping to examine certain plants. The roots and leave she chose, either for medicine or food went into a makeshift basket she'd woven from willow branches hanging from her shoulder.

Not far from this same spot, on the first day here, she had found a bearberry bush. Crushing the green leaves and stems of the bush into a liquid, she had mixed it with meadowsweet to make a poultice. Bearberry was used by her people to treat blood poisoning and Meadowsweet was good for stopping the flow of blood.

Along the fringes of the meadow, blackberries were beginning to ripen. Picking the dark black ones, from among the unripe red ones, she gathered a few hands full to but in her basket, then gathered another hand full to eat as she walked.

Tonight, using a round river rock on another cupped out stone, she would pound several cattail roots into a thick, soupy paste. After separating the stringy fibers, she would mix the remaining starchy paste with the berries and a little honey. This she would pour on a large flat rock, suspended over the hot coals of her fire to bake. It would make a tangy, sweet kind of bread, which kept well and could use for traveling. She hoped the man would be well enough to move soon. The rest of the girls would be many miles away by now.

Thinking about the other captive girls filled Laurel's mind with anguish, dampening her spirit. The sun, slowly inching its way toward the west, seemed no longer as bright or the skies quiet as blue. Guilt drove another painful splinter into her already tortured heart. She was torn between the need to help the man who'd given so much to help her and the need to be on her way, to try helping the other girls.

Drawing near the overhang, Laurel began to move more cautiously. From atop a nearby hill, a hundred yards away, she paused to study the surrounding forest. Bluejays and cardinals called out in the canopy of oak and chestnut trees. Crickets and grasshoppers chipped among the weeds and grass. It was not the sound of a forest that had been recently disturbed.

After satisfying herself that nothing was out of place, Laurel cautiously moved closer. At times it seemed strange and somehow sad, this new-found sense of caution, a fearful awareness that had become her new way of life.

At one corner of the overhang, near the end of the line of small trees and limbs she'd cut and stacked around the opening, Laurel stopped in front of one particular small cedar. Lifting it out of the way, she stepped into the shadowy semi-darkness. Even before her eyes adjusted to the gloom, she knew something was different.

Chapter 30

Matthew opened his eyes to small confined area of near darkness. Rising to his knees, he felt around the spot where he'd been laying face down in a mound of leaves. Instinctively, his first thoughts were for his guns. Unable to see or feel them at his side filled him with sudden panic. Then, as his eyes began to adjust to the weak light filtering through the brush covering the overhang, he began to notice details around him. With relief, he saw his rifle leaning against a rock, not far from his reach. His other gear lay on top of his buckskins, apparently having been washed and hung there to dry.

For the first time, Matthew became aware of being naked. Even though alone, he felt the sudden heat of embarrassment flush in his face. Someone had undressed him. From what few vague snatches of memory he could recall were, the only other person around had been the girl.

Rising to his feet, Matthew was assaulted by a multitude of sore muscles, screaming at points from all over his body. Flexing his arm, expecting his shoulder to be a hotbed of pain, he was surprised to fine it was much improved. Much better than..... The thought brought on the sudden realization that he had no idea how long he'd been asleep. A day, he speculated. Maybe two. Surely.

His buckskins were stiff. He had to work them with his hands, until they were limber enough to pull over his shoulders. Once dressed, feeling at least less embarrassed, Matthew set about checking the charges in his rifle and pistol. He did remember stumbling along in the darkness during a terrible rain storm . . . remembered being bone soaking wet.

Someone had dried and wiped off both guns with an oily rag from his shooting pouch. The flash-pan on each gun had also been dried and recharged with fresh gunpowder from his powder horn. Someone had taken precautions to insure their safety.

A slight flickering of the light filtering through the stacked brush around the opening alerted him that someone was moving around outside. Picking up his rifle, Matthew stepped back among the dark shadows at the rear of the overhang. As a section of covering brush was pulled away, he very slowly he eased back the hammer on the rifle.

"Osiyo," Matthew offered the standard Cherokee greeting, stepping out of the shadows when he realized the intruder was in fact the girl he'd journeyed so far to help. She carried something wrapped in a blanket of green leaves. In the other hand she held his belt knife. It looked huge in her small hand.

"He-l-lo," she returned in broken English, a smile brightening her face. "It is good...you are awake."

While her words surprised Matthew, they also answered a question that had been troubling him. During the past few days of fevered induced sleep he seemed to remember a voice speaking different languages. Now he realized it was neither a dream, nor

238

delusion.

"How many days was I out," he asked? Then realizing she failed to grasp his meaning, Matthew laid his head on his hand closing his eyes, pantomiming sleep.

"Four suns," she said, holding up her hand with four fingers spread away from the knife handle then pointing the blade at the mound of leaves where Matthew had been asleep.

"Four," Matthew said disbelievingly. It didn't seem impossible that he could have slept for the better part of a week. A frown creased his features as thoughts of what fate might have befallen him without the help of this tiny wisp of a girl. It was strange, and more than a little disconcerting. The idea of being helpless, of having someone else care for him was something he hadn't experienced in years. It seemed alien.

"You were very... *utivga*...sick,"she said. "The wound on our back was poisoning your blood. It had to be...reopened... cleaned. You were very...lucky."

"You must be a very good medicine woman," Matthew said, once again flexing his shoulder muscles.

Chapter 31

July, 20th 1776

Most of the men, who knew Edward Mills, referred to him simply as ***Bear***. Whether this was due to the fact that he stood a head taller and was broader in the shoulder than most men, or his massive sweep of blond, shoulder length hair and beard, or the deep growl in his voice, was all a matter of prospective. And even though he was, by nature, a very mild mannered person, few men wanted to venture arousing his bad side.

Despite being larger than the average black bear, Edward moved through the forest with less noise than a field mouse. Unfortunately, the same could not be said about the men following in his footsteps.

From somewhere, back along the column of men trailing in his wake, came the sound of another stick cracking beneath a careless boot or moccasin. Gritting his teeth in frustration, he didn't waste the effort of looking back. Another angry glare, cast in their direction, would not make their feet any less clumsy…or at least it had not on the other half dozen times he'd tried.

Carelessness was a damn good way to get the bunch of them killed. He was sure anyone with a few hundred yards could not have helped overhearing their approach, especially the band of Cherokee warriors purportedly bent of raiding the settlements a few miles further down the valley.

All he could do was to scan for any movement among the endless tree trunks ahead and reconcile himself to the fact that most of the men were not hunters, much less Indian fighters. Maybe a half dozen, among the fifty men in his patrol, were experienced frontiersman. The rest were farmers and tradesman. Good men, true of heart, Edward had no doubt. Unfortunately, it didn't make their feet move with any more skill.

Two days earlier a trader, footsore and exhausted, had arrived a Fort Caswell with a warning of an impending attack by Dragging-Canoe and his warriors.

Word had spread quickly to the nearby homesteads. The fort had rapidly filled with settlers seeking refuge behind its log walls.

Temporarily stationed at the fort were several companies of militia and over a hundred frontiersmen, Edward among them.

It had been decided to move away from the fort, confront the enemy before they could attack the walls. So now, on the purported day of the attack, half dozen groups of men moved to meet the assault.

The valley leading to the fort was several miles wide, and offered plenty of thick cover to conceal the approaching war party. By spreading out at intervals, close enough that any shots fired would alert the other patrols, the defenders hoped Dragging-Canoe would not be able to sneak his warriors past.

Somehow, Edward had found himself *volunteered* as a guide and leader. It was not a position he wanted, in fact he had loudly protested when his name had been nominated.

In the end, like a shanghaied sailor, waking up with sever hang-over, and finding himself a hundred miles out to sea, Edward reluctantly conceded to the noisy petitions of his fellow volunteers. Now, he was beginning to regret it.

His most pressing concern was for the safety of his men. If they blundered into an ambush, if any one got killed, it would be another cold gravestone to bear on his already overburdened shoulders.

No matter how far he traveled, no matter how much ale or hard liquor he drank, Edward could never seem to escape from under the weight of those two rough carved stones he'd used to make the grave of his son and wife. Sometimes it felt like the weight was slowly driving him feet first into the ground.

In truth it was a burden he would not have shed, even were he able. He needed the open fiery agony in his heart, needed to feel the hurt, to punish himself, to allow the pain to fuel his anger and his need for vengeance. Both were honed to a razors edge.

Sometimes he wasn't sure who he needed to punish the most.... the band of raiding Cherokee murderers who'd inflicted their merciless torment on his family... or himself... for not being there to protect him when he was needed the most.

Edward was tired beyond measure. The only time he'd slept in the past few months was with his arms wrapped around an empty crock jug, its fiery contents burning at his throat, stomach and mind. He hated the liquor, but it was better than the alternative.

Whenever Edward closed his, awake or asleep, he was assaulted by ghost. Each time he would relive the agony

242

of finding his homestead raided, his wife raped and scalped, her throat cut, his ten year old son missing.

Like a laden figure with arms and legs cast of lead, he would relive the slow motion agony of trailing the war party away from his home, of following their sign until at last he'd came upon the spot where they'd stopped. What he found was a scene forever carved on to the walls of his heart.

His son had been tied to a small tree in the center of a clearing. The remains of a fire still smoldered around his feet. What remained of his clothes clung in blackened tatters to his burned skin.

At first, Edward had thought the boy was dead, but when he cut the straps holding his arms up higher on the tree, a weak moan escaped from his blistered lips. He had carried the boy home in his arms, tears streaming down his face, his mind too numb to accept the scope of what had befallen his family.

His son's pain had ended a few hundred yards before they reached the cabin.

Edward dug one grave under the sheltering branches of an old white-oak tree growing on the hill above their homestead. He'd wrapped his wife's arms around her son, then he wrapped them with a quilt his mother had given them as a wedding present.

Two large water smoothed stones, carried one at a time on his shoulder, from the Catawba River, over three miles away, marked the grave. Tears streamed down his cheeks as he used his hunting knife to scratch names on the stones.

For several hours he sat staring vacantly at the two headstones. When the tears stopped flowing, Edward once again picked up his hunting knife. Using the top of his son's gravestone, he had worked the knife's blade back to a keen edge.

How do you escape the horror of finding your family brutally murdered? How do you purge those hateful images from your mind's eye?

For a long while he had wondered the forest, aimlessly, seeking answers. Was vengeance what he sought? In truth, he was not a vengeful man, nor would it bring back his family.

Time had not blunted the terrible ache in his heart and drinking himself into a black numbness lasted only until the morning sun wrought pain in his head. In the end he come to realize that what he sought was justice... *frontier justice.*

Edward's mind was pulled from these dark brooding thoughts by the sound a voice, a grumbling mumbled curse, coming from somewhere back along the column of men.

He was in the process of turning his head back find out just who the fool was, when he caught a flash of movement in the trees a hundred yards ahead.

Acting purely on instinct he began dropping to his knees, even before spotting several tell-tell puffs of gray smoke. One of the musket balls, instead of catching him where his stomach had just been, instead tore through the fringes of his buckskin shirt, cutting an angry, but shallow gash across his shoulder. Around him, flying chunks of lead cut leaves, pinged off rocks, or thumped dully into the trunks of tress.

Behind   him,   men scrambled for any cover they could find.

After a quick look around, Edward realized they had been caught in an open spot that would leave his men exposed. The volley of shots would no doubt bring reinforcements, but in the mean time all the war party had to do was pick them off one at a time. He didn't want to lose any men if he could help it.

Scrambling low, Edward headed back along the trail toward his men. He motioned them to fall back. In seconds every member of his squad was racing back along the trail.

Behind them, the fleeing frontiersmen could hear the war whoops and yells of the Cherokee giving chase.

After only a short dash, Edward spotted a place where a winter ice storm had downed several large pine trees. Quickly he motioned his men to take cover behind the trees.

Just after the last of his men had positioned themselves bulwark of dead limbs and trunks, the first warriors raced into view.

Their leader, a tall muscular warrior, brandishing a scalping knife in on hand and a musket in the other, was urging his men to give chase, to attack. The attackers rushed forward in a wave.

Close to two hundred yards away, Edward watched the big lead warrior, following him with the sights on his rifle barrel. His finger slowly tightened on the trigger. His gun was old, but he was confident in its accuracy.

245

About a year ago, a young man had passed by his homestead, offering to do work in exchange a few supplies.

A quiet, amiable young man, Edward remembered his name was Matthew, had repaired worn or broken items. Using tools from his pack, he had *freshened* the worn rifling in his old gun. It shot a good ever.

He'd even fixed a broken hinge on a locket for his wife. It had made her smile.

Gritting his teeth at the memory of that lost smile, Edward applied added pressure to the trigger. Sparks flew as the flint, held in the jaws of the hammer, skidded across the hardened frizzen igniting the powder in the pan. Smoke billowed.

Before the smoke blocked his view, Edward saw the big warrior pitch forward disappearing into the undergrowth.

Not wasting further time looking, he began reloading his rifle. Around him shots were ring out furiously, as his men picked their own targets.

A few hundred yards to the north, the sound of more shots erupted. Another detachment of volunteers arrived. Soon the valley floor was obscured by a fog of gray smoke. The sound gunfire slowly faded. The sudden quietness, settled like a blanket across the forest turned battleground. Heavy. Ominous.

Like an apparition, drifting out of the smoke, Edward spotted two warriors, half carrying, half dragging their wounded leader. Before he could take aim, they vanished back into the smoke.

In the brief instant they had been visible; Edward saw

that their leader had been wounded severely. Blood covered both sides of his body. If his wounds were not mortal, if would be a long time before he would fight again.

For more than more than an hour the wary men studied the forest around them. No further attacks came. When the smoke had thinned enough to see, the only sign that the war party had ever been there was the scattering of dead braves. Their wounded must have been carried away like their leader.

The frontiersmen had suffered a few casualties. One man dead, two more were wounded. A man, Edward recalled his name as Frazier, would likely lose his arm where a musket ball had shattered his elbow.

As most of his squad prepared for the trip back to the fort, Edward along with six other men, eased forward among the dead Cherokee. Most were men of about his own age, but a couple were young, only a few years older than his son would have been.

Deep in his heart, Edward knew these were the same men were part of the group who had murdered and raped his wife then burned his son at the stake, destroying his life.

Their deaths offered no solace to his pain. Slowly walking away, Edward realized that it never would.

Chapter 32

According to Matthew's sense of distance, he and Laurel had covered close to a hundred miles in the last four days. Travel had been slow at first, until he started to regain his strength. Much to his surprise the girl never once faltered, matching his pace, even though her legs were much shorter. With each passing mile, each day spent traveling in her company, his admiration for the girl increased.

He had always felt himself to be a good woodsman, knowledgeable in wilderness survival but he was humbled by Laurel's woodcraft, by her working knowledge of wild plants and trees, for both medicine and food.

As they moved along the trail, always heading northeast, she would bend over to pick this or that wild plant, mushroom, or berry. By nightfall, she had usually collected enough to supply their evening meal.

The journey bread she had baked, before leaving the shelter, lasted for a couple of days. Since then they had eaten what ever she had gathered. Then earlier that day Matthew had used a single arrow from his bow to kill two grouse roosting side by side in a spruce tree.

As evening neared Matthew found a level spot near a small stream, where they could spend the night. Despite having traveled hard all day, Laurel immediately began gathering wood to build a fire.

Matthew would have roasted the birds over an open

fire. A quick way to cook but also making the meat tough and stringy. Instead, Laurel had dressed the birds, filled them with various leaves and roots. Then rolling each bird in green leaves, she placed them in a hole she'd dug in the ground, then lined it with stones. Over this, she placed a layer of small washed stones from a nearby stream.

Over top of this pit, she built fire, fueling it with dry wood until she had a good bed of coals... From the items she'd collected during the day, she took a hand full of leaves, placing them into at turtle shell she had spotted beside the trail that morning.

Mathew had been curious when she had stopped to scrub it with sand and water. Now as he watched as she filed it with water, he began to understand.

Using two green sticks she picked up the hot small rocks, dropping them one by one into the water. Soon the liquid was steaming hot. To this she added the last of the honeycomb. Using the sticks again, she dipped out the stones.

Matthew, sitting on a flat rock to one side, observed all this activity in silent wonder.

"Drink," she said, picking up the makeshift bowl and handing it to Matthew.

Hesitantly he raised the steaming turtle shell to his mouth. The dark liquid had a familiar aroma. Taking a small sip, he raised his face up in surprise. It tasted like a little like coffee, only with a faint taste of ginger. The little dab of honey, Laurel had added, softened the slightly bitter taste. He took another swallow, this time

249

savoring the taste.

"This is amazing," Matthew said, handing the shell back to the girl. "What plant did you use to make this?"

"My people call it...chick-awee," she said with a smile, as she used another piece of wood to dig out the two roasted birds. "It only grows to the north of our lands, but sometime we trade for it from the Catawba's or the Creeks. I found some today"

When the leaf wrapped birds had cooled enough to handle, Laurel handed one to Matthew, taking the other for herself.

Again, Matthew was amazed. The meat had a slightly nutty flavor and was so tender it almost fell off the bones. The leaves, as well as the crisp rootstock, cooked inside had the same spicy flavor.

"You seem to have learned a great deal about making life easier," Matthew said, wiping away a tiny dribble of grease from the corner of his mouth with his sleeve.

'My grandfather is a very wise man," she replied, a look of pained longing suddenly marred her otherwise lovely face as she remembered her home and family. "When I was very small, I sometimes felt that he was being cruel, especially when he made me work, or learn things. Sometimes I would cry when the other children were out playing or swimming in the river. Only later, when I was much older, did I realize that he feared he might die before I able to care for myself. Now I know that what he did was because of his love for me."

"Judging from what I've seen of him, reflected in you," Matthew said, "he must indeed be a very good and wise man."

Watching the sun slowly drop behind the thin blue line of distant mountains, Matthew and Laurel shared a last swallow of drink from the makeshift shell bowl as they ate what remained of their evening meal in silence.

**

An hour before dawn, as the stars first began to fade in the eastern horizon. Matthew was awakened by the feel a small hand pressing firmly against his lips.

Startled, his hand instinctively wrapped around the handle his belt knife, the big blade sliding swiftly and silently from the leather sheath.

"*Nasquv toi*—Be still. Someone camps... not far away," she whispered, looking north into the dark shadows cast by countless thousands of trees standing sentinel in the night.

With her free hand, Laurel brushed aside his arm, the one with the big knife, as thought it were a harmless toy, as though certain he would never harm her with it.

Matthew however was shaken; frightened at how close she had come to hurting her by his own innate reactions. His heartbeat was pounding in his ears, his hands trembling as he eased the blade back into its buckskin sheath.

"Who? How do you know that?" Matthew asked in a throaty whisper, his voice quivering slightly, betraying the emotional turmoil of what he perceived as way too close of a call.

"Wood smoke," Laurel said, touching her finger to her

251

nose. "Someone makes a fire ... not far...downwind."

Rising to his feet, Matthew stood quietly staring into the night, his face turned into the night breeze. At last the faint slight rosin smell of burning pine pitch reached his nostrils.

"You're right," Matthew said. "About a quarter of a mile away...I'd guess."

Again he was amazed by the young Indian girl's uncanny abilities, as well as being somewhat abashed at his own lack there of. Traveling in her company was turning into a humbling experience as well as beginning to be somewhat of a strain on his pride. He wasn't however, foolish enough to let pride get the better of his brains. He would just have to swallow it, unsavory as it might be, and try to learn from her. Besides right now he had more important things to worry about...like who their neighbors were.

Matthew was fairly confident that they hadn't caught up with the raiding party this quickly, but there were plenty of other options. It could just be other travelers, traders heading back from one of the towns along the Virginia coast, or another group of Indians. It could also be something he feared, another group of warriors sent to bring the girl back, and/or to kill him. Either way, he saw no course other than to slip into the darkness and try identifying the camp before sunrise, which wasn't far off.

Almost as if reading his mind, Laurel began gathering up what few possessions they had, carefully placing them in the basket she had woven of willow limbs. She emphatically refused to let him carry the contraption, so after their first day out, he had cut strips of buckskin from the tail of his shirt to make straps so she could carry it like a pack on her shoulders.

Picking up his on pack, Matthew tucked the pistol in his belt, adjusted his slouch hat then slung his bow and quiver over the other shoulder. Picking up his rifle from where it leaned against a near by tree, he moved silently into the darkness. Behind him, he could barely make out the faint whisper of Laurels footsteps trailing in his wake.

Chapter 33

"Hello the camp," Matthew called from a hundred yards away, stepping out into the open trail where he would be clearly visible.

He had been closer. Close enough to see that the camp consisted of two Indians and two white men. The white men had the look of traders. The Indians were not Shawnee, but Matthew wasn't sure what tribe they belonged to. They didn't appear to by a threat, so he had eased back to a safe distance, to where he'd left the girl behind a crooked hemlock, before hailing the camp. It would not have been polite, or prudent, to startle them by speaking up at to close a distance.

At the sound of his voice, all four men scrambled for their weapons. A natural reaction, Matthew thought, given the current state of affairs along the frontier.

"Who ye be and what be your business," called back on of the white men. The other three keeping cautious watch in all direction of the surrounding forest.

"Travelers, just two of us," Matthew answered. "Smelled your smoke. Though we might sit a spell. Trade a little talk. Ain't jawed with no one in quiet a spell."

"Come on in, then, but slow. Keep your guns pointed at the sky."

Cautiously, Matthew walked toward the camp, hoping he wasn't walking into more trouble. Laurel silently followed his lead.

The men turned out to be friendly, and exactly as Matthew had surmised, traders, heading back into the wilderness with packs bulging with items destined to be swapped to the various tribes, for furs or anything else of value.

After introductions, they were invited to a breakfast of strong black coffee, from a real cup, thick slices of crispy fried salt pork and pone-bread fried in the grease.

Homer, the man who'd invited them into the camp, the obvious leader, was an older man, appearing to be in his late fifties, wiry, grizzled and weatherworn. He reminded Matthew, for the world of Thadis. A resemblance that started him wishing his old friend was here with him now. He missed the cantankerous old buzzard.

The other man was a big, good natured giant with broad shoulders blond hair and reddish blond beard. His name was Nicholas, but he preferred to be called Swede. He spoke very little and smiled a lot, being the obvious muscle of this bunch.

The two Indians...Jumps-High and Eats-Dog... turned out to be Choctaw. The pair was instantly enthralled with Laurel. Right away they started jabbering questions at him which he couldn't understand. Homer translated for them. They wanted to know if *his woman* was for sell or trade.

Matthew told them "no," leaving it at that, figuring it would be less troublesome if the dark skinned Romeos continued to think him and Laurel as a couple.

After they'd finished their meal, the two traders pulled

out pipes, offering Matthew a smoke, which he declined, with thanks.   As the two men lit their tobacco with brands from the fire Laurel began clearing away the pans and cups.

"Vat a good voman you got there," the Swede spoke through a halo of smoke. "

"No vonder you not vant to trade her."

With the traders relaxing with their pipes and the two Choctaw content to watch Laurel move about her work, Matthew figured it was a good time to ask a the question he been holding back.

"Have you run across sign of another larger party passing through here about," he asked?

"Party," the man named Homer coughed, almost choking on his tobacco smoke. "I'd say, it be more like an army than any party. At least a thousand men, maybe more, and I'll not be missing my guess by much."

"What did you say," Matthew asked, more than a little confused. "I meant a group of maybe fifteen; mostly women, herded along by a hand full of Shawnee warriors and one white man."

"Weren't no women folk with this bunch," Homer said in his high-pitched bird-like voice. Then removing the well chewed pipe stem from his mouth, he used it to point southeast. " They passed by a couple of days ago, headed south in an all mighty hurry. First we thought they was soldiers, headed off to fight the British. Didn't make much sense though. They was headed into Indian territory. Way I figure it, they musta been volunteers, sent by the governor of Virginia. Eats-Dog says they're headed for the Overhill villages to punish the wicked

256

Cherokee."

This was more information that Matthew had bargained for. It took him a while to ingest it and sort things out. Thadis had warned him of the possibility of an all out Cherokee/ white war as well as a possible war with England. It seemed as if both had come to pass.

"Are we fully at war with England," Matthew asked?

"Reckon so," Homer said. "Bunch political big-wigs, Thomas Jefferson, General Washington, Ben Franklin and a whole bunch more, got together and wrote it all down in fancy words. Happened some time in the first week of this month. Called it the *Deceleration of Independence*. Copies of it been nailed up in every town and printed in every newspaper all up and down the eastern seaboard. I even got a copy of it myself. Can't read it though. I learned to do my sums, but never did pick up on the reading and writing part. Wish I had though."

Rummaging around in his pack, Homer at last drew out a hand full of much battered papers.

"You ever learn to read," he asked, handing them to Matthew.

"Been a long time ago," Matthew replied. "Don't know if I remember how?"

In truth, Matthew, had always been a good reader, primarily because his Uncle had insisted he have a thorough education. And according to him reading was the cornerstone of that foundation. Matthew had especially enjoyed reading Greek mythology and even

257

some of the works of Shakespeare. That had been years ago.

Studying the words written on the first few lines, Matthew was surprised at how easily it came back to him. He began to read the words out loud

"July, 4th 1776"

"When in the course of human events, it becomes necessary for one nation to break the political bounds, that bind it to another, we hold these truths to be self-evident..............."

Matthew continued reading the pages, pausing occasionally until a word he didn't catch finally clicked in his head, until all the pages had been read.

"Well, I'll be damned," said Homer. "I guess that pretty much sums it up."

"Yes. Yes, vhis is right. Vhis why I come here," added Swede. "To be free. To live vas I choose. Not da vay someone else think I should be to live."

"What about you, Matthew," Homer asked? "You said you came here from England, said you got family there."

"I have no ill will toward the English people," Matthew said, "but I was born in Ireland. Therefore, I know full well the tyranny of English monarchy. Even to this day, no doubt there is a price on my head in

England."

"What did you do... rob a tax collector ... or maybe kill someone," Homer asked, his smile making it plain that he believed Matthew too young and gentlemanly to be a vicious criminal.

"In fact, I did kill a man," Matthew said, staring down into the coals of the fire. "But it was in self-defense. He killed a young woman I was with, then ran his sword through my shoulder. Fortunately there were witnesses. I wasn't prosecuted."

"Vell den vat did you do to vecome such a vad outlaw," Swede asked?

"I became an outlaw for killing a couple of rabbits," Matthew said, knowing how foolish it sounded, but also aware that in truth it had made him a wanted outlaw.

"Your joking with us," Homer accused.

"No, I assure you, it is not a joke," Matthew said. "I was nineteen then. The wounds to my body had healed. But the scars on my heart and soul had grown festered and corrupt. I blamed myself for her death. I hated myself, or rather what I perceived of myself. To escape this, I ran away. I had never really known my father other than through whispered stories and slanderous remarks pointedly spoken in my presence.

My mother's parents blamed him for her death. For this reason I felt something of empathy for the life he'd lived. My father was a ship's Captain, a life long sailor and I suppose he could have been labeled a pirate. When I turned fifteen, my uncle told me the story of how my father loved the sea and how had died there, along with my mother. So I decided to travel to Ireland, where I signed aboard a cargo ship, trying to find a life where I might grow to be a man. After two years, spent mostly aboard ship...homesick... and through with the sea.... I headed back to England. I wanted to visit my uncle and his family, the only members of my family I cared to see. Reaching my last port of call, my hitch over, I crossed the English Channel headed London.

Not managing to save a great deal of money while at sea, and wanting to hold on to what little I did have, I chose to slept in the forest along side the roads, roasting potatoes in the coals of my fire for food at night and the next day. It felt strange to have my feet once again on solid ground."

Mathew felt a little uneasy in offering up so much information about his past, especially to strangers, but on the other hand he felt a deep need to make them understand his pent up anger at the abuse the English monarchy was heaping on its own people. Taking a deep breath, he continued…

"One night, tired nothing but potatoes, I sat snares, catching two young rabbits. The next morning as they roasted on a spit over my fire, two burly looking men, dressed in ragged clothing, came tromping into my camp."

"What's your name boy," said the biggest man, a stocky, dour looking fellow with a scruffy beard and dirty face, carrying a well worn musket slung over his shoulder.

"Matthew Maybin,' I told him, honestly, thinking I had nothing to hide.

260

"Well, Matthew Maybin, do you know the penalty, for poaching the King's rabbits... Seventy pounds sterling or six months on the work farm."

The other man didn't say anything, just kept an ancient, rusty looking crossbow, with a very new wicked, metal tipped arrow, pointed at my belly. Seeing my disconcertion, he smiled, showing a mouth full of broken, yellowish brown teeth. The smile stopped way short of his eyes.

"They were wild rabbits. I caught them in a snare,' I said, trying to defend myself."

"Then you admit to breaking the law.'

"What law?'

"Boy you must be ignorant...or deaf and dumb. Probably both. Everyone knows that the King has decreed all wildlife...rabbits included... to be the property of the Crown. And as official gamekeeper to this county, it is my duty to bring your before the magistrate, where you will be found guilty and punished."

"I've been at sea for the past two years. I didn't know about this law.

"Won't make a bit of difference to the magistrate. You got any money, boy? Anything to pay your fine?"

I had about fifty pounds, everything I had scraped together from two long years at sea, hidden in my clothing and my pack, but I wasn't about to let these two know.

"No,' I lied.

"Well then, I guess it'll be the work farm for you."

Old snag tooth only grinned once again, shifting his aim higher to my chest.

As absurd as it sounds, I had no choice but to do as these two tyrants ordered. The mistake they made was having me carry my own gear, and the fact that they intended to eat my breakfast as we traveled along. I guess partaking of the King's wildlife, did not apply to them. Fortunately, they could not gnaw the meat off the bones and keep there weapons trained on me at the same time. At the first thick stand of trees, I bolted as fast as I could run. I knew that neither one of the two could catch me. I did however hear the dull thud of a crossbow bolt, burying itself in a tree behind which I had just dashed.

I never stopped until I got back to Ireland. I wrote my Uncle a letter, explaining what had happened. He wrote me back that the sheriff had come looking for me with a warrant for poaching as well as for assault on the gamekeeper.

I sent him another letter, asking him to ship me my personal belongings. When they arrived I paid almost all the money I had left to my name for a ticket to a country I had never seen before. I arrived in Charles Town.... it seems like a lifetime ago."

The two traders ventured neither comment, nor condemnation, only nodding their heads, as was the way the longhunter. Men living in the wilderness accepted a man's word as fact...until he proved differently. It was a story not so unlike the countless others they had heard...or lived and the reason why most of them had migrated into this rough and untamed country.

Matthew didn't know what to expect from revealing his story. It was something he had only told a few friends like Thadis. He wasn't sure why he'd told it now and to strangers at that. Maybe it had something to do with what he'd just read. The words had struck a cord that continued to resonate in his mind, to connect in a way he was not totally sure of. Maybe the Swede had the right of it. It was freedom…that men could choose their own destiny and deep inside, Matthew could sense that this would change the course of the world.

For a long time, they all sat in quiet compilation, lost in their own thoughts. It was Laurel who brought them back to the world at hand.

"Do you know of this… *nahnai*…this place, where the river…James… reaches the sea," she said looking down at the three white men.

"Yes mam," answered Homer, a smile ceasing his weathered features. "It's only about a weeks walk. I can even draw you a map, if you'd like."

Taking the sheets of paper that Matthew had returned after reading them, Homer picked up charred piece of wood and began drawing a map on the back of a copy of the Deceleration of Independence.

Chapter 34

Matthew had chosen their campsite well. Located in the middle of a dense stand of giant hemlock, a few hundred yards from a river they figured to be the James, the massive trees blocked any sight of their camp, while the thick canopy helped dissipate any smoke their small campfire might make.

Concealed among the dark shadowy trunks, Matthew watched as Laurel sat by the campfire humming softly as she prepared the fish he had caught earlier that afternoon. Four trout, stuffed with an assortment of leaves and roots that she had gathered, were roasting on a flat rock placed over the bed of coals. The smell made his empty stomach growl.

Each evening before they camped, Matthew made a long circuit of his chosen spot. He was fairly confident that no one was within a half-mile circle the spot. He'd also gotten in a habit of trying to sneak up on the camp, undetected. As usual, it didn't work.

No matter how much stealth he employed, Laurel somehow always seemed to know he was there. She might not show it. But she knew, none the less. Like now. Even though he was well concealed in the dark, she looked up, her large brown owl-like eyes, reflecting the dancing firelight. She smiled.

"Atsadi adasdayvnvdi nulisdv," she spoke softly,

reaching down to reposition the fish.

Matthew had learned more Cherokee words in the past few weeks than he had in the past four years. She said their meal would be ready soon. He smiled.

Matthew would have scoffed at the idea, would never have admitted, that he was infatuated with this young Indian woman. Yet to him, her voice sounded as sweet as running water to a man dying of thirst. He felt comfortable in her presence, somewhat like he did with his friend, Thadis, and yet vastly different

He had almost forgotten how good it felt to talk with someone close to his own age. To carry on a conversation for nothing more than expressing how he felt.

In the past few years, it had not been uncommon for Matthew to go for months without speaking to another living creature... that is if didn't count talking to the occasional chattering squirrel or quarreling bluejay. How this had come about he wasn't really sure. His life seemed filled with "it should have been's."

Few men are born with the temperament necessary to spend long periods of time away from the company of their human counterparts. Man is, by nature, a gregarious creature, ruled by instincts, by ancestral memories honed over thousands of years. A compulsion to gather into groups, to cling too one another for comfort, for safety, is a normal survival mechanism ingrained in the human subconscious. Most men cannot ignore its persistent call.

"The big lonesome." Thadis called it.

265

When he first befriended the old trader, Thadis had warned Matthew that it was the lack of hearing the human voice he had to guard against. The loneliness was what usually sent the greenhorns scampering back toward civilization after only a week or two.

Of course some would try stick it out, only to end up crazy. Talking to themselves. "Asvnilv yuwanelvhi adanvdo," the Cherokee called it. "Touched by spirits."

With out a doubt, a life spent wandering the lonely mountain trails dissecting vast sprawling wilderness of the southern Appalachian's could be filled with very real, very profound silence. It could be a double-edged sword. It either drove you crazy... or you learned to love it.

Matthew wasn't sure into which category he fit. Sometimes, in the fading light of evening, or by a flickering campfire, as he used a small sliver of charred wood to record his thoughts into a leather bound journal, he would recite the words aloud... just to hear the sound of a human voice.

Anyone spending time in the wilderness soon learns the forest is seldom ever quiet.   There is the wind whispering among the pine boughs, the chatty calls of songbirds flitting from branch to branch along the green, the lonely call of a distant loon, or the movements of crickets and grasshoppers, or nameless other insects scurrying among the leaves and grass, their chirps and squeaks, filling the day with an endless variety of noises. And at the end of the day there is always the lonesome call of a distant owl or a deer or some other small animals hurrying along leaf strewn trails...Sometimes, late at night there was only the sound of your own beating heart.

The past week following their crude map toward the mouth of the James river, had awakened in Matthew the knowledge of just how much he missed talking to someone close to his own age, to someone female. It seemed the young Cherokee girl had not only saved his life, she had rescued his heart. The bitterness that had once filled his soul, the anger that had driven him to this far distant wilderness, had gradually begun to fade.

During the day, a need for caution kept their conversation to a bare minimum. Within a couple of days they had fallen into a pattern of using sign language or simple head motions to communicate. In fact, most of the time there was little need for words. They worked well as a team, each having an almost innate understanding of what the other one was thinking.

At night, when Matthew returned from his patrols, sure they would not be overheard, they talked of many things. Some trivial...some important.

At first they had talked on what might happen if they did manage to overtake the Shawnee warriors and the captive girls. They quickly realized it was topic laced with far too many and maybe's" to even venture speculation. With no idea of where or when their journey might end, or what the circumstances it might end under, they decided there was no point worrying until the time arrived..

So Laurel talked of her life in the mountains, of her grandfather, of the hard but happy life she known. She told him about how she had been captured and the strange way her captives had acted and traveled.

Listening to her words, Matthew could sense how much she wished to return to her home, how much she worried about her grandfather. But, worried or not she never mentioned giving up on trying to free the captive girls.

While he never said so, Matthew secretly figured she might have justifiable reason to worry about her grandfather. In his patrols, he had come across sign of several large groups of men traveling toward Cherokee territory. These men were not settlers headed to the mountains. There were way too many. These men wore they wore boots, carried heavy packs and moved in long spread, but military type formations

From the tracks, he figured the numbers ranged from a couple of hundred in one group to near a thousand in another. It was an army, of that he had no doubt. And he also had no doubts about their destination.

Thadis had warned that a war against the Cherokee was inevitable and Homer had seen them. It was probably already underway. Dragging-Canoe and several other war chiefs had gotten what the wanted. The war hatchet had been bloodied.

Rising up from where he crouched among the darkened trees and moving toward the fire, Matthew could only hope that Thadis had convinced the old chiefs to move their people deeper into the wilderness, to hide until things calmed down.

"How many suns...days... ahead ...do you think they are," Laurel asked as he squatted down on the opposite side of the fire.

She handed him one of the steaming leaf rolled fish.

"They can't travel fast, because the girls are still tied together. It slows them down. I think we should catch up with them tomorrow or the next day, Matthew answered, taking the proffered food, It was hot enough to be uncomfortable in his hand, but he wasn't about to let her know it. If she could stand it... well, so could he.

Unwrapping the leaf, Matthew pulled the top layer of roasted fish away from the bones. It tasted wonderful. He felt as hungry as a half starved wolf and ate like one.

Across the fire, Laurel watched, a pleased smile etching the lines of her face.

"This morning, I smell salt air," she said, between bites of fish. "I was told that the waters of the great ocean were salty. I think we grow near."

Matthew had not noticed any difference in the air during the day, but he didn't doubt her word for he'd learned her sense of smell was far better than his own.

"I pray that we can free the other girls soon," she said with out looking up from her food. "I fear the war your people plan to make against the English King; will carry over to my people. If so, I fear our way of life will be destroyed, ground to dust, like grain between two great millstones."

"Maybe it won't come to that," Matthew answered halfheartedly.

Once again he was astonished at how well this young woman, really not much more than a girl, who'd spent her life far from the machinations of civilization, understood how the world operated.

"I fear it has already come to pass," she said flatly. "A short while back a renowned chief of the Iroquois confederacy, Corn-Stalk traveled south to the village of Chota. He tried to persuade our chiefs to join them, to fight both the English and the Colonials. Together, he said, they could drive the white man back into the sea."

Matthew listened without speaking, once again amazed at Laurel's uncanny insight. He was trying to protect her from knowledge she was already more than aware of.

"Despite being our ancient blood enemies," she continued, "Dragging-Canoe and several others would have joined with the northern tribes, but the old chiefs, had long ago sworn an oath to the English King. They would not be swayed to raise the war ax against him or his people in this land. Instead they chose not to be involved in this war, but it seems now they must fight or die."

Matthew could not help thinking about his own troubles with the King of England. If the English sovereignty treated its own subjects with such ill disdain, what little value would they place on the lives of few so-called savages in some far distant wilderness. Even though the king had sworn to be a *father* to them, in the end, it would mean nothing.

"When your people refused to take sides," Matthew said with a sigh, "I the think the English devised another way to pull your people into their war. Even if you didn't fight at the side of the British army, it would be almost as effective if you went to war with the settlers."

"Yes," she said, the anger rising in her voice. "By

270

sending their dogs, the Shawnee, disguised as settlers to steal our women."

"Even worse," Matthew spoke softly, "they took you."

"My grandfather would not long be fooled by this trick," she said defiantly.

"Maybe not," Matthew said, placating. "But it wouldn't take long to set Dragging-Canoe off on another rampage. From what I understand, he was intent on making you his bride."

"I would never agree to be his wife," she said, the fire again rising in her eyes.

"My understanding, sometimes the girls never get a choice."

"My grandfather would never have forced me to take him for my husband."

"That's not what I meant. I had heard that desperate braves sometimes steal the women they cannot win. After they are with child, it is too late."

"What you say is true," Laurel said quietly, relenting her anger. "Dragging-Canoe looks for any reason to make war on the white settlers. His followers are young fools. They think the path he travels will lead to a great victory with much blood and many white scalps." "Fools," she said again, taking a bit of her forgotten fish.

"Thadis was headed to warn the chiefs that this might happen," Matthew said, trying to lift her spirits. He desperately hated to see her unhappy.

For a while they ate in silence.

271

After a while Laurel took out the two copper cups they had gotten from the traders and placed them on the hot stones by the fire. In each one she dropped a couple of pieces of sassafras root, then filled each with water. For a while they sat without speaking, each lost in their own thoughts.

Soon the cups were steaming.

"Why do your people war with their own King," Laurel asked, handing Matthew one of the cups, then taking the other one for herself.

It was a simple question, one that had been on Matthew's mind a great deal the past few weeks. He wasn't sure there was a simple answer.

For a long time, he sat without speaking. Almost with out thinking, he took the map from his pouch, unfolded it, map side down. He studied the words had written there...like he'd done so many times before.

In Congress,   July 4,   1776

The unanimous Declaration of the thirteen united States of America,

When in the course of human events it becomes necessary for one people............

Matthew had almost memorized the words by heart, even the names written at the bottom of the page. Names like, Hancock, Adams, Jefferson, Hall, Walton and Clark, he had never heard of. Others like Franklin or Jefferson, he recalled hearing in passing conversations with traders, or at homesteads where he had occasionally stopped to trade.

Fifty-six names. He'd counted them, trying to imagine

what they would be like. He pictured individuals from all walks of life. Farmers, lawyers, blacksmiths, rich and poor, but with one thing in common, there was not a coward among them. They had, with the stroke of a pen, laid their lives on the line. If their cause failed, one and all would most likely be shot, or hanged, for treason.

Sitting there, mesmerized by the tiny flames dancing along the coals of their fire, Matthew could not help but wonder if in the same circumstance, he could offer up the same courage. Would he stand up and fight, even die, for a cause he believed in. Was he willing to die...for the right to die...free?

"Freedom," he said, louder than he intended, suddenly looking up from the coals and remembering Laurel's question. "They fight for the right to be free...to live their lives as they see fit, to not live under the tyranny of a chosen few who feel their birthright gives them leave to steal and rob or imprison anyone they choose or anyone who would defy them."

Matthew had not realized how passionately he felt about the subject until his own tongue had given voice to his innermost thoughts. He had seen, first hand, the oppression of the English Crown. Even now, in this new country calling its self-America, the heavy hand of an unjust monarchy brought pain and suffering to a people, both red and white, who had done it no harm. It was wrong, and yet what could one man do?

"My people have always had to fight to be free," Laurel said; as she swallowed the last of her drink and began prepare herself a place to sleep between two huge protruding roots at the base of a huge beech tree "It is

273

the way things are. Always, there are those from other tribes, or even from our own, who would take what is not rightfully theirs. Sometimes, then it is necessary to make war."

"Unfortunately, you are very much right," Matthew said, putting away the map and clearing his own place to sleep on the opposite side of the fire."

Later, as the coals from their fire slowly faded and the darkness enveloped them, Matthew lay back against another tree, his head propped under one arm, his other hand resting lightly on the grip of his pistol., listening to the sounds in the darkness. Along the river, bullfrogs croaked to one another. Insects could be heard scurrying along the bark of the tree he leaned against. Above him a breeze whispered through the treetops.

None of these unseen sounds spoke of danger. It should have been peaceful night, but he was restless nonetheless. His mind kept wandering back to the things Laurel had said. As a boy he had fled from injustice and tyranny. But now the man he had become was realizing that sometimes you had to stop running. As his eyes began to grow heavy, Matthew was vaguely aware of a turning point in his life having been reached. Laurel was right. Sometimes it was necessary to *make war*.

Chapter 35

Sharp fragments of broken sea shells and bits of weathered rock dug painfully in into Matthew's legs and stomach, making lying in the thick patch of stunted brush more than just a little uncomfortable. He ignored the discomfort without comment. Laurel, stretched beside him endured the same discomfort without complaint. His pride wasn't about to let him grumble, at least not where she would hear it. Besides the spot offered the only vantage point where they could study the shoreline below.

The wind chopped beach marked the boundary of the very same ocean he struggled so hard to cross only four years earlier. On that day, on unsteady sea legs, he'd walked down the gangplank into a new and untamed land, a world seemingly filled with endless possibilities. At the moment his list possibilities, even his chances of living out the day, seemed painfully slim.

After a week of hard, sometimes dangerously fast traveling, they had at last reached the end of their journey. The mouth of the James River and the vastness of the mighty Atlantic lay before them. They had overtaken the raiding party, only scant minutes away from being too late. And now having caught up with their quarry, Matthew was at a loss of what to do next. Time was running out.

Desperately, he wracked his brain for some plan of

action...anything with even a glimmer of hope. Unfortunately every idea he'd come up with so far had entailed at least one serious flaw... primarily that he and Laurel would both likely end up dead, or worse, captured.

Falling into the hands of very enemies he had dogged for several hundred miles was an eventuality he had hoped to avoid. After all the damage he'd inflicted on the war party in the last few weeks, if he and Laurel were captured, Matthew had no illusions of their deaths being anything other than painful and slow.

Damn but he wished Thadis were here. The old man would know what to do. The old trader would have everything worked out in a matter of minutes.

Right now, the only thing Matthew could come up with seemed more like a suicide pact than a workable plan, but darkness would be falling soon, for better or worse, it was time to act.

In the waning hour of daylight, Matthew watched as the girls were herded from the trees down onto the beach. From a distance they seemed no more than tiny rag doll figures, huddled in a tight cluster.

He could only imagine how frightened and alone they must feel, ripped away from their homes, brutalized, about to be thrust into a world, into a way of life of which they had no experience or possible way of understanding.

All that stood between those girls and that tragic event was his meager skills and those of one small Cherokee girl. And no matter how resourceful, she might have been in the past, and no matter how much effort they put forth, he felt a sinking certainty that it would not be

276

enough. So far they'd been lucky. Matthew couldn't help but feel their good fortune was running out.

Like a life sized chess game, all the players were scattered across the board. The game was drawing near its end and Matthew had no idea what his next move should be. He was painfully aware that the precious little time they had was rapidly slipping away with every moment of indecision and inaction.

A ship was anchored several hundred yards off shore, a twin mast schooner, riding low in the choppy sea, looked similar, though slightly smaller than the one Matthew had called home for almost two years.

The Midnight-Mary had been a large ship, used for hauling iron along the coast from Spain back to Ireland. This ship was built smaller and faster, designed to outrun or out maneuver larger ships. It was kind craft favored by pirates, or sea captains whose cargo holds were filled with items not listed on the ships bill of lading.

In the distance beyond the ship, a thunderstorm was gathering force along the horizon. Occasional angry bolts of jagged lightening fractured the slate gray sky as dark clouds, like a fleet of misty ghost ships, scudded ahead of the approaching storm

From the way things looked the storm would make landfall about the time darkness added its own gloom to the scene. Matthew hoped the arriving storm would be a distraction and work in his favor. He needed all the help he could get, however small.

From the concealment of small knoll, covered with

277

grass and brush, Matthew and Laurel watched as three small boats detached themselves from the ship, then turned their bows toward the shore. In the distance, the rise and fall of the long oars made the boats look oddly like a trio of slow-motion water spiders, skimming lazily across the surface.

Not far away, a fire ate hungrily at a mound of sun-bleached driftwood piled on the rock-strewn shore. The fire was obviously a beacon signal intended to alert the ship's crew of the arrival of their new cargo. When the burley, Shawnee warrior, the one Laurel had called Big-Neck, had used a burning pine knot to set fire to the pile of wood, it had touched off a beehive of activity onboard the ship. Now the longboats were making their way to shore.

Glancing north along the beach, Matthew saw that the girls were still clumped together at the edge of the wood line. He had to give credit to the craftiness their captors. Bound as they were, back to back, tied together in two lines, the girls could only move only by a very coordinated effort.

They were guarded by two warriors, a small wiry hatchet-faced man, who carried an old smooth bore musket, and by Big-Neck, who carried only his fearsome war ax and the knife at his side. His brutish size and snarling face seemed more than to make up for his lack of firearms.

No other warriors were in sight, but Matthew had not been fooled, he had spotted four other braves hidden at intervals among the trees. If anything went wrong they could make a hasty showing.

Matthew had spent over an hour stealing through a

thick tangle of longleaf pine and pin oaks before locating the remaining warriors. They were concealed at intervals among the trees, close enough to observe the activity on the beach and respond if needed, but out sight so as not to over intimidate the landing party.

The Englishman nervously paced back and forth along the edge of the incoming tide, watching the approaching boats, his sword in one hand, the other resting on the handle of flintlock pistol tucked in the waistband of his pants. The wind whipping at his hair and clothing carried occasional drops of rain, as well as salt spray from the churning waves, forcing him to wipe his eyes with the back of his sword hand. At his side, a leather bag swung from a strap over his shoulder. Its weight seemed to be an encumbrance to his balance as he moved along the waters edge.

The longboats, fighting against the choppy seas had completed half the trip to the shoreline. The men manning the oars had muskets strapped over their shoulders. The man standing in the front of the lead boat had his sword drawn. Obviously this was not a deal built on mutual trust.

The time to act was at hand, workable plan or not. Any further postponement would see the girls herded aboard the rowboats and taken to the ship. Then all their efforts would have been in vain.

Carefully the pair crawfished down the small hill into the concealing forest. Once they were safely out of sight, Matthew turned to face the girl. In his heart, he despaired at placing her in such danger. To look at her, she appeared small and fragile, no more than a child, but he also knew she was as tough as iron and resourceful as anyone he'd ever met. Still, he feared for her safety in what they were about to undertake. She would be pitted against harsh, seasoned warriors, men who would not for a moment be swayed by the fact that she was a girl.

"You ready," Matthew whispered, turning to face Laurel as he led the way through a stand of water oaks?

Nodding her agreement, Laurel smiled and followed without comment. For some reason her unquestioning trust in his judgment left Matthew feeling angry with himself...angry and apprehensive. Certainty not at the girl, she had been a source of inspiration. He owed his life to her.

In truth, he could not put a finger on the source of his slowly smoldering rage. Perhaps his discomposure stemmed from his own self- perceived doubts about the outcome of the impending fight, of not being able to better protect Laurel. Or as Thadis might have said, he was just working up first class, gut ripping *"mad."*

In truth his anger was fueled by a compound of many emotions. Primarily he was fed up with a world where strength and power were to often reason enough to run roughshod over others. It was the same abuse of power; he had fled England to escape. And here this ugly demon had raised its head once again. Perhaps the trappings were changed, bare and brutal instead of disguised under the pomp of an autocratic monarchy, but the same base flaws of humanity, just the same. There always seemed to be those men who were willing to enslave or subjugated their fellow men... all for a few pieces of gold.

As they trotted, through the growing gloom, the

280

whipping wind tore leaves from the oak branches above their heads, Matthew turned to glance at Laurel.

Her knuckles, white from gripping the stock of his rifle, were the only signs she might be suffering any tension. Earlier, Matthew had instructed her on how to sight and squeeze the trigger, and how to reload. She also carried his big knife, jury-rigged at her waist.

Laurel's main objective would be to free the girls. She would shoot, if she had to, but primarily the gun was to defend the girls once they were free. His own job would be to deal with the warriors.

Matthew had his bow strung, with an arrow knocked, and more metal tipped shafts hanging loosely in the quiver at his back. His pistol was primed and tucked in the belt at his waist, his tomahawk on the other side.

When Matthew broke from the dark shadows of the trees, less than a hundred yards separated him and Laurel from the girls and their captors.

Lowering his head, squinting his eyes against the wind whipped rain, Matthew charged toward the warriors on the beach, Laurel following in his footsteps. As he ran, for a time, the world seemed to take on a surreal aspect. The weakening daylight seemed to take on a strange defused quality as though he viewed the world through a hazy piece of glass. Time too, seemed altered and slowed, as the passage of sands through the hourglass diminished.

Like slow, deliberate hammer falls against an anvil, Matthew was acutely aware of the pounding of his heart. Each moccasined foot seemed to land ponderously slow against the soft sand. Around him, the world became eerily devoid of sound, other than the pounding rush of blood through his veins. He seemed to be moving in slow motion.

Halfway across the short expanse of storm swept beach, the spell was suddenly broken by an explosion of shattered wood that sent shockwaves of pain through his right hand and arm.

The upper limb of his bow was literally slung away by the tension on the string as huge musket ball splintered the wood just above his hand. The remainder of the bow fell from Matthew's hand, which had gone numb from the shock.

Ahead of him a bloom of gray gun smoke was carried away by the wind, revealing the Englishman, standing knee deep in the churning surf, holding a long barreled English dueling pistol still leveled in Matthews's direction.

Time that mere seconds ago time had seemed to move as slow molten lava, now seemed to rage like a flash flood. Around him, everything seemed to be happening at once, all the chess pieces were moving at one time.

The men in the longboats dropped their oars, replacing them with muskets. From the woods the sound of gunshots carried above the wind, thought no more bullets seemed to strike anywhere near. The girls, as well as the two warriors leading them paused to look in his direction.

Matthew focused his attention on the man he perceived as their primary threat, the huge warrior Laurel had identified as the leader of the Shawnee war party, Big Neck.

A predatory, animal like growl rumbled deep in Matthew's chest as his feet pounded against the sandy ground. From the corner of his eye he saw Laurel close at his heels. Less than a hundred yards separated them.

His bow destroyed, Matthew wrapped his numb fingers of his left hand around the handle of his tomahawk, awkwardly pulling it from his belt. His right hand reached for the pistol at his side. Using his thumb, never breaking stride, he pulled back the hammer on the pistol.

Matthew saw the hatchet-faced warrior aiming his musket in their direction. Veering sharply to the right, and hoping Laurel followed suit, he saw a puff of smoke erupt from the guns barrel. Like an angry bee, he heard the musket ball cut through the air to his left. Risking a glance back, he was relieved to see Laurel unharmed.

Fifty yards.

Hatchet-Face was busy trying to reload his gun. Big-Neck drew his tomahawk and stood waiting, a wicked grin etched across his cruel face.

Twenty-five yards.

Matthew raised the pistol, firing at the warrior with the gun before he could finish loading it. His shot clipped the edge of the gunstock, then angled up to catch the brave through the neck. He fell to his knees gripping his throat before toppling to one side.

Big-Neck, bellowing like an enraged bull, lunged to meet Matthew head on.

Matthew knew there was no way he could beat Big-

Neck in a contest of brute force. The man was huge. He also realized that his own skill with a tomahawk would be no match for a man who had carried one since he was a boy.

He would have to rely on the fighting skills he learned at sea and prayed it would be enough. In the instant before the two men collided, Matthew feigned to swing his tomahawk, but instead dropped low, passing under Big-Necks own vicious swing, then kicking out with all his strength, driving his heel into the big mans leg just below the knee.

Matthew felt bone crack under his foot.

Big-Neck let out a howl of pain and outrage, stumbled backwards and fell. Despite the pain he quickly came to his knees.

After the kick, Matthew rolled away, coming to his feet as well. Now he watched warily and amazed as the big warrior rose back to his feet. The wicked grin on his face had been replaced with a look of raw hatred. Matthew knew the man's leg was broken, he felt it snap, but if the big warrior was in pain, it was never revealed on his face.

The two faced each other. One confident that help would be coming... soon. The other knowing he would have to act before that help arrived.

Matthew saw Laurel freeing the first of the girls. Glancing toward the sea, he saw Englishman, who now seemed transfixed in the edge of the water where he fired the shot destroying Matthews bow as though he couldn't make up his mind what to do next.

A hundred yards down the beach; two warriors

emerged from the woods, moving toward them. Strangely they weren't moving as fast as he would have expected.

In that instant of distraction, Big-Neck launched his attack, throwing his tomahawk with all his bull like strength.

Matthew heard Laurels warning scream, saw the wicked ax whirling in his direction. He did the only thing he could think of. He raised his on tomahawk to block approaching missile.

The two axes collided an arms length in front of Matthews's head, deflecting the deadly blade, but the tough hickory handle flipped around smacking him squarely on the forehead.

Stunned, fighting unconsciousness, Matthew saw Big-Neck draw a wicked looking knife from a sheath at his side and start hobbling toward him. Fighting back the darkness, he saw two of the girls who had been freed, break away, charging barehanded toward their former tormentor.

Before he could call out, warn them to stay away, his legs crumpled and a black void overwhelmed him.

Chapter 36

Laurel was frightened, even more frightened than the day she'd been captured and hauled from her village. On that day there had been little time for anything other than a short, futile struggle. The Shawnee had executed their plan so flawlessly there had been no time to fight back. In less than an instant she had been grabbed by strong arms and bound with lengths of leather. The only thing her struggles achieved was to get her hit on the head, hard enough to knock her unconscious.

Draped over the shoulder of a stout warrior, she'd been trussed up then carried away like the carcass of a slain deer.

Of course, later there had been plenty of time to contemplate her fate. By then, thinking had only served to depress her. What she and Matthew were attempting was vastly different.

Running head on into the face of the enemy left you with little time to think and a lot to be frightened. Her heart fluttered against her rib cage like a wild bird caught in a trap.

Laurel's fear was not so much for herself as it was for Matthew. He was strong, she knew, and quick, but still weak from his injuries, as well as inexperienced. In a fight against a warrior as bloodthirsty and brutal as Bull-Neck, she was sure he would be out matched,

Now, racing along the shore a few steps behind Matthew, Laurel did her best to ignore these fears. At the beginning of their mad dash, she had kicked off her moccasins in order to gain a better purchase on the loose sand. Zigzagging across the open beach, she was vaguely aware of the wet sand between her toes as her feet pounded the ground, aware of cold drops of rain beginning to splatter against her face, stinging her eyes, and overwhelmingly aware that ahead, death waited in their path.

The only thing keeping her fingers from trembling was the tight grip she maintained of the rifle Matthew insisted she carry. Her other hand, holding the razor edged metal arrowhead, shook anyway.

Matthew wanted her to save the shot in his rifle for the warriors who would undoubtedly come boiling out hiding at the sound of the first shot. Laurel had doubts about this, but would do what he said. Given her choice, would have used the gun to kill Bull-Neck first.

Laurel was startled, by the sound of a gunshot and the almost simultaneous sound of a lead ball impacting against the bow Matthew carried. Splinters of wood erupted as the bow flew from his hand.

Laurel glanced to the side in time to see the Colonel Hayward lowering his still smoking pistol to his side. Almost instantly another shot rang out, this one from the direction of the captive girls. She heard the angry bee-like whine as the lead ball passed close by her, but closer to Matthew. She veered away, headed toward the girls as Matthew had instructed.

The world suddenly seemed to turn into slow motion. From the corner of her eye, she saw Matthew pull the pistol from his belt, pause long enough to aim, then fire.

Splinters of wood fly from the gunstock held by the brave who had fired at them. The warrior was trying desperately to reload his weapon when blood erupted from his throat, splattering the captive girls as he turned, then slowly fell to one side.

Never slowing her pace, Laurel plunged toward the cluster of bound girls. Stepping around the dead warrior at their feet, she dropped the rifle and began slicing away the bindings on the wrist and ankles of the first girl.

After freeing her, Laurel handed her the little blade, yelling over the sound of the approaching storm, to begin freeing the other girls.

After reaching down to recover the gun, Laurel looked up in time to see that Matthew and Bull-Neck had almost reached each other. Then something astonishing happened. When the two men were almost ready to collide, Matthew dropped low, passing feet first, a hair's breath below Bull-Necks vicious swing'

Laurel had never seen anyone fight in such a way. The heel of Matthews's foot landed squarely against Bull-Necks leg, just below the knee. She heard both men grunt with the impact.   Matthew went to the ground, then quickly scrambled backwards. Bull-Neck stumbled backwards a few yards then went to his knees.

From down the beach a shot rang out, then another barely heard above the wind and rain. The Colonel had waded waist deep into the water, waving his arms, motioning the men in the boats to come on ashore. They remained motionless.

A blur of motion brought her attention back closer. Two girls, the ones who had been raped several times before reaching the main group, were running directly toward Bull-Neck. At the same time, the big warrior had recovered enough to stand up and was in the process of hurtling his war-ax at Matthew. Her warning cry was drowned out by distant clap of thunder.

The world, which moments earlier had seemed trapped in slow motion, suddenly began to race wildly out of control.

Laurel watched, horrified as Bull-Neck's ax spun through the air toward Matthew. She saw Matthew try to deflect the oncoming blade with his own, saw the weapons meet, in a clash of sparks. Then Matthew fell. She had no idea how badly he was hurt.

Turning the gun, holding it the way Matthew had shown her, Laurel lined the sights up on Bull-Necks chest. He was fifty yards away. She could not afford to miss.

Before she could squeeze the trigger, the two young girls running toward the big warrior, launched themselves at his back like a pair of enraged rabbits attacking a wolf.

As they ran, one of the girls had pulled from beneath her ragged bloodstained buckskin dress, a long sliver of dried wood. At night, concealed between the other girls, she had used a sharp edged rock to sharpen the wooden weapon.

Holding on desperately, her small hand entangled in Bull-Neck's long raven hair, the girl reached over his shoulder and with all her strength, drove the wooden spike into his chest.

The makeshift blade penetrated Bull-Neck's chest, lodging between two breastbones. It was not a fatal blow. Because of the girls small size, and her precarious perch the dried fragment of cedar missed his lung and did not penetrate deep enough to reach his heart.

Sounding more like a wounded bear than his namesake, the big warrior let out a pain-filled roar. Reaching up with one mighty arm, Bull-Neck grabbed his tiny antagonist by the throat. Like a wolf worrying a wounded ground squirrel, he shook her until he felt the bones in her neck snap.

With a mighty heave, he tossed the girl to one side. She landed in a lifeless heap, her head turned at an unnatural angle.

Torn between bloodlust and pain, the wooden spike still protruding from his bloody chest, Bull-Neck turned around to focus his rage the remaining girl. Loosening her hold on his hair, she had dropped to the ground behind him and was busily trying to crab away from his reach.

Laurel had been trying to aim the rifle at the big Shawnee leader, but the presence of the girl had kept her from firing. With the last girl scrambling out of the way, she again took aim.

Before she had time to squeeze the trigger, something else blocked her vision.

Matthew, crouched low, his small knife gripped tightly in one hand, was charging head on toward Bull-Neck.

A sudden bolt of lightening with three separate prongs, like Poseidon's mighty Trident, split the darkening sky, close enough that the immediate clap of thunder shook the ground almost instantly.

Bull-Neck turned just as Matthew launched himself into the air.

Laurel watched, terrified as the two men collided like another thunderbolt.

**

Matthew fought against the darkness.

Rising to his knees, his vision cleared just in time to see Bull-Neck hands close around the neck of one of the young girls. How had she gotten involved?

"N -o-o-o," he screamed, a flood of sorrow ripping at his heart, helplessly watching her lifeless body tossed aside like so much worthless offal.

A dark killing rage one like he'd never known boiled through him, searing away any pain he might have felt. He wasn't aware of rising to his feet, of charging like an angry loin toward a hated enemy. He was only vaguely aware of lightning striking close by.

There was no plan to his attack. No strategy. No thoughts of survival. There was only the burning need to feel his own hands seek vengeance against this hated enemy.

Just as Bull-Neck turned to face him, Matthew leaped. Like a eagle, talons extended he flew through the air.

An instant before the two men collided, Matthew

dropped his knife, then cupping is hands together, he used them like a battering ram against the foot long wooden stake still imbedded in Bull-Necks chest.

Matthew was stunned by the impact. One hand felt like it might be broken. The other one throbbed almost as bad. His momentum had carried him several feet past Bull-Neck. He shakily regained his feet and began looking for his dropped knife.

Bull-Neck tried to rise to his feet. He made it to his knees then fell face down in the sand. The sharpened piece of cedar wood now protruded from his back.

Matthew stood looking down at Bull-Neck's still body, rainwater washing the blood from his wounds in tiny red streams. Still he was not certain that the Shawnee warrior might not again try to rise to his feet. His knees felt as shaky as the wind driven trees along the shore.

Laurel raced across the distance between them, then put her arms around his waist for support. For once he didn't mind leaning on her. Weak beyond measure, all he wanted to do was lay down and rest for a month, unfortunately he only got was a few seconds.

A hundred yards down the beach two Shawnee warriors stepped out of the woods. He took his rifle from her hand and turned to face them.

By this time the rain was falling in almost solid sheets. Rainwater and chaff, whipped to froth by the howling wind, along with the growing darkness, rendered the men barely visible. A third man stepped out of the woods behind the two warriors.

Matthew rubbed the water from his eyes, then squinted at the three men. Slowly he lowered his gun, a grin cutting at the corners of his mouth. He could hardly believe what he was seeing. The man walking up the beach, his gun trained on the two warriors, was Thadis Smith.

"Look," Laurel shouted above the wind, pointing toward the longboats fighting against the choppy sea. All three boats were retreating toward the ship.

The Colonel, frighten and desperate, waded deeper into the swelling waves. Tossing aside first his pistol then his sword, he began yelling something at the men in the boats. It went unheard over the gale. Wading even deep he began to swim toward the retreating crafts.

The boat, in which the ship's Captain rode, stopped. Apparently they would come no closer, but were willing to wait for the Englishman to swim to them.

When the floundering Colonel finally reached the boat, the Captain reached down to give him a hand. But instead of helping him aboard, he drew his sword and in one quick motion, ran it through Hayward's neck.

Reaching down, the Captain snatched the leather pouch from his victim's shoulder. Letting loose of the Englishman's hand, he mumbled a curse, then spit on the slowly reddening water.

Matthew stood in stunned silence as the boats slowly moved away.

Turning his attention back to the shoreline, Matthew watched as Thadis Smith, looking for the world like old grizzled wolf, one that had been almost drowned in river, guided two Shawnee warriors in their direction at

293

gunpoint.

As the three men drew near, Matthew sagged back against Laurel's side and waited till Thais stood at his side.

"I told you that damn big knife of yours was gonna get your drowned one of these days," he said with a weak smile. "From the looks of you, I think maybe it already did."

For the first time in many weeks, Thadis Smith smiled.

Chapter 37

Matthew sat with his back against an outcrop of sun-warmed, weather-smoothed granite. Below him a vertical rock face dropped out of sight into the valley below. The cliff marked the fall-line where the Blue Ridge Mountains of North Carolina dropped thousands of feet to the foothills of South Carolina.

Thadis had guided him to the spot a few days earlier. The old trader, along with the rest of their group, was camped in a sheltered cove a few miles away.

The view from the rocky precipice was awe inspiring as well as humbling. Matthew had returned to this spot with the intent of catching up with the entries in his journal, but first he had to sort out his emotions. He needed to filter through the events of the last few months, and to figure what path his future might take.

For more than an hour he had rested against the same rock, enthralled with the stark beauty of such vast wilderness.

Below, miles of unbroken forest stretched out of sight in any direction. The trees along the mountaintop had already taken on bright hues of fall, dark reds, brilliant yellows and orange brush strokes. In the foothills below, the color had only begun to take hold.

Through small openings in the canopy below Matthew caught an occasional glimpse of moving water. The three forks of the upper Saluda River found their origin in the countless springs and seeps scattered along the ridges below, its waters eventually joining to cut a swath through the heart of South Carolina.

To the Cherokee, the streams and rivers were more than a source of life, of food and drink. They were held in reverence, treated as living spirits. Little wonder they clung so tenaciously to this particular area.

Not only was there the watershed of the Saluda below, to the west, shouldered in the haze of the setting sun, laid the valleys of the Seneca and the Toogaloo. Together they would merge to form the mighty Savanna, a river that served as the boundary of two states as it meandered its way to the Atlantic.

A rifle shot to the north. On the western side of an area called the *flat-woods,* the head waters of Little River flowed northeast to join with the French Broad. These waters flowed north then west and eventually turned south, joining with other waters flowing along the western flanks of the Appalachian. Their journey would take them all the way to the mighty Mississippi.

On the eastern edge of the *flat-woods* the tributaries on the Green River united to begin a trek of five hundred miles across North Carolina.

It was little wonder that the Cherokee called this land, the *etsi vhnai ama ...mother of waters.* A high mountain thunderstorm venting it's fury against these lonely mountain peaks might find its raindrops, spread with time, over more than a thousand miles.

Matthew's thoughts were interrupted by a sudden gust

of wind.

A cool breeze flowing along the rim of the mountain carried with it a whirlwind of autumn leaves. They hung momentarily, suspended in midair, like an inverted kaleidoscope. After a few seconds their beautiful dance started to slowly slide down.

Matthew watched until the spinning leaves had disappeared into the depth. For some reason they reminded him of the Chimney-sweeps he had watched as a young boy, small black and white birds gathering by the thousands over English rooftops just before dark. Round and round the sweeps would circle in an ever tightening formation, until suddenly, by some unseen signal, they would drop like inverted bullets into the bores of stone or terra-cotta chimneys.

The image in his mind seemed a lifetime ago.

Matthew's leather bound journal lay in his lap. He had retrieved it, along with his pack, on the return trip from the coast of Virginia. In his right hand a quill pin.

His wrist still felt a little stiff from his fight with Bull-Neck, and the axe wound on his back still gave an occasional twinge. Fortunately, he had suffered no broken bones that day on the beach, only a sprain. The healing had been slow, primarily because he couldn't seem to stop using his hand.

So far he had not once dipped the feather in the small clay pot filled with the juice squeezed from the root of the Bloodroot flower.

Laurel had gathered and prepared the roots. She had also

brought him the feather from a gobbler that Thadis had killed. She was an amazing girl. Sometimes it seemed she knew more about his needs than he did.

The pen worked much better than the charcoal stick he had been using. Even so, he had not managed to jot down a single thought. His heart was heavy, his mind awash with a torrent of emotions, some good, but mostly sad.

It had been late October by the time he and Thadis guided their ragged band of refugees back into what had once been their wilderness stronghold. That had been two weeks ago.

Matthew had once heard a traveling preacher refer to these mountains as a dark and bloody land. It had never seemed more so than now. The journey home had begun in sadness.

Little-Flower who had died attacking Bull-Neck, was left resting in a burial mound in the dark rain drenched forests of Virginia. It had been a tearful departure.

Along the way things only got worse.

They had freed the two remaining Shawnee braves, sending them away without their weapons, before starting a long journey home.

It had been all that he and Thadis could do to keep the group fed and out of the path of scattered groups of militia that seemed to suddenly fill the woods. These groups of men, anywhere from three to twenty or more, were obviously returning from some sort of wilderness campaign.

Both he and Thadis had a fair notion of what had happened, but neither one designed to talk about it, at least not in front of the girls.

As they traveled the weather slowly took on a hint of autumn. During the day, in the brilliant sun, the air was warm enough to be comfortable. At night it often frosted and required sleeping close to campfires. Normally it was the time of year that Matthew loved the most. Now, he was too preoccupied with finding food and shelters each day, to take much notice.

The girls had stretched and tanned the hides of every squirrel, rabbit or deer that he or Thadis had managed to kill for food along the way. They wasted nothing. These hides no matter how small were stitched together to form sleeping covers for nights that were often accompanied by ice on the stream banks.

After reaching the French Broad River, they followed its course slowly making their way south and higher into the mountains. After a week, they encountered the first burned out village. It was Laurel's grandfather's encampment.

Every cabin or shelter had been torched or ransacked. Cornfields resembled nothing more than blackened scars on the land. Bushels of potatoes, squash, and beans lay trampled, rotting in the sun. A few half wild dogs, nosing about the destroyed village, fled to the woods at their approach. No other sign of life could be found.

Laurel was devastated. It was the first time Matthew had seen her cry. Even at Little-Flowers burial, she put on a strong front, if only for the sake of the other girls.

It broke Matthew's heart to see her in pain... and worse ... to not be able to do anything about it. He would have held her in his arms, offered her comfort, but he wasn't sure how she would react to his sympathy.

After salvaging what little they could, Thadis, fearful of encountering more returning militia, pushed them further up river. The next day their number increased.

Two older men, three women, and four children, one infant girl and two boys around four or five, and one about ten, made up the group.

Matthew scouting ahead, had spotted the men and the older boy, working fish traps at the mouth of a small tributary stream. Not knowing how many there were, and not wanting to alarm them, he had slipped back down stream.

They decided that Laurel should approach them alone. Matthew wanted to accompany her at least part of the way.

She would have none of it, arguing that a white man entering their camp might receive an arrow before he had the chance to offer up his intentions. Her logic, as usual, could not be disputed.

Laurel set off at a run.

Matthew knew she was anxious for any word of her grandfather. He argued with himself that there was no reason to fear for her safety. They were her people.

It didn't matter. Sitting on a moss-covered log, gritting his teeth while he kept a watchful eye for movement among the stand of sycamore trees, Matthew used his hunting knife to cut a length of green sourwood into a neat pile of shavings.

Thadis and the other girls rested at the base of a hemlock. The old trader didn't offer up any comment at his friend's obvious discomposure, but the silent smirk on his face made Matthew cut even more furiously at the offending sourwood.

After what seemed an eternity, but was really less than half an hour, Matthew spotted Laurel returning along the trail. For the first time since they had reached her village, she was smiling.

The nine people in the group ahead were from her village.

Thanks to Thadis having warned of the attack, Gray-Fox-Killer had prepared his people to abandon their village when and if an attack came. Everything that could be carried in baskets or packs had been readied for departure.

Scouts had returned with word of the approaching army. Thirty warriors had stayed behind to fight, not with any chance of winning against an army of two thousand or more. Sacrificing their lives that their families would be able to escape into the wilderness ....

Only five braves returned.

Gray-Fox-Killer had planned to hide his people in the rugged mountains to the west, thinking that such a large force would not peruse them in the rough terrain. Unfortunately he had underestimated the tenacity of the frontiersman.

In order to hide move effectively, Gray-Fox-Killer had been forced to divide his people into small scattered groups. It proved to be an effective tactic.

After wasting a few days chasing shadows, the army had departed. There were other towns and villages to be *subdue*. Most would not fare   so well.

After a few weeks Gray-Fox-Killer sent out his few remaining scouts to search for his scattered people. They were to travel west and gather for the winter at the base of a mountain called *agowadvdi inv* ...see far.

Thadis called the place **Lookout Mountain**.

Thadis suggested that they head south, spend some time at a place he knew to gather food and supplies before heading west. A place called the *flat-woods*.

After leaving Laurel's village, the size of their party increased almost daily. Every few miles or so, the forest trail turned up new refugees. Confused, weary and haggard, all but one group elected to join them. At the mouth of the Little River, they turned away from the French Broad and began the climb toward Cedar Mountain, where they would camp. By the time they arrived their numbers had increased to fifty seven. And with each new arrival, the scope of the events that had befallen the Cherokee people grew increasingly tragic.

More than thirty villages had been destroyed. No one seemed to know how many people had been killed. Probably no one ever would. Those who could escape into the forest, survived. Those who chose to stand and fight ... died.

The Lower and Middle towns had fallen first, then the Over Hill villages were burned one by one. As with Gray-Fox-Killer's village, all stores of food were torched or trampled.

No doubt, death would continue to stalk the Cherokee through out the long cold winter, but they were a resilient people. Already, the hunters were scouting the woods for deer, turkeys, and grouse, while the young boys trapped rabbits and squirrels.

The women gathered acorns and chestnuts, roasting them along with the meat and fish the men provided, over slow smoky fires.

Persimmons, blue berries and crab apples, along with other roots and berries covered every available rock around the camp, drying in the mid-day sun. The coming winter might be harsh, bellies might not be totally full, but neither would they be empty. Laurel's people were survivors. They would once again.

After establishing camp, Matthew and Thadis had set off across country to the old trader's cabin at *Flat Rock*, to retrieve anything that could be of use in the coming winter. With his mother's people forced further west, Thadis would no longer be living there.

After loading everything they could carry into packs, the two men stood for a while, each lost in his own private thoughts, when suddenly Thadis put his hand on Matthews arm.

Using hand signals the old man motioned for him to stay quiet, leading him into the shadows of a couple of huge white pines.

Thadis eased his rifle up against one of the trees, silently looking down the barrel.

It took Matthew a few seconds to catch a glimpse of slight movement, nothing more than a flash of light against a scrap of white fabric about three hundred yards away. Then came the low murmuring of human voices.

After a couple of minutes, two men appeared, walking toward them. One man carried a tall length of wood, to the top of which was tied a white rag. The other carried a satchel and some kind of contraption in his hand.

Thadis lowered his rifle.

Neither man carried a gun. Both were dressed the same, gray wool trousers, light brown cotton shirts, tall black leather boots and floppy felt hats.

They were more than a little startled when two fierce looking, unshaven, buckskin clad men suddenly appeared in their path.

The man with the pole apparently had the idea of using it for a weapon, but had second thoughts when Thadis glared at him which was indeed lucky for him.

It turned out they were surveyors, hired by a group of wealthy landowners in Charles-Town and Savannah. With the Cherokee no longer a threat, they were paying to have the area mapped out for future expansion.

Matthew, suddenly seeing trouble brewing in the in the fiery depths of his friends eyes, quickly changed the subject. He asked the men how the war with England was going.

It only took a few words for Matthew to realize that the men were Tories, loyal to the English Crown. After a short period of listening to what news they had, he and Thadis made their excuses and departed.

For most of the trip back to camp, Thadis had the disposition of an erupting volcano, grumbling under his breath with each step.

Occasionally some words would reach Matthew's ears. *Vulture* was one word often repeated. Others he hadn't heard since he left the sea. Wisely, he listened without comment.

The day after returning to camp, Thadis had shown Matthew the cliff were he now sat. He said it was a place God had created for man to think through his problems.

It seemed to work. After spending a few hours, sitting quietly, watching the sun turn the western horizon crimson and gold, his old friend had returned to his normal grumpy but loveable self.

Now Matthew was back at the same spot trying to work out his own demons.

Tomorrow Thadis would lead his new communal of refugees west, toward Look Out mountain. Matthew would head southeast to Charles-Town.

His friends were upset with his plans. He had tried to explain his reasons, but it was difficult because he wasn't even sure what those reasons were; only something he knew in his heart had to be done.

Picking up his journal, Matthew took out the map he and Laurel had followed for so long. Turning it over, he looked at the words written there. He wasn't sure why he held on to the piece of paper. It was tattered and some of the letters were smeared from the water on the beach of Virginia on that wet miserable day.

It didn't matter he'd memorized most of it anyway. Looking down, as always, the same line caught his attention: *We hold these truths to be self evident, that all men are created equal.....*

To Matthew those few words seemed vitally important.

They rang true in his heart and summed up everything he had come to believe in. That all men, white, red, black, or yellow were entitled to live free. He knew first hand the injustice of English rule and nothing would get better until this new country calling itself America, freed itself from the tyranny of one man ... King George.

From what Matthew had seen, it was the same story with all people ... even the Cherokee. One man ... Dragging-Canoe ... followed by a few others, had caused a war that devastated his own people.

When any tribe, city, or nation ruled its people by brut force alone it is the innocent who suffer the most. For this reason alone, Matthew knew that he must join in the fight against England, fight to give the seed of this new government time to sprout and mature, to give the voice of the people the chance to rule a nation.

He had heard that a man called Washington was leading the fight against the British to the north. In the south, a rice farmer turned soldier, by the name Marion, was using Indian fighting tactics to out maneuver the British along the Santee River.

Matthew had no idea what group he would join. When the time came that problem would work itself out.

Picking up his journal, he dipped the pen into the dark red ink. One day he would return to the mountains, he had no doubt about it, but for now there was something worth fighting for.

The first word he'd written in the journal in a long while was .... *Freedom*

The End. ....

Additional Historical Footnotes

In the fall of 1776, the renegade war chief, Dragging-Canoe, was shot though both hips in the battle of Carter's Valley. Carried away by his men from the fight, he would recover, eventually leading his men to the area that is now present day Chattanooga, Tennessee. For many years he would continue to ferment trouble between the Cherokee and the Whites.

On May 20th 1777, a convention of the old Cherokee chiefs, desperate for peace, negotiated a treaty with the states of Georgia and South Carolina in an attempt to end the war. To achieve this treaty, the chiefs ceded in excess of 5,000,000 acres, which included the present day counties of Greenville, Anderson, Pickens and Oconee Counties in South Carolina.

Matthew Maybin fought in a number of battles during the Revolutionary War; among these were the battles of Cowpens and King's Mountain. He was given a land grant, which he later sold, then purchased land along the headwaters of Green River, not far from Flat Rock, N.C. and only a half day's walk from an area know locally as *the Flat-Woods.* Many of his descendants still live among those beautiful, secluded mountain coves.

Thadis Smith would become a name much honored among the Cherokee. Many mothers would pass on this name to their sons... a great honor. It shows up many times on the rolls of the Cherokee people and is common, even today.

307

Personal Note

The seed of this story took root in my mind one fall day more years ago than I care to remember. On a picnic outing along the Blue Ridge Parkway, my wife and I and our two young daughters stopped at an overlook to eat and admire the beautiful fall colors.

While my wife set out our meal and the girls frolicked in the new fallen leaves, I walked out to read a historical marker, near the road.

On that cold, gray and silver metal marker were written these words:

......In 1776 Revolutionary War General Griffith Rutherford led 2,400 men through the gap below and to your left .During the war's early phases, the Cherokee, with British support, attacked the frontier settlements. Rutherford's expedition was a major frontier offensive to subdue the Cherokee. Rutherford's forces destroyed as many as 36 villages in this area, forcing the Cherokee deeper into the Great Smokey Mountains. / Although skirmishes with the Cherokee continued, the colonists' major military efforts were then directed to battles with the British on the eastern seaboard....

Reading the words written there, I could not help but think of the untold tragedy written between those cold metal lines. Thirty-six villages, with names like Cowee, Nequassee, Kanuga, Stecoee, Tuckasegee, Watauga, Nununyi, and Cherokee, destroyed and burned.

In my mind swam the images of countless hungry, cold and displaced children who suffered the aftermath of such a war. Having the benefit of hindsight, I knew this was only one sad chapter in the on going tragedy that was to befall the Cherokee people.

Walking back toward my family, the sunshine no longer seemed as bright and the sky a more subdued shade of blue.

Watching my daughters scattering leaves with their feet as they ran, I was suddenly overwhelmed with a dark sense of melancholy. As always, I was thankful for the life of peace I had been granted and yet was aware of how fleeting and fragile it can be. With mankind's propensity to destroy itself, I worried for my children's future. In all of man's wars it seems that the innocent are the one's who suffer most.

Walking back toward our picnic table, these thoughts filled my heart with a great sadness.

One day perhaps mankind would learn to overcome the desire to make war on itself, and travel a new path.

I would like to take this time to thank my family and frie3nds who always told me I could when I so often felt that I could not....all my love and gratitude...

Tom

Acknowledgments

I would like to take this opportunity to apologize to my family members, near or far, for the latitude I have taken with our mutual ancestor. While the story of Matthew Maybin is purely fictional, no more than the overzealous musings of a mountain boy who never outgrew his wonder-lust for the wilderness or a fascination for the hero's of the past, Matthew was very much a real person.

I have striven to portray him as I would like to believe many of our forefathers lived…with honor and courage.

I have tried to stay within the bounds of actual history, in the telling of this tale. If perchance, I have erred in some fact or detail….well damn, let me know and I will wonder off into the mountains and spend a few days pondering the error of my ways…It's a tough life.

About me…………

I guess I have always been a square peg in a round hole…sometimes my life just doesn't fit.

I began my journey as a writer more years ago than I care to remember, right out of high school… but a war in Vietnam, then a marriage, children and life got in the way.

Now I am a young boy trapped in an old man's body. My mind still rambles the mountains and streams of Flat, Rock N C.. where I grew up and I still dream of great men and heroic deeds. I hope this never changes.

I owe a debt of gratitude to my fifth grade teacher who opened my mind to the wonderful world of books. I cannot imagine what my life would be without them.

For these among many other reasons I write of what and how my heart dictates.

I can do nothing more….

Thomas Maybin

Made in the USA
Lexington, KY
10 October 2013